To mom
from Jeanie

may 2-10

MARY HIGGINS CLARK

SIMON & SCHUSTER

Loves Music, Loves to Dance

NEW YORK • LONDON • TORONTO • SYDNEY • TOKYO • SINGAPORE

SIMON & SCHUSTER
SIMON & SCHUSTER BUILDING
ROCKEFELLER CENTER
1230 AVENUE OF THE AMERICAS
NEW YORK, NEW YORK 10020

DESIGNED BY EVE METZ
MANUFACTURED IN THE UNITED STATES OF AMERICA

1 2 3 4 5 6 7 8 9 10

LIBRARY OF CONGRESS CATALOGING-IN-PUBLICATION DATA
CLARK, MARY HIGGINS
LOVES MUSIC, LOVES TO DANCE/MARY HIGGINS CLARK
P. CM.
I. TITLE.
PS3553.L287L6 1991
813'.54—DC20   91-10757
CIP
ISBN 0-671-67364-5

ENDLESS THANKS to all who gave so much input and encouragement in the writing of this book—my editor, Michael V. Korda; his associate, senior editor Chuck Adams; my agent, Eugene H. Winick; Robert Ressler, Associate Director of Forensic Behavioral Services. Kudos to my daughter, Carol Higgins Clark, for her research, comments and suggestions and for burning the midnight oil with me as we raced to deadline. And of course, special thanks to the rest of my family and friends, who endured my usual self-doubting about whether or not I could tell this story; their saintly patience will have the cathedrals fighting for their bones.

FOR MY BROTHER JOHNNY'S BOYS,
LUKE AND CHRIS HIGGINS,
AND FOR HIS GRANDDAUGHTER, LAURA.

WITH LOVE.

What is a friend?
A single soul dwelling in two bodies.

—Aristotle

Loves Music, Loves to Dance

I
MONDAY
February 18

*T*HE ROOM was dark. He sat in the chair, his arms hugging his legs. It was happening again. Charley wouldn't stay locked in the secret place. Charley insisted on thinking about Erin. *Only two more,* Charley whispered. *Then I'll stop.*

He knew there was no use protesting. But it was becoming more and more dangerous. Charley was becoming reckless. Charley wanted to show off. *Go away, Charley, leave me alone,* he begged. Charley's mocking laugh roared through the room.

If only Nan had liked him, he thought. If only she'd invited him to her birthday party fifteen years ago . . . He'd loved her so much! He'd followed her to Darien with the present he'd bought her at a discount house, a pair of dancing slippers. The cardboard shoebox had been plain and cheap, and he'd taken such trouble to decorate it, drawing a sketch of the slippers on the lid.

Her birthday was on March twelfth, during spring break. He'd driven down to Darien to surprise her with the present. He'd arrived to find her house ablaze with lights. Cars were being parked by valets. He'd driven slowly past, shocked and stunned to recognize students from Brown there.

It still embarrassed him to remember that he'd cried like a baby as he turned around to drive back. Then the thought of the birthday gift made him change his mind. Nan had told him that every morning at seven o'clock, rain or shine, she jogged in the wooded area near her home. The next morning he was there, waiting for her.

He remembered, still vividly today, her *surprise* at seeing him. *Surprise,* not pleasure. She'd stopped, her breath coming in gasps, a stocking cap hiding her silky blond hair, a school sweater over her running suit, her feet in Nikes.

He'd wished her a happy birthday, watched her open the box, listened to her insincere thanks. He'd put his arms around her. "Nan, I love you so much. Let me see how pretty your feet look in the slippers. I'll fasten them for you. We can dance together right here."

"Get lost!" She pushed him away, threw the box at him, started to jog past him.

It was Charley who had run after her, grabbed her, thrown her to the ground. Charley's hands squeezed her throat until her arms stopped flailing. Charley fastened the slippers on her feet and danced with Nan, her head lolling on his shoulder. Charley lay her on the ground, one of the dancing slippers on her right foot, replacing the Nike on her left.

A long time had passed. Charley had become a blurred memory, a shadowy figure lurking somewhere in the recesses of his mind, until two years ago. Then Charley had started reminding him about Nan, about her slender, high-arched feet, her narrow ankles, her beauty and grace when she danced with him. . . .

Eeney-meeney-miney-mo. Catch a dancer by the toe. Ten piggy toes. The game his mother used to play when he was small. *This little piggy went to market. This little piggy stayed home.*

"Play it ten times," he used to beg when she stopped. "One for each piggy toe."

His mother had loved him so much! Then she changed. He could still hear her voice. *"What are these magazines doing in your room? Why did you take those pumps from my closet? After all we've done for you! You're such a disappointment to us."*

When he reappeared two years ago, Charley ordered him to place ads in the personal columns. So many ads. Charley dictated what he had to say in the special one.

Now seven girls were buried on the property, each with a dancing slipper on the right foot, her shoe or sneaker or boot on the left. . . .

He'd begged Charley to let him stop for a while. He didn't want to do it anymore. He'd told Charley that the ground was still frozen—he couldn't bury them, and it was dangerous to keep their bodies in the freezer. . . .

But Charley shouted, "I want these last two to be found. I want them found just the way I let Nan be found."

Charley had chosen these last two the same way he had chosen the others after Nan. They were named Erin Kelley and Darcy Scott. They had each answered two different personal ads he'd placed. More important, they had each answered his *special* ad.

In all the replies he'd received, it was *their* letters and pictures that had jumped out at Charley. The letters were amusing, the cadence of the language attractive, almost like hearing Nan's voice, that self-deprecating wit, that dry, intelligent humor. And there were the pictures. Both were inviting in different ways. . . .

Erin Kelley had sent a snapshot of herself perched on the corner of a desk. She'd been leaning forward a bit as though speaking, her eyes shining, her long, slim body poised as though she were waiting to be asked to dance.

Darcy Scott's picture showed her standing by a cushioned windowseat, her hand on the drapery. She was half-turned toward the camera. Clearly, she'd been surprised when her picture was taken. There were swatches of material over her arm, an absorbed, but amused, expression on her face. She had high cheekbones, a slender frame, and long legs accentuated by narrow ankles, her slim feet encased in Gucci loafers.

How much more attractive they would be in dancing slippers! he told himself.

He got up and stretched. The dark shadows falling across the room no longer disturbed him. Charley's presence was complete and welcome. No more nagging voice begged him to resist.

As Charley willingly receded into the dark cave from which he had emerged, he reread Erin's letter and ran his fingertips over her picture.

He laughed aloud as he thought of the beguiling ad that had summoned Erin to him.

It began: *"Loves Music, Loves to Dance."*

II
TUESDAY
February 19

*C*OLD. *SLUSHY.* Raw. Terrible traffic. It didn't matter. It was good to be back in New York.

Darcy happily tossed off her coat, ran her fingers through her hair, and surveyed the neatly separated mail on her desk. Bev Rothhouse, skinny, intense, bright, a night student at Parsons School of Design and her treasured secretary, identified the stacks by order of importance.

"Bills," she said, pointing to the extreme right. "Deposit slips next. Quite a few of them."

"Substantial, I hope," Darcy suggested.

"Pretty good," Bev confirmed. "Messages over there. You've got requests to furnish two more rental apartments. I swear, you certainly knew what you were doing when you opened a second-hand business."

Darcy laughed. "Sanford and Son. That's me."

Darcy's Corner, Budget Interior Design was what the placard on the office door read. The office was in the Flatiron Building on Twenty-third Street.

"How was California?" Bev asked.

Amused, Darcy heard the note of awe in the other young woman's voice. What Bev really meant was, "How are your mother and father? What's it like to be with them? Are they really as gorgeous as they look in films?"

The answer, Darcy thought, is, Yes, they're gorgeous. Yes, they're wonderful. Yes, I love them and I'm proud of them. It's just that I've never felt comfortable in their world.

"When are they leaving for Australia?" Bev was trying to sound offhanded.

"They left. I caught the red-eye back to New York after seeing them off."

Darcy had combined a visit home with a business trip to Lake Tahoe, where she'd been hired to decorate a model ski house for budget-priced buyers. Her mother and father were embarking on an international tour with their play. She wouldn't see them for at least six months.

Now she opened the container of coffee she'd picked up at a nearby lunch counter and settled down at her desk.

"You look great," Bev observed. "I love that outfit."

The square-neck red wool dress and matching coat were part of the Rodeo Drive shopping tour her mother had insisted upon. "For such a pretty girl, you never pay enough attention to your clothes, darling," her mother had fussed. "You should emphasize that wonderful ethereal quality." As her father frequently observed, Darcy could have posed for the portrait of the maternal ancestor for whom she had been named. The original Darcy had left Ireland after the Revolutionary War to join her French fiancé, an officer with Lafayette's forces. They had the same wide-set eyes, more green than hazel, the same soft brown hair streaked with gold, the same straight nose.

"We've grown a bit since then," Darcy enjoyed pointing out. "I'm five eight. Darcy the First was a shrimp. That helps when you're trying to look ethereal." She had never forgotten when she was six and overheard a director comment, "How ever did two such stunning people manage to produce that mousy-looking child?"

She still remembered standing perfectly still, absorbing the shock. A few minutes later when her mother tried to introduce her to someone on the set, "And this is my little girl, Darcy," she had shouted "No!" and run away. Later she apologized for being rude.

This morning when she got off the plane at Kennedy, she'd dropped her bags at the apartment, then come directly to the office, not taking time to change into her usual working garb, jeans and a sweater. Bev waited for her to start sipping the coffee, then picked up the messages. "Do you want me to start getting these people for you?"

"Let me give Erin a quick call first."

Erin picked up on the first ring. Her somewhat preoccupied greeting told Darcy that she was already at her worktable. They'd been college roommates together at Mount Holyoke. Then Erin had studied jewelry design. Recently she'd won the prestigious N. W. Ayer award for young designers.

Darcy had also found her professional niche. After four years of working her way up in an advertising agency, she had switched careers from account executive to budget interior decorating. Both women were now twenty-eight, and they were as close as they'd been when living together in school.

Darcy could picture Erin at her worktable, dressed in jeans and a baggy sweater, her red hair held back by a clip or in a ponytail, absorbed by her work, unaware of outside distraction.

The preoccupied "hello" gave way to a whoop of joy when Erin heard Darcy's voice.

"You're busy," Darcy said. "I won't keep you. Just wanted to report that I've arrived, and, of course, I wanted to see how Billy is."

Billy was Erin's father. An invalid, he'd been in a nursing home in Massachusetts for the past three years.

"Pretty much the same," Erin told her.

"How's the necklace going? When I phoned Friday you sounded worried." Just after Darcy had left last month, Erin had landed a commission from Bertolini Jewelers to design a necklace using the client's family gems. Bertolini was on a par with Cartier's and Tiffany's.

"That's because I was still terrified the design might be off base. It really was pretty intricate. But all is well. I deliver it tomorrow morning and if I say so myself, it's sensational. How was Bel-Air?"

"Glamorous." They laughed together, then Darcy said, "Update me on Project Personal."

Nona Roberts, a producer at Hudson Cable Network, had become friendly with Darcy and Erin at their health club. Nona was preparing a documentary on personal columns—about the kind of people who placed and answered the ads; their experiences, good or bad. Nona had asked Darcy and Erin to assist in the research by answering some of the ads. "You don't have to see anybody more than once," she'd urged. "Half the singles at the network are doing it and having a lot of laughs. And who knows, you might meet someone terrific. Anyhow, think about it."

Erin, typically the more daring, had been unusually reluctant. Darcy had persuaded her it could be fun. "We won't place our own ads," she argued. "We'll just answer some that look interesting. We won't give our addresses, just a phone number. We'll meet them in public places. What's to lose?"

They had started six weeks ago. Darcy had had time for only one date before she left on the trip to Lake Tahoe and Bel-Air. That man had written he was six one. As she told Erin afterward, he must have been standing on a ladder when he measured himself. Also he'd claimed he was an advertising executive. But when Darcy threw out a few names of agencies and clients, he was totally at sea. A liar and a jerk, she reported to Erin and Nona.

Now, smiling in anticipation, Darcy asked Erin to fill her in on her most recent encounters.

"I'll save it all for tomorrow night when we get together with Nona," Erin said. "I'm writing every detail down in that notebook you gave me for Christmas. Suffice it to say, I've been out twice more since we talked. That brings the total to eight dates in the last three weeks. Most of them were nerds with absolutely no redeeming social value. One it turned out I'd met before. One of the new ones was really attractive and needless to say hasn't called back. I'm meeting somebody tonight. He sounds okay, but let's wait and see."

Darcy grinned. "Obviously, I haven't missed much. How many ads have you answered for me?"

"About a dozen. I thought it would be fun to send both our letters to some of the same ads. We can really compare notes if those dudes call."

"I love it. Where are you meeting tonight's prize?"

"In a pub off Washington Square."

"What does he do?"

"Corporate law. He's from Philadelphia. Just relocating here. You can make tomorrow night, can't you?"

"Sure." They were meeting Nona for dinner.

Erin's tone changed. "I'm glad you're back in town, Darce. I've missed you."

"Me too," Darcy said heartily. "Okay, see you then." She started to say good-bye, then impulsively asked, "What's the name of tonight's pig-in-a-poke?"

"Charles North."

"Sounds upscale, waspy. Have fun, Erin-go-bragh." Darcy hung up.

Bev was waiting patiently with the messages. Now her tone was frankly envious. "I swear, when you two talk, you sound like a couple of school kids. You're closer than sisters. Thinking about *my* sister, I'd say you're a lot closer than sisters."

"You're absolutely right," Darcy said quietly.

*T*HE *SHERIDAN GALLERY* on Seventy-eighth Street, just east of Madison Avenue, was in the midst of an auction. The contents of the vast country home of Mason Gates, the late oil baron, had drawn an overflow crowd of dealers and collectors.

Chris Sheridan observed the scene from the back of the room, reflecting with pleasure that it had been a coup to triumph over Sotheby's and Christie's for the privilege of auctioning this collection. Absolutely magnificent furniture from the Queen Anne period; paintings distinguished less by their technique than by their rarity; Revere silver that he knew would set off feverish bidding.

At thirty-three, Chris Sheridan still looked more like the linebacker he had been in college than a leading authority on antique furniture. His six-four height was accentuated by his straight carriage. His broad shoulders tapered down to a trim waist. His sandy hair framed a strong-featured face. His blue eyes were disarming and friendly. As his competitors had learned, however, those eyes could quickly take on a keen, no-nonsense glint.

Chris folded his arms as he watched the final bids on a 1683 Domenico Cucci cabinet with panels of pietra dura and central reliefs of inlaid stones. Smaller and less elaborate than the pair Cucci made for Louis XIV, it was nevertheless a magnificent, flawless piece that he knew the Met wanted desperately.

The room quieted as the bidding between the two high-stakes players, the Met and the representative of a Japanese bank, continued. A tug on his arm made Chris turn with a distracted frown. It was Sarah Johnson, his executive assistant, an art expert whom he had coaxed away from a private museum in Boston. Her expression reflected concern. "Chris, I'm afraid there's a problem," she said. "Your mother's on the phone. She says she has to talk to you immediately. She sounds pretty upset."

"The problem is that damn program!" Chris strode toward the

door, shoved it open, and, ignoring the elevator, raced up the stairs.

A month ago the popular television series *True Crimes* had run a segment about the unsolved murder of Chris's twin sister, Nan. At nineteen, Nan had been strangled while jogging near their home in Darien, Connecticut. Despite his vehement protests, Chris had not been able to prevent the camera crews from filming long shots of the house and grounds, nor from reenacting Nan's death in the nearby wooded area where her body had been found.

He had pleaded with his mother not to watch the program, but she had insisted on viewing it with him. The producers had managed to find a young actress who bore a startling resemblance to Nan. The docudrama showed her jogging; the figure watching her from the protection of the trees; the confrontation; the attempt to escape, the killer tackling her, choking her, pulling the Nike from her right foot and replacing it with a high-heeled slipper.

The commentary was delivered by an announcer whose sonorous voice sounded gratuitously horrified. "Was it a stranger who accosted beautiful, gifted Nan Sheridan? She and her twin celebrated their nineteenth birthday the night before at the family mansion. Did someone Nan knew, someone who perhaps toasted her on her birthday, become her killer? In fifteen years no one has come forward with a shred of information that might solve this hideous crime. Was Nan Sheridan the random victim of a deranged monster, or was her death an act of personal vengeance?"

A montage of closing shots followed. The house and grounds from a different angle. The phone number to call "if you have any information." The last closeup was the police photo of Nan's body as it had been found, neatly placed on the ground, her hands folded together on her waist, her left foot still wearing the Nike, her right foot in the sequined slipper.

The final line: "Where are the mates to this sneaker, to this graceful evening shoe? Does the killer still have them?"

Greta Sheridan had watched the program dry-eyed. When it was finished, she'd said, "Chris, I've gone over it in my mind so often. That's why I wanted to see this. I couldn't function after Nan died, couldn't think. But Nan used to talk to me so much about everyone at school. I . . . I just thought that seeing that program might make me recall something that could be important. Remember the day of the funeral? That huge crowd. All those young people from college. Remember Chief Harriman said that he was convinced her killer was sitting there among the mourners? Remember how they had cameras set up to take pictures of everyone in the funeral home and at church?"

Then, as though a giant hand had smashed her face, Greta Sheridan had broken into heart-rending sobs. "That girl looked so much like Nan, didn't she? Oh Chris, I've missed her so much all these years. Dad would still be alive if she were here. That heart attack was his way of grieving."

I wish I'd taken an ax to every television in the house before I let Mother watch that damn program, Chris thought as he ran down the corridor to his office. The fingers of his left hand drummed on the desk as he grabbed the phone. "Mother, what's wrong?"

Greta Sheridan's voice was tense and unsteady. "Chris, I'm sorry to bother you during the auction, but the strangest letter just came."

Another fallout from that stinking program, Chris fumed. All those crank letters. They ranged from psychics offering to conduct seances to people begging for money in exchange for their prayers. "I wish you wouldn't read that garbage," he said. "Those letters tear you apart."

"Chris, this one is different. It says that in memory of Nan, a dancing girl from Manhattan is going to die on the evening of February nineteenth in exactly the way Nan died." Greta Sheridan's voice rose. "Chris, suppose this isn't a crank letter? Is there anything we can do? Is there anyone we can warn?"

*D*OUG FOX pulled on his tie, carefully twisted it into a precise knot, and studied himself in the mirror. He'd had a facial yesterday and his skin glowed. The body wave had made his thinning hair seem abundant and the sandy rinse completely covered the touch of gray that was emerging at his temples.

A good-looking guy, he assured himself, admiring the way his crisp white shirt followed the lines of his muscular chest and slim waist. He reached for his suit jacket, quietly appreciating the fine feel of the Scottish wool. Dark blue with faint pinstripes, accented by the small red print on his Hermès tie. He looked every inch the part of the investment banker, upstanding citizen of Scarsdale, devoted husband of Susan Frawley Fox, father of four lively, handsome youngsters.

No one, Doug thought with amused satisfaction, would suspect him of his other life: that of the single freelance illustrator with an apartment in the blessed anonymity of London Terrace on West Twenty-third Street, plus a hideaway in Pawling and a new Volvo station wagon.

Doug took a final look in the long mirror, adjusted his pocket handkerchief, and with a glance to make sure he hadn't forgotten anything, walked to the door. The bedroom always irritated him. Antique French provincial furniture, damn place done by an upscale interior designer, and Susan still managed to make it look like the inside of Fibber McGee's closet. Clothes piled on the chaise, silver toilet articles haphazardly strewn over the top of the dresser. Kindergarten drawings taped on the wall. Let me out, Doug thought.

The kitchen was the scene of the usual mayhem. Thirteen-year-old Donny and twelve-year-old Beth jamming food in their mouths. Susan warning that the school bus was down the block. The baby waddling around with a wet diaper and grubby hands.

30

Trish saying she didn't want to go to kindergarten this afternoon, she wanted to stay home and watch "All My Children" with Mommy.

Susan was wearing an old flannel robe over her nightgown. She had been a very pretty girl when they were married. A pretty girl who'd let herself go. She smiled at Doug and poured him coffee. "Won't you have pancakes or something?"

"No." Would she ever stop asking him to stuff his face every morning? Doug jumped back as the baby tried to embrace his leg. "Damn it, Susan, if you can't keep him clean, at least don't let him near me. I can't go to the office looking grubby."

"Bus!" Beth yelled. "Bye, Mom. Bye, Dad."

Donny grabbed his books. "Can you come to my basketball game tonight, Dad?"

"Won't be home till late, son. An important meeting. Next time for sure, I promise."

"Sure." Donny slammed the door as he left.

Three minutes later, Doug was in the Mercedes heading for the train station, Susan's reproachful "Try not to be too late" ringing in his ears. Doug felt himself begin to unwind. Thirty-six years old and stuck with a fat wife, four noisy kids, a house in the suburbs. The American Dream. At twenty-two he'd thought he was making a smart move when he married Susan.

Unfortunately, marrying the daughter of a wealthy man wasn't the same as marrying wealth. Susan's father was a tightwad. Lend, never give. That motto had to be tattooed on his brain.

It wasn't that he didn't love the kids or that he wasn't fond enough of Susan. It was just that he should have waited to get into this paterfamilias routine. He'd thrown his youth away. As Douglas Fox, investment banker, upstanding citizen of Scarsdale, his life was an exercise in boredom.

He parked and ran for the train, consoling himself with the thought that as Doug Fields, bachelor artist, prince of the personals, his life was swift and secretive, and when the dark needs came there was a way to satisfy them.

III
WEDNESDAY
February 20

ON WEDNESDAY EVENING, Darcy arrived at Nona Roberts's office promptly at six-thirty. She'd had a meeting with a client on Riverside Drive and phoned Nona to suggest they cab over to the restaurant together.

Nona's office was a cluttered box in a row of cluttered boxes on the tenth floor of the Hudson Cable Network. It held a somewhat battered oak desk piled with papers, several filing cabinets, the drawers of which did not fully close, shelves of reference books and tapes, a distinctly uninviting-looking love seat, and an executive swivel chair which Darcy knew no longer swiveled. A plant which Nona consistently forgot to water drooped wearily on the narrow windowsill.

Nona loved that office. Darcy privately wondered why it didn't destroy itself by spontaneous combustion. When she arrived, Nona was on the phone, so she went out seeking water for the plant. "It's begging for mercy," she said when she returned.

Nona had just completed the call. She jumped up to embrace Darcy. "A green thumb I have not." She was wearing a khaki wool jumpsuit that faithfully followed the lines of her small frame. A narrow leather belt with a white-gold clasp sculpted in the form of linked hands cinched her waist. Her medium-blond hair, streaked with touches of gray, was blunt-cut and barely reached her chin. Her animated face was interesting rather than pretty.

Darcy was glad to see that the pain in Nona's dark brown eyes had been almost completely replaced by an expression of wry humor. Nona's recent divorce had hit her hard. As she put it, "It's traumatic enough turning forty without your husband bumping you for a twenty-one-year-old nymphet."

"I'm running late," Nona apologized. "We're meeting Erin at seven?"

"Between seven and seven-fifteen," Darcy said, her fingers itching to skim the dead leaves from the plant.

"Fifteen minutes to get over there, provided I throw myself in front of an empty cab. Terrific. There's one thing I'd like to do before we go. Why don't you come with me and witness the compassionate side of television."

"I wasn't aware it had one." Darcy reached for her shoulder bag.

All the offices rimmed a large central area which was crowded with secretaries and writers at their desks. Computers hummed and fax machines clattered. At the end of the room, an announcer was on camera giving a news update. Nona waved a general greeting as she passed. "There isn't a single unattached person in that maze who isn't answering the personal ads for me. As a matter of fact, I suspect there are some supposedly attached guys who are also quietly getting together with an intriguing box number."

She led Darcy into a screening room and introduced her to Joan Nye, a pretty blonde who didn't look more than twenty-two. "Joan does the obits," she explained. "She just finished updating an important one and asked me to take a look at it." She turned to Nye. "I know it will be fine," she added reassuringly.

Joan sighed. "I hope so," she said, and pushed the button to start the film rolling.

The face of film great Ann Bouchard filled the screen. The mellifluous voice of Gary Finch, the Hudson Cable anchorman, was properly subdued as he began to speak.

> "Ann Bouchard won her first Oscar at the age of nineteen, when she replaced ailing Lillian Marker in the 1928 classic *Perilous Path.* . . ."

Film clips of Ann Bouchard in her most memorable roles were followed by highlights of her personal life: her seven husbands, her homes, her well-publicized battles with studio executives, excerpts of interviews throughout her long career, her emotional response to receiving a lifetime achievement award: "I have been blessed. I have been loved. And I love you all."

It was over. "I didn't know Ann Bouchard died," Darcy exclaimed. "My God, she was on the phone with my mother last week. When did that happen?"

"It didn't," Nona said. "We prepare the celebrity obits in advance just the way the newspapers do. And we regularly update them. The farewell to George Burns has been revised twenty-two times. When the inevitable occurs, we just have to drop in the lead. The rather irreverent name for the project is the Toodle-oo Club."

"Toodle-oo Club?"

"Uh-huh. We do the final portion and say toodle-oo to the deceased." She turned to Nye. "That was terrific. I'm positively blinking back tears. Incidentally, have you answered any new personals?"

Nye grinned. "It may cost you, Nona. The other night I made a date to meet some jerk. Naturally got caught in traffic. Double-parked my car to rush in and let him know I'd be right back. Rushed out to find a cop ticketing me. Finally found a garage six blocks away and when I came back—"

"He was gone," Nona suggested.

Nye's eyes widened. "How did you know?"

"Because I've heard this from some other people. Don't take it personally. Now we'd better run." At the door Nona called over her shoulder, "Give me the ticket. I'll take care of it."

In the cab on the way to meet Erin, Darcy found herself wondering what it was that made someone pull a trick like that. Nye was genuinely attractive. Was she too young for the man she had met? When she answered the ad she must have given her age. Did he have some image in mind that Nye didn't fit?

It was a disquieting thought. As the cab bumped and lurched through Seventy-second Street traffic, she commented, "Nona, when we started answering these ads, I thought of it as a joke. Now I'm not so sure. It's like having a blind date without the security of being introduced to the guy because he's the best friend of somebody's brother. Can you imagine any man you know doing that? Even if for some reason Nye's date hated the way she dressed or wore her hair or whatever, all he had to do was have a quick drink and say he was rushing for a plane. He still gets away fast and doesn't leave her feeling like a fool."

"Darcy, let's face it," Nona said. "From all the reports I'm hearing, most of the people who place or answer these ads are pretty insecure. What's a lot more scary is that just today I got a letter from an FBI agent who'd heard about the program and said he wants to talk to me. He'd like us to include a warning that these ads are a natural for sexual psychopaths."

"What a lovely thought!"

As usual, Bella Vita offered encompassing warmth. The wonderful, familiar garlicky aroma was in the air. There was a faint hum of talk and laughter. Adam, the owner, greeted them. "Ah, the beautiful ladies. I have your table." He indicated one by the window.

"Erin should be along any minute," Darcy told him as they were seated. "I'm surprised she isn't waiting. She's always so prompt, it actually gives me a complex."

"She's probably stuck in traffic," Nona said. "Let's order wine. We know she'll have chablis."

Half an hour later, Darcy pushed her chair back. "I'm going to phone Erin. The only thing I can imagine is that when she delivered the necklace she designed for Bertolini's, there might have been some adjustment needed. She loses track of time when she's working."

The answering machine was on in Erin's studio apartment. Darcy returned to the table and realized Nona's anxious expression mirrored her own feelings. "I left a message that we're waiting for her and to call here if she can't make it."

They ordered dinner. Darcy loved this restaurant, but tonight she was hardly aware of what she was eating. Every few minutes she glanced at the door hoping that Erin would come flying in with a perfectly reasonable explanation of why she had been delayed.

She did not come.

Darcy lived on the top floor of a brownstone on East Forty-ninth Street, Nona in a co-op on Central Park West. When they left the restaurant they took separate cabs, promising that whoever heard from Erin first would contact the other.

The minute she got home, Darcy tried Erin's number again. She tried an hour later, just before she went to bed. This time she left an emphatic message. "Erin, I'm worried about you. It's Wednesday, 11:15. I don't care how late you get in, call me."

Eventually, Darcy fell into an uneasy sleep.

When she awakened at 6 a.m., her immediate thought was that Erin had not called.

*J*AY STRATTON stared out the corner window of his thirtieth-floor apartment in Waterside Plaza on Twenty-fifth Street and the East River Drive. The view was spectacular: the East River arced by the Brooklyn and Williamsburg Bridges, the twin towers to the right, the Hudson behind them, the streams of traffic, agonizingly slow in the evening rush hour, flowing well enough now. It was seven-thirty.

Jay frowned, a gesture that caused his narrow eyes to become almost invisible. A head of dark brown hair, expensively cut and attractively threaded with gray, helped to foster his cultivated look of casual elegance. He was aware of the tendency of his waistline to thicken, and exercised vigorously. He knew he looked a bit older than his age, which was thirty-seven, but that had proved to be an advantage. He'd always been considered unusually hand-some by most people.

Certainly the newspaper magnate's widow whom he'd escorted to the Taj Mahal casino in Atlantic City last week had found him attractive, though when he had mentioned that he'd like to have some jewelry created for her, her face turned to stone. "No sales pitch, please," she snapped. "Let's understand that."

He hadn't bothered with her again. Jay did not believe in wast-ing time. Today he'd lunched at the Jockey Club and while he waited for a table he'd started chatting with an older couple. The Ashtons were in New York on holiday celebrating their fortieth anniversary. Obviously well-heeled, they were somewhat at loose ends outside their familiar North Carolina surroundings and re-sponded eagerly to his conversational overtures.

The husband had looked pleased at Jay's query as to whether he'd chosen a suitable piece of jewelry for his wife to commemo-rate their forty years together. "I keep telling Frances that she ought to let me buy her some real nice jewelry but she says to save the money for Frances Junior."

Jay had suggested that at some time in the distant future, Frances Junior might enjoy wearing a lovely necklace or bracelet and telling her own daughter or granddaughter that this was a very special gift from Grampa to Nana. "It's what royal families have been doing for centuries," he explained as he handed them his card.

The phone rang. Jay hurried to answer it. Maybe it was the Ashtons, he thought.

It was Aldo Marco, the manager at Bertolini's. "Aldo," Jay said heartily. "I was planning to call you. All's well, I trust?"

"All is certainly not well." Marco's tone was icy. "When you introduced me to Erin Kelley I was most impressed with her and her portfolio. The design she submitted was superb and as you know, we gave her our client's family gems to reset. The necklace was supposed to have been delivered this morning. Miss Kelley failed to keep the appointment and has not answered our repeated messages. Mr. Stratton, I want either that necklace or my client's gems back immediately."

Jay ran his tongue over his lips. He realized the hand holding the phone was damp. He had forgotten about the necklace. He chose his answer carefully. "I saw Miss Kelley a week ago. She showed me the necklace. It was exquisite. There must be some misunderstanding."

"The misunderstanding is that she has failed to deliver the necklace, which is needed for an engagement party Friday night. I repeat, I want it or my client's gems back tomorrow. I hold you responsible to execute one or the other alternative. Is that clear?"

The sharp click of the phone sounded in Stratton's ears.

*M*ICHAEL NASH saw his last patient, Gerald Renquist, at five o'clock on Wednesday afternoon. Renquist was the retired CEO of an international pharmaceutical company. Retirement had thrown a man whose personal identity was linked to the intrigue and politics of the boardroom to the status of unwilling sideliner.

"I know I should consider myself lucky," Renquist was saying, "but I feel so damn useless. Even my wife pulled that old saw on me—'I married you for better or worse, but not for lunch.' "

"You must have had a game plan for retirement," Nash suggested mildly.

Renquist laughed. "I did. Avoid it at all cost."

Depression, Nash thought. The common cold of mental illness. He realized he was tired and not giving Renquist his full attention. Not fair, he told himself. He's paying for me to listen. Still, it was a distinct relief when at ten of six he was able to wrap up the session.

After Renquist left, Nash began to lock up. His office was on Seventy-first and Park, his apartment on the twentieth floor of the same building. He went out through the door that led to the lobby.

The new tenant in 20B, a blonde in her early thirties, was waiting for the elevator. He fought down irritation at the prospect of riding up with her. The undisguised interest in her eyes was a nuisance, as were her almost inevitable invitations to drop in for a drink.

Michael Nash had the same problem with a number of his women patients. He could read their minds. Nice-looking guy, divorced, no children, mid-to-late thirties, available. A diffident reserve had become second nature to him.

At least tonight the new neighbor did not repeat the invitation. Maybe she was learning. When they stepped from the elevator, he murmured, "Good night."

His apartment reflected the precise care he took with everything in his life. Ivory flax upholstery on the twin sofas in the living room was repeated on the dining room chairs surrounding the round oak table. That table had been a find at an antique auction in Bucks County. The area carpets had muted geometric patterns on an ivory background. A wall of bookcases, plants on the windowsills, a Colonial dry sink which served as a bar, bric-a-brac he'd gathered on trips abroad, good paintings. A comfortable, handsome room.

The kitchen and study were to the left of the living room, the bedroom suite and bath to the right. A pleasant apartment and an attractive complement to the big place in Bridgewater that had been his parents' pride and joy. Nash was often tempted to sell it, but knew he'd miss riding on weekends.

He took off his jacket and debated between watching the tail end of the six o'clock news or listening to his new compact disc, a Mozart symphony. Mozart won. As the familiar opening bars softly filled the room, the doorbell rang.

Nash knew exactly who it would be. Resigned, he answered it. The new neighbor stood holding an ice bucket—the oldest trick in the book. Thank God he hadn't started to mix his drink. He gave her the ice, explained that no, he couldn't join her, he was on his way out, and steered her to the door. When she was gone, still twittering about "Maybe next time," he made straight for the bar, mixed a dry martini, and ruefully shook his head.

Settling on the sofa near the window, he sipped the cocktail, appreciating its smooth, soothing taste, and wondered about the young woman he was meeting for dinner at eight o'clock. Her response to his ad had been downright amusing.

His publisher was ecstatic about the first half of the book he was writing, the book analyzing the people who placed or answered personal ads, their psychological needs, their flights into fantasy in the way they described themselves.

His working title was *The Personal Ads: Quest for Companionship or Departure from Reality?*

IV
THURSDAY
February 21

*D*ARCY SAT at the dinette table, sipping coffee and staring unseeingly out the window at the gardens below. Barren now, scattered with unmelted snow, in the summer they were exquisitely planted and manicured to perfection. The prestigious owners of the private brownstones they backed included the Aga Khan and Katharine Hepburn.

Erin loved to come over when the gardens were in bloom. "From the street you'd never guess they exist," she'd sigh. "I swear, Darce, you sure lucked out when you found this place."

Erin. Where was she? The minute she woke up and realized that Erin had not phoned, Darcy had called the nursing home in Massachusetts. Mr. Kelley's condition was unchanged. The semi-comatose state could go on indefinitely, although he was certainly getting weaker. No, there had been no emergency call to his daughter. The day nurse really couldn't say if Erin had made her usual phone call last evening.

"What should I do?" Darcy wondered aloud. Report her missing? Call the police and inquire about accidents?

A sudden thought made her shiver. Suppose Erin had had an accident in the apartment. She had a habit of tilting back in her chair when she was concentrating. Suppose she'd been lying there unconscious all this time!

It took her three minutes to throw on a sweater and slacks, grab a coat and gloves. She waited agonizing minutes on Second Avenue before getting a cab.

"One-oh-one Christopher Street, and please hurry."

"Everybody says 'hurry.' I say take it easy, you'll live longer." The cabbie winked into the rearview mirror.

Darcy turned her head. She was in no mood to banter with the driver. Why hadn't she thought of the possibility of an accident? Last month, just before she went to California, Erin had dropped by for dinner. They'd watched the news. One of the commercials showed a frail old woman falling and getting help by touching the emergency signal on a chain around her neck. "That'll be us in fifty years," Erin had said. She'd imitated the commercial, moaning, "Hel-l-l-p, hel-l-l-p! I've fallen, and I can't get up!"

Gus Boxer, the superintendent of 101 Christopher Street, had an eye for pretty women. That was why when he hurried to the lobby to answer the persistent ring of the doorbell, his annoyed scowl was quickly replaced by an ingratiating twist of his mouth.

He liked what he saw. The visitor's light brown hair was tossed by the wind. It fell forward on her face, reminding him of the Veronica Lake movies he stayed up to watch. Her hip-length leather jacket was old but had that classy look that Gus had come to recognize since taking this job in Greenwich Village.

His appraising eyes lingered on her long, slim legs. Then he realized why she looked familiar. He'd seen her a couple of times with 3B, Erin Kelley. He opened the vestibule door and stepped aside. "At your service," he said in what he considered to be a winning manner.

Darcy walked past him, trying not to show her distaste. From time to time, Erin complained about the sixty-year-old Casanova in dirty flannel. "Boxer gives me the creeps," she'd said. "I hate the idea he has a master key to my place. Once I walked in and found him there and he gave me some cock-and-bull story about a leak in the wall."

"Was anything ever missing?" Darcy had asked.

"No. I keep any jewelry I'm working on in the safe. There's nothing else worth pocketing. It's more that he has a nasty, flirtatious way about him that makes my skin crawl. Oh well. I've got a safety bolt when I'm inside and the place is cheap. He's probably harmless."

Darcy came straight to the point. "I'm concerned about Erin Kelley," she told the superintendent. "She was supposed to meet me last night and didn't show up. She doesn't answer her phone. I want to check her apartment. Something may have happened to her."

Boxer squinted. "She was okay yesterday."

"Yesterday?"

Thick lids drooped over faded eyes. Parted lips were moistened with his tongue. His forehead collapsed into erratic lines. "No, I'm wrong. I seen her Tuesday. Late afternoon. She come in with some groceries." His tone became virtuous. "I offered to carry 'em up for her."

"That was Tuesday afternoon. Did you see her go out or return Tuesday evening?"

"Nope. Can't say I did. But listen, I'm not a doorman. Tenants have their own keys. Delivery guys gotta use the intercom to get let in."

Darcy nodded. Knowing it was useless, she had rung Erin's apartment before she buzzed for the superintendent. "Please. I'm afraid there may be something wrong. I've got to get into her place. Do you have your passkey?"

The twisted smile returned. "You gotta understand, I don't normally let people into an apartment just because they wanna go in. But I seen you with Kelley. I know you're friends. You're like her. Classy. Good-lookin'."

Ignoring the compliment, Darcy started up the stairs.

The stairs and landings were clean but dreary. The patched walls were battleship gray, the tiles on the steps uneven. Walking into Erin's apartment had the effect of going from a cave into daylight. When Erin moved here three years ago, Darcy had helped her paint and paper. They'd hired a U-Haul and made forays into Connecticut and New Jersey for garage-sale furnishings.

They'd painted the walls a stark white. Colorful Indian rugs were scattered over the scratched but polished parquet floor. Framed museum posters were arranged over a studio couch that was covered in bright red velour and piled with vividly assorted throw pillows.

The windows faced the street. Even though the sky was overcast, the light was excellent. Under the windows a long worktable held Erin's supplies neatly placed side by side: torch, hand drill, files and pliers, ring clamps and spring tweezers, soldering block, gauges, drills. Darcy had always been fascinated to watch Erin at work, her slender fingers skillfully handling delicate gems.

Next to the table was Erin's one extravagance, a tall chest with several dozen narrow drawers. A nineteenth-century pharmaceutical cabinet, the bottom drawers were a facade concealing a safe. One easy chair, a television, and a good stereo system completed the pleasant room.

Darcy's immediate impression was a surge of relief. There was nothing out of order here. Gus Boxer at her heels, she walked swiftly into the tiny kitchen, a small windowless cubicle that they'd painted a bright yellow and decorated with framed tea towels.

The narrow hallway led to the bedroom. The pewter and brass bed and a two-on-three dresser were the only furniture in the closet-sized room. The bed was made. There was nothing out of place.

Clean, dry towels were on the rack in the bathroom. Darcy opened the medicine chest. With a practiced eye, she noted that Erin's toothbrush, cosmetics and creams were all there.

Boxer was becoming impatient. "Looks okay to me. You satisfied?"

"No." Darcy went back into the living room and walked over to the worktable. The message machine showed twelve calls had come in. She pressed playback.

"Hey, I don't know—"

She cut off Boxer's protest. "Erin is missing. Have you got that straight? She's *missing*. I'm going to listen to these messages and see if they might somehow give me an idea of where she might be. Then I'm going to call the police and inquire about accidents. For all I know, she's unconscious in a hospital somewhere. You can stay here with me or if you're busy, you can go. Which is it?"

Boxer shrugged. "I guess it's okay to leave you here."

Darcy turned her back on him, reached into her purse, and took out her notebook and pen. She did not hear Boxer leave as the messages began. The first one had come on Tuesday evening at six forty-five. Someone named Tom Swartz. Thanks for answering his ad. Just discovered a great little inexpensive restaurant. Could they meet for dinner? He'd phone again.

Erin was supposed to meet Charles North on Tuesday evening at seven o'clock at a pub near Washington Square. By quarter of seven she had undoubtedly already left, Darcy thought.

The next call came in at seven twenty-five. Michael Nash. "Erin, I certainly enjoyed meeting you and hope you might be free for dinner sometime this week. If you have a chance, call me back this evening." Nash left both his home and office numbers.

Wednesday morning the calls began at nine o'clock. The first few were run-of-the-mill business-related. The one that made Darcy's throat close was from an Aldo Marco of Bertolini's. "Miss

Kelley, I am disappointed you did not keep our ten o'clock appointment. It is essential that I see the necklace and be sure there is no last-minute adjustment necessary. Please get back to me immediately."

That call had come in at eleven. There were three more follow-ups from the same man, increasing in irritation and urgency. Besides Darcy's own messages, there was another one concerning the Bertolini assignment.

"Erin, this is Jay Stratton. What's going on? Marco's bugging me for the necklace and holding me responsible for bringing you to him."

Darcy knew that Stratton was the jeweler who had given Erin's portfolio to Bertolini's. His message came in around seven Wednesday evening. Darcy started to push the rewind button, then paused. Maybe it would be better not to erase these. She looked in the phone book for the number of the nearest precinct. "I want to report someone missing," she said when the call was answered. She was told that she would have to come in personally, that this kind of information about a competent adult could not be accepted over the phone.

I'll stop there on my way home, Darcy thought. She went into the kitchen and made coffee, noting that the only milk container was unopened. Erin started her day with coffee and always drank it light. Boxer had seen her with groceries Tuesday afternoon. Darcy looked into the garbage pail under the sink. There were a few odds and ends, but no empty milk container. She wasn't here yesterday morning, Darcy thought. She never got back Tuesday night.

She brought the coffee back to the worktable. A daily reminder was in the top drawer. She flipped through it, starting with today. There were no appointments listed. Yesterday, Wednesday, there were two: Bertolini's, 10 A.M.; Bella Vita, 7 P.M. (Darcy and Nona).

In the preceding weeks, there were notations of dates with

names of men unfamiliar to Darcy. They were usually scheduled between five and seven o'clock. Most of them had the meeting place listed: O'Neal's, Mickey Mantle's, P. J. Clarke's, the Plaza, the Sheraton . . . all hotel cocktail lounges and popular pubs.

The phone rang. Let it be Erin, Darcy prayed as she grabbed it. "Hello."

"Erin?" A man's voice.

"No. This is Darcy Scott. Erin's friend."

"Do you know where I can reach Erin?"

Disappointment, intense and overwhelming, swept over Darcy. "Who is this?"

"Jay Stratton."

Jay Stratton had left the message about the Bertolini jewelry. What was he saying?

". . . if you have any idea where Erin is, please tell her that if they don't get that necklace, they'll file a criminal complaint."

Darcy's eyes flickered to the pharmaceutical cabinet. She knew that Erin kept the combination in her address book under the name of the safe company. Stratton was still talking.

"I know Erin kept that necklace in a safe in her studio. Is there any possibility you can check to see if it's there?" he urged.

"Hold on a minute." Darcy put her hand over the speaker, then thought, What a dumb thing to do. There's no one here I can ask. But in a way she was asking Erin. If the necklace wasn't in the safe, it might mean that Erin had been the victim of a robbery when she attempted to deliver it. If it was there, it was almost certain proof that something had happened to her. Nothing would have kept Erin from delivering the necklace on time.

She opened Erin's address book and turned to D. Next to Dalton Safe was the series of numbers. "I have the combination," she told Stratton. "I'll wait for you to come here. I don't want to open Erin's safe without a witness. And in case the necklace is here, I'll want a receipt for it from you."

He said he'd be right over. After she replaced the receiver, Darcy

50

decided that she'd ask the superintendent to be present as well. She didn't know anything about Jay Stratton except that Erin told her he was a jeweler and the one who got her the Bertolini commission.

While she waited, Darcy went through Erin's files. Under "Project Personal," she found sheets of personal columns torn from magazines and newspapers. On each page a number of the ads were circled. Were these the ones Erin had answered, or had thought about answering? Dismayed, Darcy realized that there were at least two dozen of them. Which, if any of them, had been placed by Charles North, the man Erin was to meet on Tuesday evening?

When she and Erin agreed to answer the personal ads, they'd gone about it systematically. They'd had inexpensive letterheads made with only their names at the top. They'd each chosen a favorite snapshot to send when requested. They'd spent a hilarious evening composing letters they had no intentions of sending. "I love to clean clean clean," Erin had suggested, "my favorite hobby is doing the wash by hand. I inherited my grandmother's scrub board. My cousin wanted it too. It caused a big family fight. I get a little nasty during my period, but I'm a very good person. Please call soon."

They had finally come up with what they decided were reasonably alluring responses. When Darcy was leaving for California, Erin had said, "Darce, I'll send yours out about two weeks before you're due back. I'll just change a sentence here or there to fit the ad."

Erin didn't own a computer. Darcy knew she typed out the responses on her electric typewriter but did not Xerox them. She kept all the input in the notebook she carried in her purse: the box numbers of the ads she answered, the names of the people she called, her impressions of the ones she dated.

. . .

Jay Stratton leaned back in the cab, his eyes half-closed. The speaker behind his right ear was blaring rock music. "Will you turn that down?" he snapped.

"Man, you trying to deprive me of my music?" The cabbie was in his early twenties. Wispy, snarled hair hung around his neck. He glanced over his shoulder, caught the look on Stratton's face, and, muttering under his breath, lowered the volume.

Stratton felt sweat forming in his armpits. He had to pull this off. He tapped his pocket. The receipts Erin had given him for the Bertolini gems and for the diamonds he'd given her last week were in his wallet. Darcy Scott sounded smart. He mustn't arouse the slightest suspicion.

The nosy superintendent must have been watching for him. He was in the foyer when Stratton arrived. Obviously, he recognized him. "I'll bring you up," he said. "I'm supposed to stay while she opens the safe."

Stratton swore to himself as he followed the squat figure up the stairs. He didn't need two witnesses.

When Darcy opened the door for them, Stratton's face was set in a pleasant, somewhat-concerned expression. He had planned to sound reassuring, but the worry in Scott's eyes warned him against banalities. Instead, he agreed with her that something must be dreadfully wrong.

Smart girl, he thought. Darcy had obviously memorized the combination of the safe. She was not about to let anyone know where Erin kept it. She had a pad and pen ready. "I want to itemize everything we find in there."

Stratton deliberately turned his back while she twisted the dial, then crouched beside her as she pulled the door open. The safe was fairly deep. Boxes and pouches lined the shelves.

"Let me hand everything out to you," he suggested. "I'll describe what we find. You write it down."

Darcy hesitated, then realized it was a sensible suggestion. He was the jeweler. His arm was brushing against hers. Instinctively, she moved aside.

Stratton looked over his shoulder. An irritated-looking Boxer was lighting a cigarette and glancing around the room, probably searching for an ashtray. It was Stratton's only chance. "I think that velvet case is the one Erin kept the necklace in." Reaching for it, he deliberately knocked a small box onto the floor.

Darcy jumped as she saw the glitter of stones scattering around her and scrambled to collect them. An instant later Stratton was beside her, cursing his carelessness. They searched the area thoroughly. "I'm sure we got them all," he said. "These are semiprecious, suitable for good costume jewelry. But more important . . ." He opened the velvet case. "Here's the Bertolini."

Darcy stared down at the exquisite necklace. Emeralds, diamonds, sapphires, moonstones, opals, and rubies were set in an elaborate design that reminded her of the medieval jewelry she'd seen in portraits at the Metropolitan Museum of Art.

"Lovely, isn't it?" Stratton asked. "You can understand why the manager at Bertolini's was so upset at the prospect of something happening to it. Erin is remarkably gifted. She not only managed to create a setting that made those stones look ten times their own considerable value, but she did it in the Byzantine style. The family who commissioned the necklace was originally from Russia. These gems were the only valuable possessions they were able to take when they fled in 1917."

Darcy could visualize Erin sitting at this worktable, her ankles around the rungs of the chair, the way she used to sit when she was studying in college. The sense of impending disaster was overwhelming. Where would Erin willingly go without delivering this necklace on time?

Nowhere *willingly,* she decided.

Biting her lip to keep it from quivering, she picked up the pen. "Will you describe this for me and I think we should identify every precious stone in it so there's no question that any are missing."

As Stratton removed other pouches, velvet cases, and boxes from the safe, she noticed that he was becoming increasingly more agitated. Finally he said, "I'm going to open the rest all at once, then we'll list them." He looked directly at her. "The Bertolini necklace is here, but a pouch I gave Erin with a quarter of a million dollars worth of diamonds is gone."

Darcy left the apartment with Stratton. "I'm going to the police station to file a missing-person report," she told him.

"You're absolutely right," he said. "I'll take care of getting the necklace to Bertolini's immediately and if we haven't heard from Erin in a week, I'll contact the insurance company about the diamonds."

It was exactly noon when Darcy entered the Sixth Precinct on Charles Street. At her insistence that something was terribly wrong, a detective came out to see her. A tall black man in his mid-forties with military bearing, he introduced himself as Dean Thompson and listened sympathetically as he tried to allay her fears.

"We really can't file a missing-person report for an adult woman simply because no one has heard from her for a day or two," he explained. "It violates freedom of movement. What I will do if you give me her description is check it against accident reports."

Anxiously, Darcy gave the information. Five feet seven, one hundred and twenty pounds, auburn hair, blue eyes, twenty-eight years old. "Wait, I have her picture in my wallet."

Thompson studied it, then handed it back. "A very attractive woman." He gave her his card and asked for hers. "We'll keep in touch."

SUSAN FRAWLEY Fox hugged five-year-old Trish and guided her reluctant feet to the waiting school bus that would take her to the afternoon session of kindergarten. Trish's woebegone face was on the verge of crumbling into tears. The baby, firmly held under Susan's other arm, reached down and pulled Trish's hair. It gave the needed excuse. Trish began to wail.

Susan bit her lip, torn between annoyance and sympathy. "He didn't hurt you and you're not staying home."

The bus driver, a matronly woman with a warm smile, said coaxingly, "Come on, Trish. You sit right up here near me."

Susan waved vigorously and sighed with relief as the bus pulled away. Shifting the baby's weight, she hurried from the corner back to their rambling brick and stucco home. Patches of snow still covered isolated sections of the lawn. The trees seemed stark and bloodless against the gray sky. In a few months the property would be lush with flowering hedges and the willows would be heavily laden with cascades of leaves. Even as a small child Susan had studied the willows for the first hint of spring.

She shoved the side door open, heated a bottle for the baby, brought him to his room, changed him, and put him down for a nap. Her quiet time had begun: the hour and a half before he woke up. She knew she should get busy. The beds weren't made. The kitchen was a mess. This morning Trish had wanted to make cupcakes, and spilled batter was still lumped on the table.

Susan glanced at the baking pan on the countertop and half-smiled. The cupcakes looked delicious. If only Trish wouldn't carry on so about kindergarten. It's almost March, Susan worried. What's it going to be like when she's in the first grade and has to be gone all day?

Doug blamed Susan for Trish's reluctance to go to school. "If

55

you'd go out more yourself, have lunch at the club, volunteer for some committees, Trish would be used to being minded by other people."

Susan put the kettle on, sponged the table, and fixed a grilled cheese and bacon sandwich. There is a God, she thought gratefully as she reveled in the blessed silence.

Over a second cup of tea, she permitted herself to face the anger that was burning inside her. Doug hadn't come home again last night. When he stayed in for late meetings he used the company suite at the Gateway Hotel near his office in the World Trade Center. He got furious when she called him there. "Damn it, Susan, unless there's an earth-shattering emergency, give me a break. I can't be called out of meetings and by the time they're over it's usually well past midnight."

Taking the tea with her, Susan got up and walked down the long hall to the master bedroom. The antique full-length standing mirror was in the right-hand corner opposite the wall of closets. Deliberately, she stood in front of it and appraised herself.

Thanks to the baby's exploring fingers, her short, curly brown hair was disheveled. She seldom bothered with makeup during the day but really didn't need it. Her skin was clear and unlined, her complexion fresh. At five feet four she could certainly afford to lose fifteen pounds. She'd been one hundred and five when she and Doug were married fourteen years ago. Sweats and sneakers had become her daily wardrobe, especially since Trish and Conner were born.

I am thirty-five years old, Susan told herself. I could lose some weight, but contrary to what my husband thinks, I am not fat. I'm not a great housekeeper, but I know I'm a good mother. A good cook, too. I don't want to spend my time outside the house when I have young children who need me. Especially since their father won't give them the time of day.

She swallowed the rest of the tea, her anger building. Tuesday night when Donny came home from the basketball game, he had been in the never-never land between ecstasy and misery. He had sunk the winning shot. "Everybody stood up and cheered for me, Mom!" Then he added, "Dad was practically the only father who wasn't there."

Susan's heart had wrenched at the pain in her son's eyes. The babysitter had canceled at the last minute, which was why she hadn't been able to be at the game either. "This is an earth-shattering event," she'd said firmly. "Let's see if we can reach Dad and tell him all about it."

Douglas Fox was not registered at the hotel. There was no conference room in use. The suite kept for personnel of Keldon Equities was not being occupied.

"Probably some dumb new operator," Susan had told Donny, trying to keep her tone even.

"Sure, that's it, Mom." But Donny wasn't fooled. At dawn, Susan had awakened to the sound of muffled sobs. She'd stood outside Donny's door, knowing that he wouldn't want her to see him crying.

My husband doesn't love me or his children, Susan told her reflected image. He lies to us. He stays in New York a couple of nights a week. He's bullied me into almost never calling him. He's made me feel like a fat, frowsy, dull, useless clod. And I'm sick of it.

She turned from the mirror and analyzed the cluttered bedroom. I could be a lot more organized, she acknowledged. I used to be. When did I give up? When did I become so damn discouraged that it wasn't worth trying to please him?

Not hard to answer. Nearly two years ago, when she was pregnant with the baby. They'd had a Swedish au pair, and Susan was sure that Doug had had an affair with her.

Why didn't I face it then? she wondered as she began to make the bed. Because I was still in love with him? Because I hated to admit my father was right about him?

She and Doug had been married a week after she was graduated from Bryn Mawr. Her father offered her a trip around the world if she'd change her mind. "Under that schoolboy charm, there's a foul-tempered sneak," he had warned her.

I went into it with my eyes open, Susan acknowledged, as she returned to the kitchen. If Dad had known the half of it, he'd have had a stroke, she thought.

There was a pile of magazines on the wall desk in the kitchen. She riffled through them until she found the one she was looking for. An issue of *People* with an article about a female private investigator in Manhattan. Professional women hired her to check out the men they were considering marrying. She also handled divorce cases.

Susan got the phone number from information and dialed it. When she reached the investigator, she was able to make an appointment for the following Monday, February 25th. "I believe my husband is seeing other women," she explained quietly. "I am thinking of divorce, and I want to know all about his activities."

When she hung up she resisted the temptation to simply sit and continue to think things through. Instead, she attacked the kitchen vigorously. Time to shape up this place. By summer, with any luck, it would be on the market.

It wouldn't be easy raising four children alone. Susan knew that Doug would pay little if any attention to the kids after the divorce. He was a splashy spender but cheap in hundreds of little ways. He'd balk at adequate child support. But it would be a lot easier to live on a tight budget than to go on with this farce.

The telephone rang. It was Doug, complaining again about the damn late meetings these last two nights. He was exhausted today and they still hadn't settled everything. He'd be home tonight, but late. Real late.

"Don't worry, dear," Susan said soothingly. "I understand perfectly."

THE COUNTRY road was narrow, winding, and dark. Charley didn't pass a single other car. His driveway was almost hidden by brush at the point where it intersected the road. A secret and quiet place, removed from curious eyes. He'd bought it six years ago. An estate sale. Estate giveaway was more like it. The place had been owned by an eccentric bachelor who as a hobby renovated it himself.

Built in 1902, the exterior was unpretentious. Inside, the renovation had consisted of turning the entire first floor into one open room, complete with a kitchen area and fireplace. Wide plank oak flooring shone with a satiny finish. The furniture was Pennsylvania Dutch, austere, handsome.

Charley had added a long upholstered couch covered in maroon tapestry, a matching chair, an area rug between the couch and fireplace.

The second floor was exactly as he'd found it. Two small rooms made into one decent-sized bedroom. Shaker furniture, a carved headboard bed and tall chest. Both made of pine. The original tub, free-standing on claw feet, had been left in the modernized bath.

Only the basement was different. The eight-foot freezer that no longer held an ounce of food, the freezer where, when necessary, he left the bodies of the girls. Here, ice maidens, they'd waited for their graves to be dug under the warming rays of the spring sun. There was a worktable in the basement as well, the worktable with a stack of ten cardboard shoe boxes. There was only one left to decorate.

A charming house nestled in the woods. He'd never brought anyone here until two years ago when he'd begun to dream about Nan. Before that, owning the house had been enough. When he wanted to escape, this was his retreat. The aloneness. The ability to pretend that he was dancing with beautiful girls. He'd play old movies on the VCR, movies in which he became Fred Astaire and danced with Ginger Rogers and Rita Hayworth and Leslie Caron. He'd follow Astaire's graceful movements until he could step with his every step, mimic the way Astaire would turn his body. Always he sensed Ginger and Rita and Leslie and Fred's other partners in his arms, their eyes worshipful, loving the music, loving the dance.

Then one day, two years ago, it was over. In the middle of the dance, Ginger drifted away and Nan was in Charley's arms again. Just like the moments after he killed her, waltzing on the jogging path, her light, svelte body so easy to hold, her head lolling on his shoulder.

When that memory came back, he'd run to the basement and taken the mates of the sequined dancing slipper and the Nike that he'd left on her feet from the shoe box and cradled them in his arms while he swayed to the music on the stereo. It was like being with Nan again, and he'd known what he had to do.

First he'd set up a hidden video camera so he could relive every single moment of what was to happen. Then he'd begun to bring the girls here one by one. Erin was the eighth to die here. But Erin would not join the others in the wooded fields that surrounded the house. Tonight he would move Erin's body. He had decided exactly where he would leave her.

The station wagon moved silently down the driveway, around to the back of the house. He stopped at the metal doors that led to the basement.

Charley's breath began to come in short, excited gasps. He reached for the handle to open the back door of the wagon, then stood irresolutely. Every instinct warned him not to delay. He must lift Erin's body from the freezer, carry it to the car, drive back to the city, leave it on the abandoned Fifty-sixth Street dock bordering the West Side Highway. But the thought of watching the video of Erin, of dancing with her just one more time, was irresistible.

Charley hurried around the house to the front door, let himself in, snapped on the light, and without bothering to remove his overcoat ran across the room to the VCR. Erin's tape was on top of the others on the cabinet. He popped it in and sat back on the couch, smiling in anticipation.

The tape began to play.

Erin, so pretty, smiling, coming in the door, exclaiming with delight over the house. "I envy you this haven." He fixing a drink for them. She sitting curled on the couch. He sitting across from her in the easy chair, getting up and setting a match to the kindling in the fireplace.

"Don't bother to light a fire," she'd told him. "I really must get back."

"Even for half an hour it's worth it," he'd assured her. Then he'd turned on the stereo, muted, soft, and pleasant, the songs of the forties. "Our next date is going to be at the Rainbow Room," he said. "You enjoy dancing as much as I do."

Erin had laughed. The lamp beside her accentuated the glints of red in her auburn hair. "As I wrote when I answered your ad, I love to dance."

He'd stood up, held out his arms. "How about now?" Then, as though struck by a thought, said, "Wait a minute. Let's do this right. What shoe size are you? Seven? Seven and a half? Eight?"

"Seven and a half narrow."

"Perfect. Believe it or not, I have a pair of evening slippers that should fit you. My sister asked me to pick up a pair she had ordered in that size. Like the good big brother I did as I was told. Then she phoned and told me to take them back. She'd found a pair she liked better."

Erin had laughed with him. "Just like a kid sister."

"I'm not going to be bothered running around returning them." *The camera stayed on her, catching her smiling, content expression as she looked around the room.*

He'd gone up to the bedroom, opened the closet where boxes of new evening shoes were lined up on the shelf. He'd bought the ones he'd chosen for her in a variety of sizes. Pink and silver. Open toes and backs. Heels as narrow as stilettos. A gossamer ankle strap. He reached for the pair that were seven and a half narrow and carried them down, still wrapped in tissue.

"Try these on, Erin."

Even then, she wasn't suspicious. "They're lovely."

He'd knelt and slipped off her ankle-top leather boots, his hands impersonal. She'd said, "Oh, really, I don't think . . ." Ignoring her protest, he'd fastened the slippers on her feet.

"Will you promise to wear these next Saturday when we go to the Rainbow Room?"

She had lifted her right foot a few inches off the carpet and smiled at the sheer beauty of the shoes. "I can't accept these as a gift . . ."

"Please." He had smiled up at her.

"Well, let me buy them from you. The funny thing is, they'd go perfectly with a new dress I've only worn once."

It had been on the tip of his tongue to say, "I saw you in that dress." Instead, he'd murmured, "We'll talk about payment later." Then he'd put his hand on her ankle, letting it linger just enough to begin to alert her. He'd stood up, gone over to the stereo. The cassette he had specially prepared was already in place. "Till There Was You" was the first song. The Tommy Dorsey orchestra began to play and the unforgettable voice of the young Frank Sinatra filled the room.

He walked back to the couch and reached for Erin's hands. "Let's practice."

The look he'd been waiting for came into Erin's eyes. That tiny first flicker of awareness that something wasn't quite right. She recognized the subtle change in his tone and manner.

Erin was like the others. They all reacted the same way. Speaking too quickly, nervously. "I think I really had better start back. I have an early appointment tomorrow morning."

"Just one dance."

"All right." Her tone had been reluctant.

When they began to dance, she seemed to relax. All the girls had been good dancers, but Erin was perfection. He'd felt disloyal thinking she might even be better than Nan. She was weightless in his arms. She was grace. But when the last notes of "Till There Was You" faded away, she stepped back. "Time to go."

Then when he said, "You're not going anywhere," Erin began to run. Like the others, she slipped and slid on the floor he had polished so lovingly. The dancing slippers became her enemy as she scurried to escape him, raced toward the door to find it bolted, pushed the panic button on the alarm system to learn it was a farce. It emitted a hollow maniacal laugh when touched, a little extra bit of irony that set most of them sobbing as he reached for their throats.

Erin had been particularly satisfying. At the end she seemed to know it was useless to plead and in an animal burst of strength she fought him, clawing at the hands that gripped her slender neck. It was only when he twisted that heavy gold necklace around her throat and she began to lose consciousness that she had whispered, "Oh God, please help me, oh Daddy. . . ."

When she was dead, he danced with her again. No resistance now in that lovely body. She was his Ginger, his Rita, his Leslie, his Nan, and all the others. When the music stopped, he took off her left slipper and replaced it with her boot.

The video ended as he carried her body down to the basement, where he laid her in the freezer and placed the other slipper and boot in the waiting shoe box.

Charley got up from the sofa and sighed. He rewound the videotape, removed it, and turned off the VCR. The cassette tape he had prepared for Erin was still in the stereo. He pressed "Play."

As the music filled the room, Charley hurried downstairs and opened the freezer. Lovely, lovely, he sighed as he saw the still face, the bluish veins that showed in the ice-blue skin. Tenderly, he reached for her.

It was the first time he'd danced with one of the girls whose body he had frozen. It was a different but thrilling experience. Erin's limbs weren't pliant now. Her back would not bend in a dip. Her cheek pressed against his neck, his chin rested on the auburn hair. That hair once so soft, now beaded with frost. Minutes passed. Finally, as the third song was ending, he twirled her around one last time, then, satisfied, glided to a halt and bowed.

It had all begun with Nan fifteen years ago on March thirteenth, he thought. He kissed Erin's lips just the way he had kissed Nan's. March thirteenth was three weeks away. By then he would have brought Darcy here and it would be over.

He realized that Erin's blouse was beginning to feel damp. He must get her to the city. Holding her in one arm, he half-dragged her to the stereo.

As he turned off the dials, Charley did not notice that an onyx ring with a gold *E* slipped from Erin's frozen finger. Neither did he hear the faint ping as it landed on the floor and lay almost hidden in the fringe on the rug.

V
FRIDAY
February 22

DARCY STARED unseeingly at the blueprint of the apartment she was decorating. The owner was spending a year in Europe and was specific about her needs. "I want to rent the place furnished, but I'm putting my own things in storage. I don't want some klutz burning a hole in my carpets or upholstery. Fix the place up tastefully but cheaply. I hear you're a genius at that."

Yesterday after she'd left the police station, Darcy had forced herself to follow up a "Moving/Everything Must Go" sale in Old Tappan, New Jersey. She'd hit a bonanza of good furniture that was practically a giveaway. Some of it would exactly suit this apartment; the rest she'd store for future jobs.

She picked up her pen and sketching pad. The sectional should be on the long wall, arcing to face the windows. The . . . She laid down the pen and put her face in her hands. I have got to get this job finished. I've got to concentrate, she thought desperately.

A memory came unbidden. The week of finals of their sophomore year. She and Erin holing up in their room, cracking the books. The music of Bruce Springsteen coming from the stereo in the next room, echoing through the walls, tempting them to join the celebrants whose exams were over. Erin lamenting, "Darce, when Bruce is playing, I can't concentrate."

"You've got to. Maybe I can buy us earplugs."

Erin, a mischievous look on her face: "I've got a better idea." After dinner they'd gone to the library. When it was closing, they hid in stalls in the bathroom until the security guards left. They'd settled themselves on the seventh floor at the desks by the elevator, where fluorescent lights burned all night, and studied in perfect peace, letting themselves out through a window at dawn.

Darcy bit her lip, realizing she was on the verge of tears again. Impatiently, she dabbed at her eyes, reached for the phone, and called Nona. "I tried you last night, but you were out." She told her about going to Erin's apartment, about Jay Stratton, about finding the Bertolini necklace, about the missing diamonds.

"Stratton's going to wait a few days to see if Erin shows up before he makes a report to the insurance company. The police can't accept a missing-person report because it interferes with Erin's right to freedom of movement."

"That's nonsense," Nona said flatly.

"Of course it's nonsense. Nona, Erin was meeting someone Tuesday night. She'd answered his ad. That's what worries me. Do you think you should call that FBI agent who wrote to you and talk to him?"

A few minutes later, Bev poked her head in Darcy's office. "I wouldn't bother you, but it's Nona." There was sympathetic understanding in her face. Darcy had told her about Erin's disappearance.

Nona was brief. "I left a message for the FBI guy to call. I'll get back to you when he does."

"If he wants to meet you, I'd like to be there." When Darcy hung up, she looked across the room at the coffee brewer on a side table near the window. She made a new pot, deliberately heaping a generous amount of ground coffee into the filter.

Erin had brought along a thermos of strong, black coffee that night they had hidden in the library. "This makes the gray cells stand at attention," she had announced after the second cup.

Now, after the second cup, Darcy was finally able to fully concentrate on the apartment plan. You're always right, Erin-go-bragh, she thought as she reached for her sketchpad.

*V*INCE D'AMBROSIO returned to his twenty-eighth-floor office from the conference room in the FBI headquarters on Federal Plaza. He was tall and trim, and no one observing him would doubt that after twenty-five years he still held the record for the mile run at his high school alma mater, St. Joe's, in Montvale, New Jersey.

His reddish-brown hair was cut short. His warm brown eyes were wide-set. His thin face broke easily into a smile. People instinctively liked and trusted Vince D'Ambrosio.

Vince had served as a criminal investigative officer in Vietnam, completed his master's degree in psychology on his return, then entered the Bureau. Ten years ago, at the FBI training academy on the Quantico Marine Base near Washington, D.C., he'd helped set up the Violent Criminal Apprehension Program. VICAP, as it was called, was a computerized national master file with a particular emphasis on serial killers.

Vince had just conducted an update session on VICAP for detectives from the New York area who had taken the VICAP course at Quantico. The purpose of today's meeting had been to alert them that the computer which tracked seemingly unrelated crimes had sent out a warning signal. There was a possible serial killer loose in Manhattan.

It was the third time in as many weeks Vince had delivered the same sobering news: "As you all are aware, VICAP is able to establish patterns in what heretofore have been considered isolated cases. The VICAP analysts and investigators have recently alerted us to a possible connection between six young women who have vanished in the past two years.

"All of them had apartments in New York. No one is sure whether they were actually *in* New York when they disappeared. They're all still officially listed as missing persons. We now believe that is a mistake. Foul play is a probability.

"The similarities between these women are striking. They are all slender and very attractive. They range in age from twenty-two to thirty-four. All are upscale in background and education. Outgoing. Extroverted. Finally, every one of them had begun to regularly answer personal ads. I am convinced we have another personal-ad serial killer out there, and a damn clever one.

"If we are right, the profile of the subject is the following: well-educated; sophisticated; late twenties to early forties; physically attractive. These women wouldn't have been interested in a diamond-in-the-rough. He may never have been arrested for a violent crime but could have a juvenile history of being a Peeping Tom, maybe stealing women's personal items at school. His hobby could be photography."

The detectives had left, all promising to be on the lookout for any reports of missing young women who fit that category. Dean Thompson, the detective from the Sixth Precinct, lingered behind the others. Vince and he had met in Vietnam and had remained friends over the years.

"Vince, a young woman came in yesterday, wanting to file a missing-person report on a friend of hers, Erin Kelley, who hasn't been seen since Tuesday night. She's a young woman who fits the profile you've described. *And* she was answering a personal ad. I'll stay on top of it."

"Keep me posted."

Now, as Vince flipped through the messages on his desk, he nodded with satisfaction when he saw that Nona Roberts had called him. He dialed her, gave his name to her secretary, and was immediately put through.

He frowned as Nona Roberts's troubled voice explained, "Erin Kelley, a young woman I talked into answering personal ads for my documentary, has been missing since Tuesday night. There is no way Erin would have dropped out of sight unless she'd been in an accident, or worse. I'd stake my life on that."

Vince looked at his list of appointments. He had meetings in the building the rest of the morning. He was due at the Mayor's office at one-thirty. Nothing he could skip. "Would three o'clock work out for you?" he asked Roberts. After he replaced the receiver, he said aloud, "Another one."

A MOMENT AFTER she telephoned Darcy about the three o'clock appointment with Vincent D'Ambrosio, Nona received an unexpected visit from Austin Hamilton, CEO and sole owner of Hudson Cable Network.

Hamilton had an icy, sarcastic manner which his staff regarded with intense apprehension. Nona had managed to talk Hamilton into the personal-ads documentary despite the fact that his initial reaction had been: "Who cares about a bunch of losers meeting other losers?"

She had secured his reluctant go-ahead by showing him the pages upon pages of personal ads in magazines and newspapers. "It's the social phenomenon of our society," she'd argued. "These ads aren't cheap to place. It's the old story. Boy wants to meet girl. Aging executive wants to meet wealthy divorcée. The point is, does Prince Charming find Sleeping Beauty? Or are these ads a colossal and even humiliating waste of time?"

Hamilton had grudgingly agreed that there might be a story there. "In my day," he'd pointed out, "you met people socially at prep school and college and at coming-out parties. You acquired a select group of friends and through them met other social equals."

Hamilton was a sixty-year-old professional preppie, and the consummate snob. He had, however, singlehandedly built Hudson Cable and his innovative programming was a serious challenge to the three big networks.

When he stopped in Nona's office his mood was frosty. Even though he was as always impeccably dressed, Nona decided that he still managed to remain remarkably unattractive. His Savile Row suit did not quite conceal his narrow shoulders and thickening waist. His sparse hair was tinted a silvery blond shade that did not succeed in looking natural. His narrow lips, which were capable of selectively breaking into a warm smile, were set in an almost invisible line. His pale blue eyes were chilly.

He got right to the point. "Nona, I'm damn sick of this project of yours. I don't think there's an unattached person in this building who isn't placing or answering personal ads and wasting time comparing results ad nauseam. Either wrap this project up fast or forget it."

There was a time to placate Hamilton; a time to intrigue him. Nona chose the second option. "I had no idea how explosive this personal-ads business might be." She fished on her desk for the letter from Vincent D'Ambrosio and handed it to Hamilton. His eyebrows went up as he read it.

"He's coming here at three o'clock." Nona swallowed. "As you can see, he points out that there's a dark side to these ads. A good friend of mine, Erin Kelley, answered one on Tuesday night. She's missing."

Hamilton's instinct for news overcame his petulance. "Do you think there's a connection?"

Nona turned her head, abstractly noted that the plant Darcy had watered two days ago was beginning to droop again. "I hope not. I don't know."

"Talk to me after you meet with this guy."

Disgusted, Nona realized Hamilton was salivating over the potential media value of Erin's disappearance. With a visible effort to sound sympathetic, he said, "Your friend's probably fine. Don't worry."

When he was gone, Nona's secretary, Connie Frender, poked her head in the door. "Are you still alive?"

"Barely." Nona tried to smile. Had she ever been twenty-one? she wondered. Connie was the black counterpart of Joan Nye, the Toodle-oo Club president. Young, pretty, bright, smart. Matt's new wife was now twenty-two. And I'll be forty-one, Nona thought. With neither chick nor child. Lovely thought.

"This single black female wishes to meet anyone who breathes," Connie laughed. "I've got a whole new batch of responses from some of the box numbers you wrote to. Ready to look at them?"

"Sure."

"Want some more coffee? After Awesome Austin, you probably need it."

This time Nona knew her smile was almost maternal. Connie did not seem to know that offering the boss a cup of coffee was frowned upon by some feminists. "I'd love one."

She returned with it five minutes later. "Nona, Matt's on the phone. I told him you were in conference and he said it was vital that he talk to you."

"I'm sure it is." Nona waited for the door to close and took a swig of coffee before she reached for the phone. Matthew, she thought. Meaning of the name? Gift of God. For sure. "Hi, Matt. How are you and the prom queen?"

"Nona, is it possible for you to stop being nasty?" Had he always sounded this querulous?

"No, it really isn't." Damn, Nona thought. After nearly two years, it still hurts to talk with him.

"Nona, I was wondering. Why don't you buy me out of the house? Jeanie doesn't like the Hamptons. The market's still lousy so I'll give you a real break on the price. You know you can always borrow from your folks."

Matty the moocher, Nona thought. Marriage to the child-bride had reduced Matt to this. "I don't want the house," she said quietly. "I'm going to buy my own place when we unload this one."

"Nona, you love that place. You're just doing this to punish me."

"See you." Nona broke the connection. You're wrong, Matt, she thought. I loved the house because we bought it together and cooked lobsters to celebrate our first night in it and every year we did something else to make it even greater. Now I want to start absolutely fresh. No memories.

She began to go through the new batch of letters. She'd sent out over a hundred to people who had placed recent ads requesting them to share their experiences. She'd also persuaded the cable anchorman, Gary Finch, to invite people to write in about the results of personal ads they'd either placed or answered and the reason they no longer would do it.

The result of the on-air announcement was proving to be a bonanza. A relatively small number wrote ecstatically about meeting "the most wonderful person in the world and now we're engaged" . . . "living together" . . . "married."

Many others expressed disappointment. "He said he was an entrepreneur. Meaning he's broke. Tried to borrow money the first time I met him." From Bashful Single White Male: "She criticized me all through dinner. Said I had a nerve putting in the ad that I was attractive. Boy, did she make me feel lousy." "I started getting obscene phone calls in the middle of the night." "When I got back home from work I found him sitting on my doorstep sniffing coke."

Several letters were unsigned. "I don't want you to know who I am, but I'm sure one of the men I met through a personal column is the man who burglarized my house." "I brought a very attractive fortyish executive home and found him trying to kiss my seventeen-year-old daughter."

Nona felt heartsick at the final letter in the pile. It was from a woman in Lancaster, Pennsylvania. "My twenty-two-year-old daughter, an actress, disappeared almost two years ago. When she did not return our calls, we went to her New York apartment. It was obvious that she had not been there in days. She was answering personal ads. We are frantic. There has been absolutely no trace of her."

Oh God, Nona thought, oh God. Please let Erin be all right. Her hands trembling, she began to sort through the letters, adding the most interesting to one of three files: *Happy About Ads. Disappointed. Serious Problem.* The last letter she held out to show Agent D'Ambrosio.

At one o'clock Connie brought her in a ham and cheese sandwich. "Nothing like a little cholesterol," Nona commented.

"There's no point in ordering tuna for you when you never eat it," Connie commented.

By two, Nona had dictated letters to potential guests. She made a note to herself to invite a psychiatrist or psychologist to be on the program. I ought to have someone who can do a wrap-up analysis of the whole personal-ads scene, she decided.

Vincent D'Ambrosio arrived at quarter of three. "He knows he's early," Connie told Nona, "and doesn't mind waiting."

"No, that's fine. Ask him to come in."

In less than one minute, Vince D'Ambrosio forgot the remarkable discomfort of the green love seat in Nona Roberts's office. He considered himself a good judge of people and liked Nona immediately. Her manner was straightforward, pleasant. He liked her looks. Not pretty but attractive, especially those large reflective brown eyes. She wore little if any makeup. He also liked the touches of gray in her dark blond hair. Alice, his ex-wife, was also blond but her sunny tresses were the result of regular appointments at Vidal Sassoon. Well, at least now she was married to a guy who could afford them.

It was obvious that Roberts was desperately worried. "Your letter coincides with the most recent responses I've been receiving," she told him. "People writing about meeting thieves, moochers, addicts, lechers, perverts. And now . . ." She bit her lip. "And now, someone who never would have dreamed of answering a personal ad and did it as a favor to me, is missing."

"Tell me about her."

Nona was fleetingly grateful that Vince D'Ambrosio did not waste time with empty reassurances. "Erin is twenty-seven or -eight. We met six months ago in our health club. She, Darcy Scott, and I were in the same dance classes and became friendly. Darcy will be here in a few minutes." She picked up the letter from the woman in Lancaster and handed it to Vince. "This just arrived."

Vince read it quickly and whistled silently. "Somebody didn't file a report with us. This girl isn't on our list. She brings the count up to seven missing."

In the cab on the way to Nona's office, Darcy thought of the time she and Erin had gone skiing at Stowe their senior year of college.

The slopes had been icy, and most people had headed for the lodge early. At her urging, she and Erin went for one last run. Erin hit a patch of ice and fell, her leg snapping under her.

When the patrol came with the meat wagon for Erin, Darcy skied beside her, then accompanied her in the ambulance. She remembered Erin's ashen face, Erin trying to joke. "Hope this doesn't affect my dancing. I plan to be queen of the stardust ballroom."

"You will be."

At the hospital, when the X-rays were developed, the surgeon raised his eyebrows. "You really did a job on yourself, but we'll fix you up." He'd smiled at Darcy. "Don't look so worried. She'll be fine."

"I'm not just worried. I feel so damn guilty," she'd told the doctor. "Erin didn't want to make the last run."

Now as she entered Nona's office and was introduced to Agent D'Ambrosio, Darcy realized she was experiencing exactly the same reaction. The same relief that somebody was in charge, the same guilt that she had urged Erin to answer the ads with her.

"Nona only asked if we wanted to *try* them. I was the one who pushed Erin to do it," she told D'Ambrosio. He took notes as she talked about the phone call on Tuesday, about Erin's saying she was meeting someone named Charles North in a pub near Washington Square. She noticed the change in D'Ambrosio's manner when she spoke about opening the safe, about giving the Bertolini necklace to Jay Stratton, about Stratton's claim that there were diamonds missing.

He asked her about Erin's family.

Darcy stared at her hands.

Remember arriving at Mount Holyoke first day of freshman year? Erin already there, her suitcases piled neatly in the corner. They'd sized each other up, both liked what they saw. Erin's eyes widening as she recognized Mother and Dad but not losing her composure.

"When Darcy wrote to me this summer introducing herself, I

76

didn't realize that her parents were Barbara Thorne and Robert Scott," she'd said. "I don't think I ever missed one of your films." Then she added, "Darcy, I didn't want to settle in until you were here. I thought you might have a preference about which closet or bed you wanted."

Remember the look Mother and Dad exchanged. They were thinking, what a nice girl Erin is. They asked her to join us for dinner.

Erin had come to college alone. Her father was an invalid, she explained. We wondered why she never even mentioned her mother. Later she told me that when she was six, her father developed multiple sclerosis and needed a wheelchair. Her mother took off when she was seven. "I didn't bargain for this," she'd said. "Erin, you can come with me if you want."

"I can't leave Daddy all alone. He needs me."

Over the years, Erin completely lost touch with her mother. "The last I heard she was living with some guy who owned a charter sailboat in the Caribbean." She was at Mount Holyoke on a scholarship. "As Daddy says, being immobilized gives you plenty of time to help your kid with her homework. If you can't pay for college, at least you can help her get a free ride." Oh Erin, where are you? What's happened to you?

Darcy realized that D'Ambrosio was waiting for her to answer his question. "Her father's been in a nursing home in Massachusetts for the last few years," she said. "He's not aware of much anymore. I guess I'm the closest thing Erin has to a relative besides him."

Vince saw the pain in Darcy's eyes. "In my business I've observed that having one good friend can beat having a passel of relatives."

Darcy managed a smile. "Erin's favorite quote is from Aristotle. 'What is a friend? A single soul dwelling in two bodies.' "

Nona got up, stood beside Darcy's chair, and put her hands reassuringly on her shoulders. She looked squarely at D'Ambrosio. "What can we do to help find Erin?"

A LONG TIME ago, Petey Potters had been a construction worker. *"Big jobs,"* as he liked to boast to anyone whose ear he could get. "World Trade Center. I usta be out on one of them girders. Tell ye, the wind wuz whippin' so ye wondered if ye were gonna stay up there." He'd laugh, a wheezy chortle. "Some view, lemme tell ye, some view."

But at night the thought of going back up on the girder began to get to Petey. A coupla shots of rye, a coupla beer chasers, and the warmth would flow into the pit of his stomach and spread through his body.

"You're just like your father," his wife began to scream at him. "A no-good drunk."

Petey never got insulted. He understood. He'd start to laugh when his wife ranted about Pop. Pop had been some card. He'd disappear for weeks at a time, dry out in a flophouse on the Bowery, and then come back home. "When I'm hungry, it's no problem," he'd confided to eight-year-old Petey. I go to the Salvation Army shelter, take a dive, get a meal, a bath, a bed. Never fails."

"What's 'take a dive' mean?" Petey had asked.

"When you go to the shelter, they tell you about God and forgiveness and we're all brothers and we want to be saved. Then they ask anyone who believes in the good book to come forward and acknowledge his Maker. So you get religion. You run up, fall on your knees, and shout something about being saved. That's taking a dive."

Nearly forty years later the memory still tickled the homeless derelict Petey Potters. He'd created his own shelter, a combination of wood and tin and old rags that he'd piled together into a tentlike structure against the sagging, shuttered terminal on the abandoned West Fifty-sixth Street pier.

Petey's needs were simple. Wine. Butts. A little food. Litter baskets were a constant supply of cans and bottles that could be redeemed for the deposits. When he was ambitious, Petey took a squeegee and a bottle of water and stood at the Fifty-sixth Street exit of the West Side Highway. No drivers wanted their car windows smeared by his efforts, but most people were afraid to wave him away. Only last week he'd heard an old bat explode to the driver of a Mercedes, "Jane, why do you allow yourself to be held up like this?"

Petey had loved the answer. "Because, Mother, I don't want to have the side of this car scratched if I refuse."

Petey didn't scratch anything when he was rejected. He just went on to the next car, armed with his squirt bottle, a coaxing smile on his face.

Yesterday had been one of the good days. Just enough snow so that the highway became messy and windshields got sprayed with dirty slush from the tires of cars ahead of them. Few people had refused Petey's ministrations at the exit ramp. He'd made eighteen bucks, enough for a hero sandwich, butts, and three bottles of dago red.

Last night he'd settled inside his tent, wrapped in the old army blanket the Armenian church on Second Avenue had given him, a ski cap keeping his head warm, a tattered greatcoat, its moth-eaten fur collar cozy around his neck. He'd finished the hero with the first bottle of wine, then settled down to puffing and sipping, content and warm in an inebriated haze. Pop taking a dive. Mom coming back to the apartment on Tremont Avenue, worn out from scrubbing other people's houses. Birdie, his wife. *Harpie,* not Birdie. That's what they shoulda called her.

Petey shook with mirth at the play on words. Wonder where she was now. How about the kid? Nice kid.

Petey wasn't sure when he heard the car pull up. He tried to force himself to wakefulness, instinctively wanting to protect his territory. It better not be cops trying to knock over his place. Nah.

Cops didn't bother with this kind of shack in the middle of the night.

Maybe it was a druggie. Petey gripped the neck of an empty wine bottle. Better not try to come in here. But nobody came. After a few minutes he heard the car start up again; he peered out cautiously. Taillights were disappearing onto the deserted West Side Highway. Maybe somebody had to take a leak, Petey decided as he reached for the last bottle.

It was late afternoon when Petey opened his eyes again. His head had that empty, throbbing feeling. His gut burned. His mouth felt like the bottom of a birdcage. He pulled himself up. The three empty bottles offered no consolation. He found twenty cents in the pockets of the greatcoat. I'm hungry, he whined silently. Poking his head from behind the piece of tin sheeting that served as door for his shelter, he decided that it must be late afternoon. There were long shadows on the dock. His eyes moved to focus on something that was clearly not a shadow. Petey squinted, muttered a profanity under his breath, and dragged himself to his feet.

His legs were stiff and his gait clumsy as he made his unsteady way to whatever was lying on the pier.

It was a slim woman. Young. Red hair curling around her face. Petey was sure she was dead. A necklace was twisted into her throat. She was wearing a blouse and slacks. Her shoes didn't match.

The necklace sparkled in the fading light. Gold. Real gold. Petey licked his lips nervously. Bracing himself for the shock of touching the dead girl he reached around the back of her neck for the clasp of the elaborate necklace. His fingers fumbled. Thick and unsteady, they could not get the clasp to release. Christ, she felt cold.

He didn't want to break anything. Was the necklace long enough to pull over her head? Trying to ignore the bruised, blue-veined throat, he tugged at the heavy chain.

Grimy fingerprints streaked Erin's face as Petey freed the necklace and slipped it in his pocket. The earrings. They were good, too.

From a distance, Petey heard the whine of a police siren. Like a startled rabbit he jumped up, forgetting the earrings. This was no place for him. He'd have to take his stuff, get himself a new shelter. When the body was found, just his being around here would be enough for the cops.

An awareness of his potential danger sobered Petey. On stumbling feet he rushed back to the shelter. Everything he owned could be tied in the army blanket. His pillow. A couple pairs of socks, some underwear. A flannel shirt. A dish and spoon and cup. Matches. Butts. Old newspapers for cold nights.

Fifteen minutes later, Petey had vanished into the world of the homeless. Panhandling on Seventh Avenue netted four dollars and thirty-two cents. He used it to buy wine and a pretzel. There was a young fellow on Fifty-seventh Street who sold hot jewelry. He gave Petey twenty-five dollars for the necklace. "This is good, man. Try to get more like this."

At ten o'clock Petey was asleep on a subway grating that radiated warm, dank air. At eleven, he was being shaken awake. A not-unkind voice said, "Come on, pal. It's going to be real cold tonight. We're going to take you to a place where you can have a decent bed and a good meal."

*A*T QUARTER OF SIX on Friday evening, Wanda Libbey, snugly secure in her new BMW, was inching her way along the West Side Highway. Complacent in the excellent shopping she'd done on Fifth Avenue, Wanda was still annoyed at herself that she'd gotten such a late start back to Tarrytown. The Friday night rush hour was the worst of the week, a time when many quit New York for their country homes. She'd never want to live in New York again. Too dirty. Too dangerous.

Wanda glanced at the Valentino purse on the passenger seat. When she'd parked in the Kinney lot this morning, she'd tucked it firmly under her arm and kept it there all day. She wasn't fool enough to have it dangling from her arm where someone might grab it.

Another damn traffic light. Oh well, in a few blocks she'd be on the ramp and past this miserable section of so-called highway.

A tap on the window made Wanda look swiftly to the right. A bearded face grinned in at her. A rag began to make swishing movements on the windshield.

Wanda's lips snapped into a rigid line. Damn. She shook her head vigorously. No. No.

The man ignored her.

I am not going to be held up by these people, Wanda fumed, jamming her finger on the button that opened the passenger window. "I don't want—" She began to shriek. The rag was thrown against the windshield. The bottle of fluid pinged off the hood. A hand reached into the car. She watched her purse disappear.

A squad car was heading west on Fifty-fifth Street. The driver suddenly straightened up. "What's that?" On the approach to the highway he could see traffic stopped, people getting out of cars. "Let's go." Siren blaring, lights flashing, the squad car lurched forward, skillfully weaving through the maze of moving traffic and double-parked vehicles.

Still screaming with rage and frustration, Wanda pointed to the pier a block away. "My purse. He ran there."

"Let's go." The squad car turned left, then made a sharp right as they roared onto the pier. The cop in the passenger seat turned on the spotlight, revealing the shack Petey had abandoned. "I'll check inside." Then he snapped, "Hey, over there. Past the terminal. What's that?"

The body of Erin Kelley, glistening with sleet, the silvery slipper flashing under the powerful beam from the spotlight, had been discovered again.

*D*ARCY LEFT Nona's office with Vince D'Ambrosio. They took a cab to her apartment and she gave him Erin's daily reminder and her personal-columns file. Vince studied them carefully. "Not much here," he commented. "We'll find out who placed the ads she circled. With any luck, Charles North is one of them."

"Erin isn't the greatest record keeper," Darcy said. "I could go back to her apartment and look through her desk again. It's possible I missed something."

"That could help. But don't worry. If North's a corporate lawyer from Philadelphia, it'll be easy to trace him." Vince stood up. "I'll get on this right away."

"And I'm going back to her apartment now. I'll leave with you." Darcy hesitated. The light on the answering machine was blinking. "Can you wait just a minute till I check the messages?" Attempting a smile she said, "There's always the chance Erin left one."

There were two messages. Both were about personal ads. One

was genial. "Hi, Darcy. Trying you again. Enjoyed your note. Hope we can get together sometime. I'm Box 4358. David Weld, 555-4890."

The other was sharply different. "Hey, Darcy, why do you waste *your* time answering ads and *my* time trying to reach you. This is the fourth time I've called. I don't like to leave messages, but here's this one. Drop dead."

Vince shook his head. "That guy has a short leash."

"I didn't leave the answering machine on while I was away," Darcy said. "I suppose if anyone tried to reach me in response to the few letters I sent myself, they probably gave up. Erin started answering ads in my name about two weeks ago. Those are the first calls I've gotten."

Gus Boxer was surprised and not especially pleased to respond to the buzzer and find the same young woman who had wasted so much of his time yesterday. He was prepared to absolutely refuse to allow her to enter Erin Kelley's apartment again but did not get the chance. "We've reported Erin's disappearance to the FBI," Darcy told him. "The agent in charge has asked me to go through her desk."

The FBI. Gus felt a nervous tremor go through his body. But that was so long ago. He had nothing to worry about. A couple of people had left their names recently just in case a vacancy came up. One good-looking gal said it would be worth a thousand bucks under the table if he put her at the top of the list. So if Kelley's friend was able to find out something happened to her, it would mean a nice piece of change in his pocket.

"I'm just as worried about that girl as you are," he whined, the unfamiliar sympathetic tone catching in his vocal cords. "Come on up."

In the apartment, Darcy immediately turned on all the lights against the impending dusk. Yesterday, the place had seemed cheerful enough. Today, Erin's continued absence was leaving its mark. A faint edging of soot was visible on the windowsill. The long worktable needed dusting. The framed posters that always gave brightness and color to the room seemed to mock her.

The Picasso from Geneva. Erin had bought it on her one school trip abroad. "I love this even though it isn't my favorite theme," she'd commented. It depicted a mother and child.

There were no further messages on Erin's machine. A search of the desk revealed nothing significant. There was a new cassette for the answering machine in the drawer. Possibly Agent D'Ambrosio would want the old tape, the one that contained messages. Darcy switched the two.

The nursing home. This was around the time Erin usually called it. Darcy looked up the number and dialed. The head nurse on Billy Kelley's floor came to the phone. "I spoke to Erin as usual on Tuesday night around five. I told her I think her father is quite near the end. She said she would spend the weekend in Wellesley." Then she added, "I understand she's missing. We're all praying that she's all right."

There's nothing more I can do here, Darcy thought, and suddenly felt an overwhelming desire to go home.

It was quarter of six when she got back to her own place. A hot shower was called for, she decided, and a hot toddy.

At ten past six, wrapped in her favorite flannel robe, steam rising from the toddy, she settled on the couch and pushed the remote control for the television.

A story was breaking. John Miller, the investigative crime reporter for Channel 4, was standing at the entrance to a West Side pier. Behind him in a roped-off area a dozen policemen were silhouetted against the cold waters of the Hudson. Darcy turned up the volume.

". . . body of an unidentified young woman was just discovered on this abandoned Fifty-sixth Street pier. She appears to have been the victim of strangulation. The woman is slim, in her mid-twenties with auburn hair. She is wearing slacks and a multicolored blouse. A bizarre twist is that she is wearing mismatched shoes, a brown leather ankle boot on her left foot, an evening slipper on her right."

Darcy stared at the television. Auburn hair. Mid-twenties. Multicolored blouse. She'd given Erin a multicolored blouse for Christmas. Erin had been delighted. "It has all the colors of Joseph's coat," she'd said. "I love it."

Auburn. Slim. Joseph's coat.

The biblical Joseph's coat had been stained in blood when his treacherous brothers showed it to their father as proof of his death.

Somehow, Darcy managed to find in her purse the card Agent D'Ambrosio had given her.

Vince was just about to leave his office. He was meeting his fifteen-year-old son Hank at Madison Square Garden. They were going to have a quick dinner, then take in a Rangers game. As he listened to Darcy he realized that he had been expecting this call; he just hadn't thought it would come quite this soon.

"It doesn't sound good," he told her. "I'll phone the precinct where the body was found. Sit tight. I'll get back to you."

When he hung up, he called Hudson Cable. Nona was still in her office. "I'll get right over to be with Darcy," she said.

"She'll be asked if she can identify the body," Vince warned.

He called the Midtown North precinct and was put through to the head of the homicide squad. The body had not yet been removed from the crime scene. When it reached the morgue, they'd send a squad car for Miss Scott. Vince explained his interest in the case. "We'd be grateful for your assistance," he was told. "Unless this turns out to be an open-and-shut case, we'd like to have it run through VICAP."

Vince called Darcy back, told her about the squad car and that Nona was on the way. She thanked him, her tone flat and unemotional.

*C*HRIS SHERIDAN left the gallery at ten past five and with long strides walked the fourteen blocks from Seventy-eighth and Madison to Sixty-fifth and Fifth. It had been a busy and highly successful week and he savored the luxurious freedom of knowing that he had the whole weekend to himself. Not a single plan.

His tenth-floor apartment faced Central Park. "Directly across from the zoo," as he told his friends. Eclectic in taste, he'd mixed antique tables, lamps, and carpets with long, comfortable upholstered couches that he'd covered in a heraldic pattern, copied from a medieval tapestry. The paintings were English landscapes. Nineteenth-century hunting prints and a silk-on-silk Tree of Life wall hanging complemented the Chippendale table and side chairs in the dining area.

It was a comfortable, inviting room, a room which in the past eight years many young women had eyed with hope.

Chris went into the bedroom, changed into a long-sleeved sport shirt and chinos. A very dry martini, he decided. Maybe later he'd go out for a plate of pasta. Drink in hand, he switched on the six o'clock news and saw the same broadcast Darcy was watching.

His compassion for the dead girl and identification with the grief her family would experience was instantly replaced by horror. Strangled! A dancing shoe on one foot! "Oh, God," Chris said aloud. Could whoever murdered that girl have been the one who sent the letter to his mother? The letter that said a dancing girl who lived in Manhattan would die on Tuesday night exactly the way Nan died.

Tuesday afternoon, after his mother called, he'd contacted Glenn Moore, the police chief of Darien. Moore had gone to see Greta, had taken the letter, reassuring her it was probably from a crank. He'd then called Chris back. "Chris, even if it's on the level, how do you begin to protect all the young women in New York?"

Now Chris dialed the Darien police station again and was put through to the chief. Moore had not yet heard about the death in New York. "I'll call the FBI," he said. "If that letter is from the killer, it's physical evidence. I have to warn you, the FBI will probably want to talk to you and your mother about Nan's death. I'm sorry, Chris. I know what that does to her."

*A*T THE ENTRANCE to Beefsteak Charlie's restaurant in Madison Square Garden, Vince threw an arm around his son's shoulders. "I swear you've grown since last week." He and Hank were now eye to eye. "One of these days, you'll be eating your blue plate off my head."

"What the heck is a blue plate?" Hank's lean face with a sprinkling of freckles across the nose was the one Vince remembered seeing in the mirror nearly thirty years ago. Only the color of his gray-blue eyes had come from his mother's genes.

The waiter beckoned to them. When they were seated, Vince explained, "A blue plate used to be the special of the evening at a cheap restaurant. Seventy-nine cents bought you a hunk of meat, a couple of vegetables, a potato. The plate was sectioned to keep the juices from running together. Your grandfather loved that kind of bargain."

They decided on hamburgers with everything piled on, french fries, salads. Vince had a beer, Hank a cola. Vince forced himself not to think about Darcy Scott and Nona Roberts going to the morgue to view the body of the murder victim. Rough as hell for both of them.

Hank filled him in about his track team. "We're running at Randall's Island next Saturday. Think you can make it?"

"Absolutely, unless . . ."

"Oh, sure." Unlike his mother, Hank understood the demands of Vince's job. "You working on anything new?"

Vince told him about the concern that a serial killer was on the loose, about the meeting in Nona Roberts's office, about the belief that Erin Kelley might be the dead woman found on the pier.

Hank listened intently. "You think you ought to be in on this, Dad?"

"Not necessarily. This may be a local homicide solely for the NYPD, but they have requested assistance from the Behavioral Science Unit at Quantico and I'll help them as much as I can." He signaled for the check. "We'd better get started."

"Dad, I'm coming in again Sunday. Why don't I go to the game alone? You know your gut is telling you to follow up on this case."

"I don't want to pull that on you."

"Look, the game is sold out. I'll make a deal with you. No scalping, but if I sell your ticket for exactly what you paid for it, I get to keep the money. I've got a date tomorrow night. I'm broke, and I can't stand to ask Mom for a loan. She sends me to that hunk of blubber she married. So anxious for us to be buddies."

Vince smiled. "I swear you've got the makings of a con man. See you Sunday, pal."

*O*N THE WAY to the morgue, Darcy and Nona clasped hands in the squad car. When they arrived, they were taken to a room off the lobby. "They'll come for you when they're ready," the cop who had driven them explained. "They're probably taking photographs."

Photographs. *Erin, don't worry. Send your picture if they request it. In for a penny, in for a pound.* Darcy stared straight ahead, barely conscious of the room, of Nona's arm around her. Charles North. Erin had met him at seven o'clock on Tuesday night. A little more than a few short days ago. Tuesday morning she and Erin had joked about that date.

Darcy said aloud, "And now I'm sitting in the New York City morgue waiting to look at a dead woman who I'm sure is going to be Erin." Vaguely she felt Nona's arm tighten around her.

The cop returned. "An FBI agent's on the way. Wants you to wait for him before you go downstairs."

Vince walked between Darcy and Nona, his hands firmly under their elbows. They stopped at the glass window that separated them from the still form on the stretcher. At Vince's nod, the attendant pulled the sheet back from the victim's face.

But Darcy already knew. A strand of that auburn hair had escaped concealment. Then she was seeing the familiar profile, the wide blue eyes now closed, the lashes dark shadows, the always smiling lips so still, so quiet.

Erin. Erin. Erin-go-bragh, she thought, and felt herself begin to sink into merciful darkness.

Vince and Nona grabbed her. "No. No. I'm all right." She fought back the waves of dizziness and made herself straighten up. She pushed away the supporting arms and stared at Erin, deliberately studying the chalky whiteness of her skin, the bruises on her throat. "Erin," she said fiercely, "I swear to you I will find Charles North. I give you my word he is going to pay for what he did to you."

The sound of racking sobs echoed in the stark corridor. Darcy realized they were coming from her.

*F*RIDAY had been an extremely successful day for Jay Stratton. In the morning, he'd stopped at the Bertolini office. Yesterday, when he brought in the necklace, Aldo Marco, the manager, had still been furious at the delay. Today, Marco was singing a different tune. His client was ecstatic. Miss Kelley had certainly executed the concept they had in mind when they'd decided to have the gems reset. They looked forward to continuing to work with her. At Jay's request, the twenty-thousand-dollar check was made out to Jay as Erin Kelley's manager.

From there, Stratton went to the police station to file a complaint about the missing diamonds. The copy of the official report in his hand, he'd headed for the midtown office of his insurance company. The distressed agent told him that Lloyd's of London had reinsured this packet of gems. "They'll undoubtedly post a reward," she said nervously. "Lloyd's is getting terribly upset about the theft of jewelry in New York."

At four o'clock, Jay had been in the Stanhope having drinks with Enid Armstrong, a widow who'd answered one of his personal ads. He'd listened attentively as she told him about her overwhelming loneliness. "It's been a year," she'd said, her eyes glistening. "You know, people are sympathetic and they take you out occasionally, but it's a fact of life that the world goes two-by-two and an extra woman is a nuisance. I went on a Caribbean cruise alone last month. It was absolutely miserable."

Jay made the appropriate clucking sounds of understanding and reached for her hand. Armstrong was mildly pretty, in her late fifties, good clothes but no style. He'd run into the type often enough. Married young. Stayed home. Raised the kids and joined the country club. Husband who became successful but mowed his own lawn. The kind of guy who made sure his wife was well provided for after he keeled over.

Jay studied Armstrong's wedding and engagement rings. All the diamonds were top quality. The solitaire was a beauty. "Your husband was very generous," he commented.

"I got these for our twenty-fifth anniversary. You should have seen the pinpoint he gave me when we got engaged. We were such kids." More glistening eyes.

Jay signaled for another glass of champagne. By the time he left Enid Armstrong, she was excited about his suggestion that they get together next week. She'd even agreed to consider having him redesign her rings. "I'd like to see you with one important ring that incorporates all these stones. The solitaire and baguettes in the center, banded on either side by alternating diamonds and emeralds. We'll use the diamonds in your wedding ring and I can get some fine quality emeralds for you at a very reasonable price."

Over a quiet dinner at the Water Club, he pondered the pleasure of substituting a cubic zirconia for the solitaire in Armstrong's ring. Some of them were so good even a jeweler's naked eye could be fooled. But of course he'd have the new ring appraised for her with the solitaire still in place. Amazing how single women fell for that. "How thoughtful of you to take care of the appraisal for me. I'll take it right to my insurance company."

He lingered at the bar of the Water Club after dinner. Good to relax. The business of being attentive and charming with these old girls was exhausting even though the results were lucrative.

It was nine-thirty when he walked the few blocks from the restaurant back to his apartment. At ten he was wearing pajamas and a robe newly purchased at Armani's. He settled on the couch with a bourbon on the rocks and turned on the news.

The glass shook in Stratton's trembling hands and liquor spilled unheeded on his robe as he stared at the screen and learned of the discovery of the body of Erin Kelley.

*M*ICHAEL NASH wondered ruefully if he should offer free analysis to Anne Thayer, the blonde who so unfortunately had bought the apartment next to his. When he left the office at ten of six on Friday afternoon, she was at the desk in the lobby, speaking to the concierge. As soon as she saw him, she dashed to stand beside him and wait for the elevator. On the way up, she chatted nonstop, as though she was on a countdown to ensnare him before they reached the twentieth floor.

"I went over to Zabar's today and got the most marvelous salmon. Fixed a platter of hors d'oeuvres. My girlfriend was supposed to come over but can't make it. Can't bear to see them go to waste. I was wondering . . ."

Nash cut her off. "Zabar's salmon is great. Put it away. It'll keep for a few days." He was aware of the commiserating glance of the elevator operator. "Ramon, I'll see you in a few minutes. I'm on my way out."

He said a firm good night to the crestfallen Miss Thayer and disappeared into his own apartment. He *was* going out, but not for an hour or so. And if he bumped into her then, maybe she'd start to get the message to leave him alone. "Dependent personality, probably neurotic, could get vicious when crossed," he said aloud, then laughed. Hey, I'm off work. Forget it.

He was spending the weekend in Bridgewater. There was a dinner party at the Balderstons' tomorrow night. They always had interesting guests. More important, he intended to use the better part of the next two days working on his book. Nash acknowledged to himself that he'd become so interested in the project that he was becoming impatient with distractions.

Just before he left, he tried Erin Kelley's number. He half-smiled as he heard the message in her lilting voice: "This is Erin. Sorry to miss your call. Please leave a message."

"This is Michael Nash. I'm sorry to miss you, too, Erin. Tried you the other day. Guess you're away. Hope there isn't a problem with your father." He left his office and home number again.

The drive to Bridgewater on Friday night was as usual a traffic-clogged nuisance. It was only when he passed Paterson on Route

80 that it began to let up. Then with each mile the terrain became more countrylike. Nash felt himself begin to relax. By the time he had driven through the gate of Scotshays, he had a total sense of well-being.

His father had bought the estate when Michael was eleven. Four hundred acres of gardens, woods, and fields. Swimming pool, tennis courts, stable. The house copied from a manor in Brittany. Stone walls, red-tiled roof, green shutters, white portico. Twenty-two rooms in all. Half of them Michael hadn't bothered with in years. Irma and John Hughes, the housekeeping couple, ran the place for him.

Irma had dinner waiting. She served it in the study. Michael settled in his favorite old leather armchair to study the notes he would use tomorrow when he wrote the next chapter of his book. That chapter would concentrate on the psychological problems of people who, when they answered personal ads, sent in pictures of themselves that had been taken twenty-five years ago. He would concentrate on what factors made them try that ploy and how they explained themselves when the date showed up.

That sort of thing had happened to a number of the girls he had interviewed. A couple of them had been indignant. Some had been downright funny describing the encounter.

At quarter of ten, Michael turned the television on in anticipation of the news, then went back to his notes. The name Erin Kelley made him look up, startled. He grabbed the remote control and pressed the volume frantically, causing the announcer's voice to shout through the room.

When the segment was finished, Michael flipped off the set and stared at the dark screen.

"Erin," he said aloud, "who could do that to you?"

*D*OUG FOX stopped for a drink at Harry's Bar on Friday evening before heading home to Scarsdale. It was a watering hole for the Wall Street crowd. As usual the bar was four deep and the news on the television set was ignored. Doug did not see the bulletin about the body that had been found on the pier.

If she was sure he was coming home, Susan usually fed the kids first, then waited to eat with him, but tonight, when he arrived at eight, Susan was in the den reading. She barely raised her eyes when he came into the room and turned away from the kiss he tried to press on her forehead.

Donny and Beth had gone to the movies with the Goodwyns, she explained. Trish and the baby were asleep. She did not offer to prepare anything for him. Her eyes went back to her book.

For a moment Doug stood uncertainly over her, then turned and went into the kitchen. She had to pull this attitude act the one night I'm hungry, he thought bitterly. She's just sore because I didn't get home for a couple of nights and was so late last night. He opened the door of the refrigerator. The one thing Susan could do was cook. With mounting anger he decided that when he was able to make it home, the least she could do was to have something ready for him.

He yanked out packets of ham and cheese and went to the bread box. The weekly community newspaper was on the kitchen table. Doug made a sandwich, poured a beer, and began to skim the paper as he ate. The sports page caught his eye. Scarsdale had unexpectedly defeated Dobbs Ferry in the midschool tournament. The sudden-death winning basket had been sunk by second-stringer Donald Fox.

Donny! Why didn't anyone tell him?

Doug felt his palms begin to sweat. Had Susan tried to phone him Tuesday night? Donny had been disappointed and sullen when Doug told him he couldn't make the game. It would be just like Susan to suggest they call with the news.

Tuesday night. Wednesday night.

The new telephone operator at the hotel. She wasn't like the young kids who willingly accepted the hundred bucks he slipped them from time to time. "Remember, any calls come in for me when I'm not here, I'm in a meeting. If it's real late, I left a do-not-disturb."

The new operator looked like she posed for a moral majority ad. He'd been still trying to figure out how to snow her into lying for him. He hadn't worried too much, however. He'd trained Susan not to phone him when he stayed in "for meetings."

But she *had* tried him Tuesday night. He was sure of it. Otherwise, she'd have had Donny phone him at the office Wednesday afternoon. And that dumb operator had probably told her there was no meeting and no one was staying in the company suite.

Doug looked around the kitchen. It was surprisingly neat. They'd had the whole house renovated when they bought it eight years ago. The kitchen was a chef's dream. Center island with sink and chopping board. Plenty of counter space. Latest appliances. Skylight.

Susan's old man had lent them the money for the renovation. He'd also lent them most of the down payment. *Lent.* Not given.

If Susan got really sore . . .

Doug tossed the rest of the sandwich in the compactor and brought his beer into the den.

Susan watched him enter the room. My handsome husband, she thought. She'd deliberately left the newspaper on the table, knowing Doug would probably read it. Now he's sweating bullets. He figured I probably called the hotel to let Donny give him the news. Funny, when you finally faced reality, it was amazing how clearly you could see things.

Doug sat on the couch opposite her. He's afraid to give me an opening, she decided. Tucking her book under her arm, she got up. "The kids will be back about half past ten," she told him. "I'm going to read in bed."

"I'll wait for them, honey."

Honey! He must be worried.

Susan settled in bed with the book. Then, knowing she was not able to focus on the print, she laid it down and turned on the television.

Doug came into the bedroom just as the ten o'clock news began. "It's too lonesome out there." He sat on the bed and reached for her hand. "How's my girl?"

"Good question," Susan said. "How is she?"

He attempted to pass it off as a joke. Tilting her chin, he said, "She looks pretty good to me."

They both turned to watch the screen as the anchorman gave the headline news. "Erin Kelley, a prize-winning young jewelry designer, was found strangled on the West Fifty-sixth Street pier. More after this."

A commercial.

Susan glanced at Doug. He was staring at the screen, his pallor a ghastly white. "Doug, what is it?"

He did not seem to have heard her.

". . . Police are searching for Petey Potters, a drifter who was known to have been living in this shack and may have observed the body when it was abandoned on this cold, debris-strewn pier."

When the segment was completed, Doug turned to Susan. As though he had just heard her question, he snapped, "Nothing's the matter. Nothing." Beads of perspiration were forming on his forehead.

At three in the morning, Susan was awakened from her own uneasy sleep by Doug thrashing beside her. He was mumbling something. A name? ". . . no, can't . . ." The name again. Susan propped herself up on one arm and listened intently.

Erin. That was it. The name of the young woman who'd been found murdered.

She was about to shake Doug awake when he suddenly quieted. With growing horror, Susan realized why the newscast had so upset him. Undoubtedly, he'd linked it to that terrible time in college when he was one of the students questioned about the girl who had been strangled.

VI

SATURDAY
February 23

ON SATURDAY morning, Charley read the *New York Post* with intense fascination. COPYCAT MURDER was the banner-sized headline.

The similarity of Erin Kelley's death to the *True Crimes* program about Nan Sheridan was the focus of the story on the inside pages.

Someone had tipped an investigative reporter from the *Post* about the letter to Nan Sheridan's mother warning that a young woman from New York would be murdered on Tuesday night. The reporter, quoting an unidentified source, wrote that the FBI was on the trail of a possible serial killer. In the past two years, seven young women from Manhattan had disappeared after answering personal ads. Erin Kelley had been answering personal ads.

The circumstances of Nan Sheridan's death were rehashed in full.

Erin Kelley's background; interviews with colleagues in the jewelry business. Their responses identical. Erin was a warm, lovely person, immensely talented. The picture the *Post* used was the one Erin had sent Charley. That delighted him.

The network was going to repeat the *True Crimes* episode about Nan's death Wednesday night. That would be so interesting to watch. Of course he'd taped it last month, but even so, to see it again, knowing that hundreds of thousands of people would be playing amateur detective. *Who did it? Who was smart enough to get away with it?*

Charley frowned. *Copycat.*

Copycat meant they thought someone else was imitating him. Anger rushed through him, stark, raging anger. They had no right not to credit him. Just as Nan had had no right not to invite him to her party fifteen years ago.

He'd go back to the secret place in the next few days. He needed to be there. He'd turn on the video and dance in step with Astaire. It wouldn't be Ginger, or Leslie, or Ann Miller in his arms.

His heart began beating faster. This time it wouldn't even be Nan. It would be Darcy.

He picked up Darcy's picture. The soft brown hair, the slender body, the wide, inquiring eyes. How much lovelier would that body be when he held it, rigid and cold in his arms?

Copycat.

Again he frowned. The anger was pounding at his temples, causing one of the terrible headaches to begin. It is I, Charley, alone who has the power of life and death over these women. I, Charley, broke through the prison of the other soul and now dominate him at will.

He would take Darcy and crush the life from her as he had crushed it from the others. And he would confound the authorities with his genius, confuse and bewilder their tiresome minds.

Copycat.

The people who wrote that should see the shoe boxes in the basement. Then they'd know. Those boxes that contained one shoe and one dancing slipper from the foot of each of the dead girls beginning with Nan.

Of course.

There was a way to prove he wasn't a copycat. His body shook with silent, mirthless laughter.

Oh yes, indeed. There was a way.

VII
SATURDAY
February 23
THROUGH
TUESDAY
February 26

*T*HE NEXT WEEK for Darcy passed as though she was a robot who had been wound up and programmed to perform specific tasks.

Accompanied by Vince D'Ambrosio and a detective from the local precinct, she went to Erin's apartment on Saturday. There were three more calls that had been received after she'd been in the apartment on Friday morning. Darcy rewound the answering machine. One was from the manager at Bertolini's. "Miss Kelley, we gave your check to your manager, Mr. Stratton. We cannot tell you how pleased we are with the necklace."

Darcy raised her eyebrows. "I never heard Erin refer to Stratton as her manager."

The second call was from someone who identified himself as Box 2695. "Erin, it's Milton. We went out last month. I've been away. I'd like to see you again. My phone number is 555–3681. And listen, I'm sorry if I came on a little too strong last time."

The third call was from Michael Nash. "He left a message the other night," Darcy said.

Vince copied the names and numbers. "We'll leave the tape on for the next few days."

Vince had told Darcy that forensics experts from the NYPD would arrive shortly to go over Erin's apartment for possible evidence. She had asked Vince if she could come with him and get Erin's private papers. "My name is on her bank account and insurance policies as trustee for her father. She told me the papers were in her file under his name."

Erin's instructions were simple and explicit. If anything happened to Erin, as agreed, Darcy would use her insurance to pay nursing home expenses. She had contracted with a funeral director in Wellesley that when the time came he would handle her father's arrangements. Everything in her apartment, all her personal jewelry and clothing, were left to Darcy Scott.

There was a brief note for Darcy: "Darce, this is surely a just-in-case. But I know you'll keep your promise to look after Dad if I'm not around. And if that ever should happen, thanks for all the great times we had together, and have fun for both of us."

Dry-eyed, Darcy looked at the familiar signature.

"I hope you'll follow her advice," Vince said quietly.

"I will someday," Darcy told him. "But not yet. Would you make a copy for me of that personal ads file I gave you?"

"Sure," Vince said, "but why? We're going to look up the people who placed the ads she circled."

"But you're not going to date them. She answered some ads for both of us. Maybe I'll get calls from people who took her out."

Darcy left as the forensics crew arrived. She went directly home and began to make phone calls. The funeral director in Wellesley. Sympathy, then practicality. He would send a hearse to the morgue when Erin's body was released. What about clothing? Open casket?

Darcy thought about the bruises on Erin's throat. Undoubtedly, there'd be media at the funeral parlor. "Closed casket. I'll bring up clothing for her." Visitation on Monday. Funeral mass on Tuesday at St. Paul's.

St. Paul's. When she'd stayed with Erin and Billy, she had gone to St. Paul's with them.

She went back to Erin's apartment. Vince D'Ambrosio was still there. He accompanied her into the bedroom and watched as she opened the closet door.

"Erin had so much style," Darcy said unsteadily as she searched for the dress she had in mind. "She used to tell me that she felt so out of it when I walked in the room with my folks that first day at college. I was wearing a designer suit and Italian boots my mother had forced on me. I thought she looked smashing in chinos and a sweater and marvelous jewelry. Even then she was designing her own pieces."

Vince was a good listener. Abstractly, Darcy was aware that she was glad he was letting her talk. "No one's going to see her," she said, "except maybe I will, just for a minute. But I want to feel that she'd be pleased with what I chose for her. . . . Erin urged me to be more daring about clothes. I taught her to trust her own instincts. She had impeccable taste."

She pulled out a two-piece cocktail dress: pale pink fitted jacket, delicate silver buttons, flowing pink and silver chiffon skirt. "Erin just bought this to wear to a benefit, a dinner dance. She was a wonderful ballroom dancer. That was something else we shared. Nona too. We met Nona in a ballroom dancing class at our health club."

Vince remembered Nona had told him that. "From what you tell me, this dress sounds like something Erin would want to wear now."

He didn't like the fact that Darcy's pupils were so enlarged. He wished he could call Nona Roberts. She had told him she absolutely had to be on a shoot in Nanuet today. Darcy Scott ought not to be alone too much.

Darcy realized she could read D'Ambrosio's thoughts. She also realized there was no use reassuring him. The best service she could perform was to get out of here and let the fingerprint experts and God knows who else do their thing. She tried to make her voice and manner matter-of-fact as she asked, "What are you doing to find the man Erin was meeting Tuesday night?"

"We've found Charles North. What Erin told you checks out. It was a lucky break you happened to ask her about him. He moved last month from a law firm in Philadelphia to one on Park Avenue. He left yesterday for a trip to Germany. We'll be waiting for him when he gets back Monday. Detectives from this precinct are going around pubs and bars in the Washington Square area with Erin's picture. We want to see if some bartender or waiter can remember seeing her on Tuesday evening and possibly can identify North when we get him."

Darcy nodded. "I'm going to Wellesley. I'll stay there till after the funeral."

"Nona Roberts is going to join you there?"

"On Tuesday morning. She can't get up before then." Darcy tried to smile. "Please don't worry. Erin had loads of friends. I've heard from so many of the Mount Holyoke grads. They'll be there. So will a lot of our buddies from New York. And she lived in Wellesley all her life. I'm staying with the people who used to be her next-door neighbors."

She went home to pack. A call came from Australia. Her mother and father. "Darling, if only we could be with you. You know we thought of Erin as our second daughter."

"I know." *If only we could be with you.* How many times had she heard that over the years? Birthdays. Graduations. But there had been lots of times when they *were* with her. Any other kid would have been so happy to have the golden couple as parents. Why had she been a throwback to the cottage-with-a-picket-fence mentality? "It's so good to talk with you. How's the play going?"

Now they were on safe ground.

The funeral was a media event. Photographers and cameras. Neighbors and friends. Curiosity seekers. Vince had told her that hidden cameras would be recording everyone who came to the funeral parlor, the church, and the interment, in case Erin's killer was there.

The white-haired Monsignor who had known Erin all her life. "Who can forget the sight of that little girl pushing her father's wheelchair into this church?"

The soloist. ". . . All I ask of you is forever to remember me as loving you . . ."

The interment. "When every tear shall be wiped away. . . ."

The hours she spent with Billy. I'm glad you don't know, she thought. Holding his hand. If he understands anything, I hope he thinks it's Erin with him.

Tuesday afternoon the Pan Am shuttle back to New York, Nona beside her. "Can you take a couple of days off, Darce?" Nona asked. "This has been a pretty awful time for you."

"As soon as I know they have Charles North in custody, I will go away for a week. A couple of my friends have a condo in St. Thomas. They want me to visit."

Nona hesitated. "That's not the way it's going to work, Darcy. Vince called me last night. They picked up Charles North. Last Tuesday evening he was in a board meeting at his law firm with twenty partners. Whoever met Erin was using his name."

*A*FTER HE SAW the broadcast and spoke to Chief Moore, Chris decided to go to Darien for the weekend. He wanted to be around when the FBI talked to his mother.

He knew Greta was planning to attend a black-tie dinner at the club. He stopped to eat at Nicola's, arrived at the house around ten and decided to watch a film. A classic movie buff, he put on *Bridge of San Luis Rey* and then wondered at his choice. The idea of lives drawn together to one particular moment in time always intrigued him. How much was fate? How much was happenstance? Was there some kind of inevitable, inexorable plan to it all?

He heard the whirring of the garage door shortly before midnight and walked to the head of the basement stairs to wait for Greta, wishing once again that she had live-in help. He did not like the idea of her coming into this big house alone late at night.

Greta adamantly refused that suggestion. Dorothy, the daily housekeeper of three decades, suited her fine. That and the weekly cleaning service. If she had a dinner party, her caterer was excellent. And that was that.

As she approached the stairs, he called down, "Hi, Mother."

Her gasp was audible. "What! Oh dear God, Chris. You startled me. I'm a bundle of nerves." She looked up, trying to smile. "I was so glad to see your car." In the dim light her fine-boned face reminded him of Nan's delicate features. Her hair, shimmering silver, was pulled back in a French knot. A sable jacket fell loosely from her shoulders. She was wearing a long black velvet sheath. Greta would be sixty on her next birthday. An elegant, beautiful woman whose smile never fully removed the sadness from her eyes.

It suddenly struck Chris that his mother always appeared to be poised waiting or listening for something, some sort of signal. When he was a kid, his grandfather had told him a World War I story about a soldier who had lost the message warning of an imminent enemy attack. Afterward the soldier always blamed himself for the terrible casualties and went through life looking in gutters and under stones for the lost message.

Over a nightcap, he told Greta about Erin Kelley and understood why the simile had occurred to him. Greta always felt that there was something Nan had told her before she died that had set off an instinctive alarm. Last week, once again, she had received a warning and been powerless to prevent a tragedy.

"The girl they found had a high-heeled evening shoe on?" Greta asked. "Like Nan? The sort of shoe you would dance in? That note said a dancing girl would die."

Chris chose his words carefully. "Erin Kelley was a jewelry designer. From what I understand, the feeling is that this is a copycat murder. Somebody got the idea from watching that *True Crimes* program. An FBI agent wants to talk to us about it."

Chief Moore phoned on Saturday. An FBI agent, Vincent D'Ambrosio, would like to drop in on the Sheridans on Sunday.

Chris was glad that D'Ambrosio emphasized that no one could have acted on the letter Greta had received. "Mrs. Sheridan," he told her, "we get tips much more specific than that one and still can't prevent a tragedy from happening."

Vince asked Chris to walk outside with him. "The Darien police have the files on your sister's death," he explained. "They're going to copy them for me. Would you mind taking me to the exact place where she was found?"

They walked down the road that led from the Sheridan property to the wooded area with the jogging path. The trees had grown higher, their branches thicker in the fifteen years, but otherwise, Chris commented, the place was pretty much the same.

A bucolic scene in a wealthy town, contrasted with an abandoned West Side pier. Nan Sheridan had been a nineteen-year-old kid. A student. A jogger. Erin Kelley was a twenty-eight-year-old career woman. Nan had come from a well-to-do social family. Erin was on her own. The only two similarities were in the manner of death and the footwear. They both had been strangled. They both had been wearing one fancy shoe. Vince asked Chris if while Nan was at school, she did any blind dating through personal ads.

Chris smiled. "Believe me, Nan had enough guys flocking around that she didn't need to answer ads to get a date. Anyhow, there was none of that personal-ads stuff when we were in college."

"You went to Brown?"

"Nan did. I was at Williams."

"I assume any special boyfriends were checked out?"

They were walking along the path that threaded through the woods. Chris stopped. "This is where I found her." He shoved his hands in the pockets of his windbreaker. "Nan thought anyone who got tied up with one guy was crazy. She was something of a flirt. She liked to have a good time. She never willingly missed a party, and she danced every dance."

Vince turned to face him. "This is important. You're sure the fancy slipper your sister was wearing when she was found was not one of her own."

"Absolutely. Nan hated spike heels. She simply wouldn't have bought that shoe. And of course, there was no trace of the mate in her closet."

As he drove back to New York, Vince continued to weigh the comparisons and differences between Nan Sheridan and Erin Kel-

ley. It's got to be a copycat murder, he told himself. *Dancing girl.*
That's what was bugging him. The note Greta Sheridan had received. Nan Sheridan had danced every dance. Had that come out
on the *True Crimes* program? Erin Kelley had met Nona Roberts
in a dancing class. Was it a coincidence?

*O*N TUESDAY afternoon, Charles North was in-
terrogated for the second time by Vincent D'Ambrosio. He had
been met at Kennedy Airport on Monday evening and his aston-
ishment at being greeted by two FBI agents had been quickly
replaced by anger. "I never heard of Erin Kelley. I never answered
a personal ad. I think they're ridiculous. I cannot imagine who
would use my name."

It was a simple matter to ascertain that North had been in a
board meeting at seven o'clock on the previous Tuesday evening,
the hour Erin Kelley supposedly planned to meet him.

This time the questioning was in FBI headquarters on Federal
Plaza. North was of medium height with a stocky build. A slightly
florid face suggested a three-martini drinker. Nevertheless, Vince
decided, he had a distinct air of authority and sophistication that
probably appealed to women. Forty years old, he had been married twelve years prior to his recent divorce. He made it very clear
that he deeply resented the request that he drop in at Vince's office
for a second interview.

"I think you must understand that I have just become a partner in a prestigious law firm. It certainly will be a great embarrassment if I am in any way linked to that young woman's death. An embarrassment for me personally and most certainly for my firm."

"I'm very sorry to embarrass you, Mr. North," Vince said coldly. "I can assure you that at this moment you are not a suspect in Erin Kelley's death. But Erin Kelley is dead, the victim of a brutal homicide. It is possible that she is one of a number of young women who have answered personal ads and disappeared. Someone used your name to place that ad. A very clever someone who knew you would have left your Philadelphia firm by the time he arranged to meet Erin Kelley."

"Will you please tell me why that would matter to anyone?" North snapped.

"Because some women who answer personal ads are smart enough to check out the man they agree to date. Suppose Erin Kelley's killer thought she might be that careful. What better name to use than someone who had just left his law firm in Philadelphia to relocate in New York. Suppose Erin had looked you up in the Pennsylvania Bar Register and called your old office. She would have been told that you just left the firm to relocate in New York. She might even have been able to ascertain that you're divorced. Now she has no qualms about meeting Charles North."

Vince leaned forward across his desk. "Like it or not, Mr. North, you are a link to Erin Kelley's death. Someone who knows your activities used your name. We're going to be following up a lot of leads. We're going to contact the people whose ads Erin Kelley may have answered. We're going to pump her friends' memories to see if she mentioned any names we don't have. In each and every case, we're going to talk to you to see if that person is someone who somehow is connected to you."

North stood up. "I see that I'm being told, not asked. Just one thing. Has my name been released to the media?"

"No, it has not."

"Then see that it isn't. And when you call at the office, don't identify yourself as FBI. Say," he smiled mirthlessly, "say it's personal business. Not personal *ad* business, of course."

When he left, Vince leaned back in his chair. I don't like wise guys, he thought. He picked up the intercom. "Betsy, I want a complete background check on Charles North. I mean everything. And here's another one. Gus Boxer, the superintendent at 101 Christopher Street. That's the apartment building where Erin Kelley lived. His face has been bugging me since Saturday. We've got a file on him, I'm sure of it."

Vince snapped his fingers. "Wait a minute. That's not his name. I remember. It's *Hoffman*. He was the super ten years ago in the building where a twenty-year-old woman was murdered."

DR. MICHAEL NASH was not surprised when on his return to Manhattan Sunday night there was a call on his answering machine asking him to contact FBI agent Vincent D'Ambrosio. Obviously, they were following up on the people who had left messages for Erin Kelley.

He returned the call on Monday morning and arranged for Vince to stop by before his first appointment on Tuesday.

Vince arrived at Nash's office promptly at 8:15 Tuesday morning. The receptionist was waiting for him and ushered him in to where Nash was already at his desk.

It was a clubby kind of room, Vince decided. Several comfortable chairs, walls a sunny yellow, curtains that let the daylight in but shielded the occupants from the view of passersby on the sidewalk. The traditional couch, a leather version of the chaise longue Alice had bought years ago, was at a right angle to the desk.

A restful room, and the expression in the eyes of the man at the desk was both kind and thoughtful. Vince thought of Saturday afternoons. Confession. "Bless me, Father, for I have sinned." The transgressions evolved from disobeying his parents to recitation of more lusty offenses in teenage years.

It always bothered him to hear someone say that analysis had replaced confession. "In confession you blame yourself," he'd point out. "In analysis you blame everyone else." His own master's degree in psychology had only strengthened that viewpoint.

He had the feeling Nash sensed his gut-level hostility to most shrinks. Sensed it and understood it.

They eyed each other. Well-dressed in an unobtrusive way, Vince thought. Vince was aware that he was no good at picking out the right tie for his suit. Alice used to do that for him. Not that he cared. He'd rather wear a brown tie with a blue suit than hear her harping at him all the time. "Why don't you leave the Bureau and get a job where you can earn some real money?" Today he'd grabbed the nearest tie and pulled it on in the elevator. It was brown and green. His suit was a blue pinstripe.

Alice was now Mrs. Malcolm Drucker. Malcolm wore Hermès ties and custom-made suits. Recently, Hank told Vince that Malcolm had blown up to size fifty-two. Fifty-two short.

Nash was wearing a gray tweed jacket, a red and gray tie. Nice-looking guy, Vince conceded. Strong chin, deep-set eyes. Skin a touch windburned. Vince liked a man to look as though he didn't hide indoors in lousy weather.

He got right to the point. "Dr. Nash, you left two messages for Erin Kelley. They suggest that you knew her, had dated her. Is that the case?"

"Yes. I am in the process of writing a book analyzing the social phenomenon of the personal ad situation. Kearns and Brown is my publisher; Justin Crowell, my editor."

Just in case I thought he was really trying to get a date, Vince thought, then warned himself to knock it off. "How did you come to go out with Erin Kelley? Did you answer her ad or did she answer yours?"

"She answered mine." Nash reached in his drawer. "I was anticipating your question. Here is the ad she answered. Here is her letter. I met her for a drink on January thirtieth at the Pierre. She was a lovely young woman. I expressed surprise that anyone so attractive would need to seek companionship. She quite frankly told me that she was answering ads at the behest of a friend who is doing a documentary. I don't usually acknowledge that I'm doing research on these meetings, but I was up-front with her."

"And that was the only time you saw her?"

"Yes. I've been terribly busy. I'm almost at the end of my book and wanted to get it finished. I'd planned to call Erin again when I turned it in. Last week I realized that it's going to take another month to complete and rushing it simply didn't work."

"And so you called her."

"Yes, early in the week. Then again last Thursday. No, it was Friday, just before I left for the weekend."

Vince studied the letter Erin had written to Nash. His ad was clipped to it: DWM, Physician, 37, 6'1", attractive, successful, good sense of humor. Enjoys skiing, riding, museums, and concerts. Seeking creative, attractive s/d/wf. Box 3295.

Erin's typewritten note had said,

Hi, Box 3295. Perhaps I'm all of the above. No, not quite. I do have a good sense of humor. I'm twenty-eight, 5'7", 120 pounds, and my best friend tells me I'm very attractive! I'm a jewelry designer on my way to being successful. I'm a good skier; can ride if the horse is slow and fat. Definitely a museum-goer. In fact, I get a lot of ideas for my jewelry by haunting them. And music is a must. See you? Erin Kelley, 212–555–1432.

"You can understand why I called," Nash said.

"And you never saw her again."

"I never got the chance." Michael Nash stood up. "I'm sorry. I have to cut this short. My first patient is arriving earlier than usual. But I'm here if you want me. If there's any way I can help, please allow me."

"How do you think you can help, Doctor?" Vince got to his feet as he asked the question.

Nash shrugged. "I don't know. I suppose it's the instinctive desire to want a killer brought to justice. Erin Kelley obviously loved life and had much to offer. She was only twenty-eight years old." He held out his hand. "You don't think much of us shrinks, do you, Mr. D'Ambrosio? Your version is that neurotic, self-centered people pay good money to come in here and complain. Let me explain how I view my job. My professional life is devoted to trying to help people who for whatever reason are in danger of sinking. Some cases are easy. I'm like a lifeguard who swims out because he notices that someone is over his head and simply escorts him back in. Other cases are much tougher. It's as though I'm trying to rescue a shipwreck victim during a hurricane. It takes a long time to get close to him and tidal waves are forcing me back. It's pretty satisfying when I'm able to complete the rescue."

Vince put Erin's letter in his briefcase. "You may be able to help us, Doctor. We're going to be tracking down the people Erin met through personal ads. Would you be willing to interview some of them and give your professional opinion of what makes them tick?"

"Absolutely."

"By any chance, are you a member of AAPL?" Psychiatrists who belonged to the American Association of Psychiatry and the

Law, Vince knew, were particularly skilled in dealing with psycho-paths.

"No, I'm not. But, Mr. D'Ambrosio, my research has shown that the vast majority of people who place or answer these ads do so because of loneliness or boredom. Others may have more sin-ister motives."

Vince turned and walked to the door. As he twisted the knob, he looked back. "I'd say that was true in Erin Kelley's case."

*O*N *TUESDAY* night, Charley drove to the retreat and went directly to the basement. He took down the stack of shoe boxes and laid them on top of the freezer. Clipped onto each of them was the name of the girl who belonged with them. Not that he needed reminding, of course. He remembered every single one in perfect detail. Besides that, except for Nan, he had a video-tape of each of them. And he had videotaped the *True Crimes* program about Nan's death. They'd done a good job of finding a girl who looked like her.

He opened Nan's box. The scuffed Nike and the black sequined satin slipper. The slipper was garish. His taste had improved since then.

Should he send Nan's and Erin's things back at the same time? Carefully, he considered the idea. It was such an interesting deci-sion.

No. If he did that the police and the media would realize immediately that their theory about a copycat murder was wrong. They'd know that one set of hands had snuffed out both lives.

Maybe it would be more fun to toy with them for a while.

Maybe start by returning Nan's shoe and the one from the first of the other girls. That had been Claire, two years ago. An ash-blond musical-comedy actress from Lancaster. She could dance so beautifully. Gifted. Really gifted. Her wallet was in the box with her white sandal and the gold slipper. Surely by now her family had given up her apartment. He'd send the package to the address in Lancaster.

Then every few days he'd send another package. Janine. Marie. Sheila. Leslie. Annette. Tina. Erin.

He'd time it so they'd all be delivered by March thirteenth. Fifteen days from now.

On that night, no matter how he accomplished it, Darcy would be here dancing with him.

Charley stared at the freezer. Darcy was going to be the last one. Maybe he'd keep her with him always. . . .

*W*HEN DARCY got back to her apartment from the airport Tuesday evening, there were a dozen messages on the answering machine. Condolences from old friends. Seven calls had come in from personal ads Erin must have answered for her. The pleasant-voiced David Weld again. This time he left a number. So did Len Parker, Cal Griffin, and Albert Booth.

A call from Gus Boxer saying he had a tenant for Erin Kelley's apartment. Could Miss Scott get the place cleared out by the weekend? If she did, she wouldn't have to pay the March rent.

Darcy rewound the tape, wrote down the names and phone numbers of the personal ad callers, and changed cassettes. Vince D'Ambrosio might want to have a record of those voices.

She heated a can of soup, ate it on a tray in bed. When she was finished she reached for the phone and the list of men who had called for a date. She dialed the first number. As it began to ring she slammed the phone back in the cradle. Tears gushed down her cheeks as she sobbed, "Erin, I want to call *you*."

VIII
WEDNESDAY
February 27

*A*T NINE O'CLOCK, Darcy went to the office. Bev was already there. She had coffee brewing and fresh juice and warm bagels. A new plant was on the windowsill. Bev hugged her briefly, her extravagantly mascaraed eyes filled with sympathy. "You can guess everything I want to say."

"Yes, I can." Darcy realized the coffee aroma was enticing. She reached for a bagel. "I didn't know I was hungry."

Bev assumed a businesslike attitude. "We had two calls in yesterday. People who saw the magic you did on the Ralston Arms apartment. Want you to redo for them. Also, would you take on that residential hotel on Thirtieth and Ninth? New owners. Claim they have more taste than money."

"Before I do anything else, I have to clear out Erin's apartment." Darcy took a gulp of coffee and pushed back her hair. "I dread it."

It was Bev who suggested she simply move all the furniture to the warehouse. "You told me it was a terrific setup. Could you use Erin's things piece by piece on jobs? One of the women who called wants to redo her daughter's bedroom in a really special way. The kid's sixteen and is coming home from the hospital after a long siege. She'll be laid up for quite a while."

It was good to think of Erin's pewter and brass bed being enjoyed by a girl like that. It made it easier. "I'd better check that it's all right for me to move everything out." She called Vince D'Ambrosio.

"I know the NYPD is finished going over the place," he told her.

Bev arranged for the van to go to Christopher Street the next day. "I'll meet it. Just show me what you want." At noon she went with Darcy to Erin's apartment. Boxer let them in.

"Sure appreciate you releasing the place," he whined. "Nice person taking it."

I wonder how much you got under the table, Darcy thought. I never want to come here again.

There were a few blouses and scarves that she decided to keep as mementos. The rest of Erin's clothes she gave to Bev. "You're Erin's size. Just please don't wear them to the office."

The jewelry Erin had made. Swiftly she gathered it, not wanting to think now about Erin's talent. What else was bothering her? Finally she laid all the jewelry on the worktable. Earrings, necklaces, pins, bracelets. Gold. Silver. Semiprecious stones. All imaginative, whether formal or fun pieces. *What was bothering her?*

The new necklace Erin had completed with the chunky gold copies of Roman coins. Erin had joked about it. "It'll retail for about three thousand dollars. I designed it for a fashion show in April. Can't afford to keep it for myself, but until then I'm going to wear it a few times."

Where was that necklace?

Had Erin been wearing it when she went out that last time? That and her initial ring and her watch. Were they with the clothes she'd been wearing when her body was found?

Darcy scooped Erin's personal jewelry into a suitcase along with the contents of the safe. She'd have the loose gems appraised and sold for Billy's nursing home expenses. She did not look back when she closed the door of apartment 3B for the last time.

*O*N *WEDNESDAY AFTERNOON* at four o'clock, a detective from the Sixth Precinct, armed with Erin Kelley's picture, was making the rounds of the pubs in the Washington Square area. So far his search had been fruitless. Several bartenders freely acknowledged knowing Erin. "She'd drop in once in a while. Sometimes with a date. Sometimes meeting someone. Last Tuesday. No. Didn't see her at all last week."

Charles North's picture produced no effect at all. "Never saw that one."

Finally, at Eddie's Aurora on West Fourth Street, a bartender positively stated: "Yeah, that girl was here last Tuesday. I went to Florida Wednesday morning. Just got back. That's why I'm sure about the date. I started talking to her. Told her I was finally getting away for some sun. She said she was a typical redhead, her skin always burned. She was expecting to meet someone and waited around for about forty minutes. He never showed up. Nice girl. Finally, she paid her bill and left."

The bartender was sure it was Tuesday; sure Erin Kelley had come in at seven o'clock; sure she had been stood up. He accurately described the clothes she had been wearing, including an unusual necklace that resembled old Roman coins. "Necklace was

126

real different. Looked expensive. I told her not to wander around outside without pulling her coat collar over it."

The detective reported to Vince D'Ambrosio from the pay phone in the bar. Vince immediately phoned Darcy, who verified that Erin had had a gold coin necklace. "I thought it might have been found on her." She told Vince that Erin's initial ring and watch were also missing.

"She was wearing a watch and earrings when she was found," Vince said quietly, and asked if he could come over.

"Sure," Darcy said. "I'll be working late."

When Vince arrived at the office, he was carrying a copy of Erin's personal ad file. "We did an exhaustive examination of all Erin's papers. In them we found a receipt for one of those private safe deposit boxes that are accessible twenty-four hours a day. Erin signed up for that only last week. She told the manager that she was a jewelry designer and was uncomfortable about the value of some of the stones she was keeping in her apartment."

Darcy listened attentively as Vince D'Ambrosio told her that Erin had been stood up on Tuesday night. "She left that bar alone at about quarter of eight. We're leaning to the theory that it was a felony murder. She was wearing the necklace Tuesday night, but not when she was found. We don't know about the ring."

"She always wore that ring," Darcy said.

Vince nodded. "She may have had the pouch of diamonds in her possession." He wondered if he was getting through to Darcy Scott. She was sitting at her desk, a pale yellow sweater accentuating the blond highlights in her brown hair, her expression totally controlled, her eyes more green than hazel today. He hated to be giving her copies of Kelley's personal ads file. He was sure that she was going to start writing to the ones that were circled.

Unconsciously, his voice deepened as he stressed, "Darcy, I know the sense of rage you're feeling at losing a friend like Erin.

The point is, I beg you not to answer these personal ads with some crazy idea that you'll find the man who called himself Charles North. We're going to do everything we can to find Erin's killer. But the fact remains that even though Erin may not have been one of his victims, there is a serial murderer using these ads to meet young women, and I don't want you to be his next date."

*D*OUG FOX had not strayed from Scarsdale over the weekend. He'd devoted himself to Susan and the children and been pleasantly compensated for his efforts by having Susan tell him that she'd arranged for a babysitter Monday afternoon. She wanted to do some shopping and proposed that they meet for dinner in New York that night and ride home together.

She had not told him that before shopping, she had the appointment with an investigative agency.

Doug had taken her to San Domenico for dinner and made it his business to be especially charming, even telling her that sometimes he forgot how really pretty she was.

Susan had laughed.

Tuesday night Doug had arrived home at midnight. "Damn late meetings," he'd sighed.

Wednesday morning he felt secure enough to tell Susan he'd be taking clients out to dinner and might as well stay at the Gateway. He was relieved at how understanding she was. "A client is a client, Doug. Just don't wear yourself out."

Wednesday afternoon when he left the office, he went straight to the apartment in London Terrace. He was meeting a divorced thirty-two-year-old real estate broker in SoHo for drinks at seven-thirty. But first he wanted to change into casual clothes and make a phone call.

He hoped that tonight he'd reach Darcy Scott.

*O*N WEDNESDAY AFTERNOON, Jay Stratton received a call from Merrill Ashton of Winston-Salem, North Carolina. Ashton had been thinking long and hard about Stratton's suggestion that he buy Frances an important piece of jewelry for their fortieth wedding anniversary. "If I discuss it with her, she'll talk me out of it," Ashton said, a smile in his voice. "Point is, I have to be in New York next week on business. You got anything to show me? I was thinking maybe a diamond bracelet."

Jay assured him that he most certainly did have something to show him. "I just bought some particularly fine diamonds which are being set in a bracelet right now. It would be perfect on your wife."

"I'd want an appraisal."

"Of course you would. If you like the bracelet, you can take it to a jeweler in Winston-Salem whom you trust and if he doesn't agree that the value is there, we don't have a deal. Are you prepared to spend forty thousand dollars? One for each year of your marriage?"

He heard the hesitation in Ashton's reply. "Well, that's a bit steep."

"A truly exquisite bracelet," Jay assured him. "Something that Frances Junior will proudly leave to her own daughter."

They arranged to meet for a drink next Monday, March fourth.

Was it all going too well, Stratton wondered as he laid the portable phone on the coffee table. The twenty-thousand-dollar check for the Bertolini necklace. Would anyone think to come looking for it? The insurance on the pouch of diamonds. With Erin's body found, the chance that she had been robbed could not be disputed. He'd give Ashton the gemstones at a reasonable but not questionable price. A jeweler in Winston-Salem wasn't going to be looking for stones listed as missing or stolen.

A wave of pure pleasure swept over him. Stratton laughed, remembering what his uncle had said to him twenty years ago. "Jay, I've sent you to an Ivy League school. You've got the brains to get good marks on your own, and you still cheat. Your father will never be dead while you're around."

When he told his uncle that he'd conned the dean at Brown into letting him reapply if he joined the Peace Corps for two years, his uncle had sarcastically snapped, "Be careful. There's nothing to steal in the Peace Corps and you might actually have to do some work."

Not that much work. At twenty he'd started over at Brown as a freshman. Never get caught, his father had warned him. And if you do, no matter how you fix it, make sure you don't have a record.

He'd of course been older than the other students. They'd all looked like babyfaced kids, even the ones who were obviously rich.

Except for one.

The phone rang. It was Enid Armstrong. Enid Armstrong? Of course, the teary-eyed widow.

She sounded excited. "I talked to my sister about your suggestion of what I should do to my ring and she said, 'Enid, if that will give you a lift, do it. You deserve to pamper yourself.' "

*O*N THE CHANNEL 4 six o'clock news, reporter John Miller had an ongoing report about Erin Kelley. It had been learned that a quarter of a million dollars in diamonds was missing from her safe. Lloyd's of London had posted a fifty-thousand-dollar reward for their return. The police still believed that she had been the victim of a copycat murderer who might not have known that she was carrying valuables. The report ended with a reminder that the *True Crimes* dramatization of Nan Sheridan's death was being repeated at eight o'clock.

Darcy snapped the off button on the remote control. "It had nothing to do with a robbery," she said aloud. "It had nothing to do with a copycat murder. No matter what they say, it had everything to do with a personal ad."

Vince D'Ambrosio would undoubtedly learn the identity of some of the people Erin had dated. But Erin had been meeting for the first time the man who called himself Charles North, and he hadn't shown up. Suppose he'd been just coming into the bar and met her at the door? Suppose he'd been one of the ones to whom she'd sent a picture? Suppose he'd said, "Erin Kelley, I'm Charles North. I got stuck in traffic. This place looks crowded. Let's go somewhere else."

It makes sense, Darcy thought. If there is a serial killer out there and if he's been responsible for other deaths, he won't stop now. If only she knew which ads Erin had actually answered, which ads she'd answered for both of them.

It was seven o'clock, a good time to try returning the calls that had been left on her machine. In the next forty minutes she reached three people, left messages for the other four. Now she had a date for drinks with Len Parker at McMullen's on Thursday, drinks with David Weld at Smith and Wollensky's Grill on Friday, and brunch with Albert Booth at the Victory Café on Saturday.

What about the guys who had left messages on Erin's machine? A couple of them had given phone numbers that she'd taken down. Maybe she'd call them back, tell them about Erin in case they didn't already know, and try to get a date with them. If they were meeting a lot of girls, they might have heard someone talk about a date who turned out to be weird.

The first two didn't answer. The next one picked up immediately. "Michael Nash."

"Michael, I'm Darcy Scott, a good friend of Erin Kelley's. I imagine you know what happened to her."

"Darcy Scott." The pleasant voice deepened with concern. "Erin told me about you. I'm so terribly sorry. I spoke with an FBI agent yesterday and assured him I'd like to help in any way I can. Erin was a lovely girl."

Darcy realized her eyes were filling with tears. "Yes, she was."

Obviously, he caught the catch in her voice. "This is terribly rough for you. Can I take you out for dinner some night soon? Talking about it may help."

"I'd like that."

"Tomorrow?"

Darcy thought swiftly. She was meeting Len at six. "If eight o'clock is all right with you."

"It's fine. I'll make a reservation at Le Cirque. Incidentally, how will I know you?"

"Medium brown hair, five eight. I'll wear a blue wool dress with a white collar."

"I'll be the most average-looking guy in the place. I'll be waiting at the bar."

Darcy hung up feeling somehow comforted. At least I'll get some use out of the Rodeo Drive clothes, she thought, and realized that instinctively she was making a mental note to call Erin and tell her that.

She got up and massaged the back of her neck. A dull headache made her realize she hadn't eaten since noon. It was now quarter of eight. A quick, hot shower, she decided. Then I'll heat some soup and watch that program.

The soup, appetizing enough when piping hot, slumped into a thick concoction of bits of vegetables swimming in tomato stock as Darcy stared at the screen. The photograph of the dead nineteen-year-old, her one foot in a scuffed Nike, the other in a sequined black satin pump, was horrifying. Was that the way Erin had looked when she'd been found? Hands folded on her waist, the tips of the mismatched shoes pointing in the air? What kind of sick brain could see that picture and want to duplicate it? The program closed with a reference to the fact that a copycat murderer might be responsible for the death of Erin Kelley.

When it was over, she snapped off the set and buried her face in her hands. Maybe the FBI was right about the copycat murder. It could not have been sheer coincidence that a few weeks after that program was shown, Erin had died in the same way.

But why Erin? And did the slipper she was wearing fit? If it did, how did her killer know her size? Maybe I'm crazy, she thought. Maybe I should back off and leave this to people who know what they're doing.

The phone rang. She was tempted not to answer it. Suddenly

she felt too tired to talk to anyone. But it might be news about Billy. The nursing home had her number to call for emergencies. She picked up the receiver. "Darcy Scott."

"In person. Well, *at last.* I've been trying you every few days. I'm Box 2721. Doug Fields."

IX

THURSDAY
February 28

ON THURSDAY MORNING, Nona, working with her assistant producer, Liz Kroll, completed the planning of the documentary. Liz, a thin-faced, sharp-featured young woman, had interviewed the potential guests, culling the duds as she put it.

"We've got a nice mix," she assured Nona. "Two couples who ended up married. The Cairones fell in love at first sight and are mushy enough to satisfy the romantic slobs. The Quinlans answered each other's ads and are pretty funny telling how their letters crossed in the mail. We've got someone who looks like young Abe Lincoln confiding how shy he is and that he's still hunting for the perfect girl. We've got a gal whose ad mistakenly read that she was a wealthy divorcée. She got seven hundred answers and has dated fifty-two of them so far. We've got a woman who had dinner with her date and at the end he picked a fight with her, stalked off, and stuck her with the check. The next guy practically attacked her when he drove her home. Now he hangs around her house. She woke up one morning and saw him looking in her bedroom window. If your friend Erin Kelley had actually met her date that night, we'd have a heck of a terrific wrap-up."

"Wouldn't we ever," Nona said quietly, and realized that she had never liked Liz.

Kruse did not seem to notice. "That FBI agent, Vince D'Ambrosio, is cute. I talked to him yesterday. He's going to show pictures of those missing girls on the program and warn people that they all answered personal ads. Then he'll ask if anybody has any information, that kind of thing. That worries me a little. We don't want to sound like *True Crimes,* but what can you do?" She got up to go. "One more thing. You know that Barnes woman from Lancaster whose daughter Claire has been missing for two years? I had a brainstorm yesterday. What about having her on the show? Just a brief segment. I bumped into Hamilton and he thought it was a great idea but said to check with you."

"Nobody bumps into Austin Hamilton." Nona felt anger cut through the dull lethargy that had been encompassing her with each passing day. Not for a single minute could she get Erin out of her mind. That face, always ready to break into a smile, that slender, graceful body. Like the others in the waltz class where they'd met, Nona was a pretty good dancer, but both Erin and Darcy were outstanding. Particularly Erin. Everyone else stopped to watch when she waltzed with the instructor. And I got friendly with them and told them about this great idea I had for a personal ad documentary. If only Vince D'Ambrosio were right. He believed Erin had been the random victim of a copycat murderer. Please God, let it be that, Nona prayed. Let it be that.

But if Erin had died because she'd answered personal ads, let this program help to save someone else. "I'll call Mrs. Barnes in Lancaster," she told Kroll, her tone a clear dismissal.

*D*ARCY SAT on the windowsill of the bedroom she was redecorating for the teenager who would soon be coming home from the hospital. Erin's pewter and brass bed would be perfect. The charming turn-of-the-century lady's vanity that she'd picked up in Old Tappan last week had deep drawers. It really was like a small dresser and wouldn't crowd the room. The present double dresser, a battered mahogany veneer object, was a horror. More overhead shelves in the closet would take care of bulky items like sweaters.

She was aware that the girl's mother, a weary look on her pleasant face, was studying her anxiously. "Lisa's been in a dreary room in the hospital for such a long time that I thought having her room done over might give her a lift. She's in for so much therapy, but she's spunky. She told the doctors she'll be back in dancing class in another couple of years. Ever since she could toddle, the minute she heard music she'd start to dance."

Lisa had been run over by a messenger on a bike who'd been cycling at top speed against the traffic on a one-way street. He'd smashed into her, breaking her legs, ankles, and foot bones. "She loves to dance," her mother added wistfully.

"Loves music, loves to dance." Darcy smiled, thinking of the framed poster with that title that had been in Erin's bedroom. Erin always said that it was the first thing she saw in the morning and it brightened her day. She firmly squelched the instinctive desire to keep it as a memoir. "I have just the thing for that wall," she said, and felt the constant pain ease a little. It was almost as though Erin was nodding in approval.

*T*HE HARKNESS AGENCY on East Forty-fifth Street was the discreet investigative firm Susan Fox retained to probe into the nocturnal wanderings of her husband, Douglas. The retainer of fifteen hundred dollars had seemed symbolic to her. That was just what she had squirreled away in a personal account, saving for Doug's August birthday. She'd smiled sadly as she wrote the check.

On Wednesday she had called Carol Harkness. "My husband has one of his famous nonmeetings tonight."

"We'll have Joe Pabst, one of our best people, following him," she was assured.

On Thursday, Pabst, jovial-featured, heavy-set, reported to his boss. "This guy's a piece of work. He leaves his office, cabs up to London Terrace. He's got an apartment there; been subletting from the owner, an engineer named Carter Fields, for two years. He's registered as Douglas Fields. Pretty neat. That way, nobody questions an illegal sublet and he don't run into anyone tracking him down at work or at home. Same initials, too. That's lucky. Don't have to worry about his monogrammed cufflinks."

Pabst shook his head in reluctant admiration. "The neighbors think he's an illustrator. Super tells me he's got a lot of signed pen-and-ink stuff framed in the apartment. I gave the super the garbage about him being up for a government assignment. Slipped the usual twenty bucks to keep the mouth shut."

At thirty-eight, Carol Harkness looked like one of the women executives in the AT&T commercials. Her well-cut black suit was brightened only by a gold lapel pin. Her ash-blond hair was shoulder length. Her hazel eyes had a cool, impersonal expression. The daughter of a New York City detective, the love of police work was in her blood.

"Did he stay there or go out?" she asked.

"Went out. About seven o'clock. You should have seen the difference in him. Hair combed so it looked real curly. Turtleneck sweater. Jeans. Leather jacket. Don't get me wrong, not cheap-looking. Kind of the way the arty types with money dress. He met some gal in a bar in SoHo. Attractive. Thirty or so. Classy. I got the table behind them. They had a coupla drinks, then she said she had to leave."

"Anxious to dump him?" Harkness asked quickly.

"No way. She had big eyes for him. He's a good-looking guy and can turn on the charm. They have a date Friday night. They're going dancing at some nightclub downtown."

*H*IS FOREHEAD CREASED in concentration, Vince D'Ambrosio studied the autopsy report on Erin Kelley. It stated that she had eaten approximately an hour before she died. Her body showed no sign of decomposition. Her clothing had been soaked through. These facts were initially attributed to the sleet and cold the day she was found. The autopsy revealed that her organs were partially thawed. The medical examiner concluded that her body had been frozen immediately after her death.

Frozen! Why? Because it was too dangerous for the killer to dispose of the body immediately? Where had she been kept? Had she died on Tuesday night? Or was it possible that she had been held captive somewhere and died as late as Thursday?

Had she been planning to put the pouch of diamonds in the security vault? From all accounts, Erin Kelley was a level-headed young woman. Certainly, she didn't seem like the kind who would confide to a stranger that she was carrying a fortune in jewels in her purse.

Or would she?

They'd been running down the identity of the people who'd placed some of the ads they believed Erin answered. So far they'd all been like that lawyer, North. Absolute proof of where they'd been Tuesday night. Some of them picked up their own mail at the magazines or newspapers where they'd run the ads. Three of the forwarding addresses for the others turned out to be mail drops. Probably married guys who didn't want to take any chance of their wives opening the mail.

It was nearly five when Vince received a call from Darcy Scott. "I've been wanting to talk to you all day, but I've been out of the office on jobs," she explained.

Best thing for her, Vince thought. He liked Darcy Scott. After Kelley's body was found, he'd asked Nona Roberts about Scott's family and had been astonished to learn that she was the offspring of two superstars. Nothing Hollywood about that girl. Genuine. It was amazing some guy hadn't snapped her up yet. He asked her how it was going.

"It's going okay," Darcy said.

Vince tried to analyze what he was hearing in her voice. The first time he met her in Nona's office her low, strained tone suggested acute worry. At the morgue, until she'd broken down, she'd spoken in the emotionless monotone of a person in shock. Now there was a certain briskness. Determination. Vince knew instantly that Darcy Scott was still convinced that Erin's death was the result of answering personal ads.

He was about to talk to her about that when she asked, "Vince, something has been bothering me. Did that high-heeled shoe Erin was wearing fit? I mean, was it her size?"

"It was the same size as her boot, seven and a half narrow."

"Then how did whoever put it on her happen to have a shoe exactly her size?"

Smart girl, Vince thought. Carefully, he weighed his words. "Miss Scott, that's something we're working on now. We're trying to trace that shoe through the manufacturer to learn where it was purchased. It's not cheap, in fact the pair probably cost several hundred dollars. That narrows considerably the number of outlets in the New York area that might carry it. I promise I'll keep you posted on developments." He hesitated, then added, "I hope you've given up the idea of following up any personal ads Erin Kelley answered for you."

"As a matter of fact," Darcy told him, "I have my first date with one of them in an hour."

*L*EN PARKER at six. They were meeting at McMullen's on Seventy-sixth and Third. A trendy place, Darcy thought, and certainly safe. A favorite with the New York "in" crowd. She'd been there on dates a few times and liked the owner, Jim McMullen. She was only going to have a glass of wine with Parker. He'd told her he was meeting some friends at the Athletic Club to play basketball.

She had told Michael Nash that she would be wearing a blue wool dress with a white collar. Now that she had it on, she felt overdressed. Erin always teased her about the clothes her mother showered on her. "When you get around to wearing them, you make the rest of us look as though we shop in John's Bargain Store."

Not true, Darcy thought as she applied another smidgen of midnight-gray eye shadow. Erin always looked great, even in college when she had so little money to buy clothes.

She decided to wear the silver and azurite pin Erin had given her for her birthday. "Funky but fun," Erin had pronounced it. The pin was shaped like a bar of music. The notes were lined in azurite, exactly the sea-blue shade of the dress. Silver bracelets and earrings and narrow suede boots completed the outfit.

Carefully, Darcy appraised herself in the mirror. On the trip to California, her mother had bullied her into going to her personal hairdresser. He'd changed her part, cut off a few inches, then accentuated the natural blond highlights in her hair. She had to admit that she liked the results. She shrugged. Okay, I look good enough that Len Parker probably won't walk out on me when I show up.

Parker was tall, bone-thin, but not unattractive. A college teacher, he told her he had recently moved to New York from Wichita, Kansas, and didn't know many people. Over a glass of wine he confided that a friend had suggested he place a personal ad. "They're really expensive. You'd be surprised. It makes a lot more sense to answer other people's ads, but I'm sure glad you answered mine." His eyes were light brown but large and expressive. He stared at Darcy. "I really have to say this. You're very pretty."

"Thank you." Why was it that something about him made her uncomfortable? Was he really a teacher, or was he like the one date she'd had before she went to California? That guy had claimed to be an advertising executive and didn't know the first thing about the agencies she brought up with him.

Parker fidgeted on the bar stool, rocking it slightly. His voice was low and with the hubbub of conversation from the people nearby, Darcy had to lean over to hear him.

"Very pretty," he emphasized. "You know, not all the girls I've met are pretty. When you read the letters they send, you'd think they were Miss Universe. And who shows up? Olive Oyl."

He signaled for another glass of wine. "You?"

"I'm fine." Carefully, she chose her words. "Surely all of them weren't that bad. I bet you've met some really pretty girls."

He shook his head emphatically. "Not like you. No way."

It was a long hour. Darcy heard about Parker's trouble finding an apartment. The prices, wow. Some girls think you should take them out for fancy dinners. Come on. Who can keep that up?

Finally, Darcy was able to get Erin's name in. "I know. My friend and I both met some strange people through these ads. Her name was Erin Kelley. Did you meet her by any chance?"

"Erin Kelley?" Parker swallowed convulsively. "Wasn't that the girl who got murdered last week? No, I never met her. And she was your friend? Gee, I'm sorry. That's lousy. Did they find the killer yet?"

She did not want to discuss Erin's death. There was no way, even if Erin met this man once, that she'd have gone out with him a second time. She looked at her watch. "I have to run. And you'll be late for your basketball game."

"Oh, that's all right. I'll skip it. Stay for dinner. They have good hamburgers here. Expensive, but good."

"I really can't. I'm meeting someone."

Parker frowned. "Tomorrow night? I mean, I know I'm not much to look at and teachers are famous for not making much money, but I'd really like to see you again."

Darcy slipped her arms into her coat. "I really can't. Thank you."

Parker stood up and punched the bar. "Well, you can pay for the drinks. You think you're too good for me. I'm too good for you."

She was relieved to see him stalk out of the restaurant. When the bartender came with the check, he said, "Miss, don't bother with that nut. Did he pull his college-professor stuff? He's on the maintenance staff at NYU. He gets more free drinks and meals through those ads he places. You got off cheap."

Darcy laughed. "I think I did, too." A thought struck her. She reached in her purse for Erin's picture. "By any chance, did he ever show up with this girl?"

The bartender, who looked as though he might be an actor, studied the picture carefully, then nodded. "He sure did. Around two weeks ago. She was a knockout. She walked out on him."

*A*T SIX O'CLOCK, Nona was surprised and pleased to receive a call from Vince D'Ambrosio. "You're obviously another one who doesn't keep regular hours," he said. "I'd like to talk to you about your program. Are you free for dinner in about an hour?"

She was.

"Okay, make a reservation at a good steak place in your neighborhood."

Smiling, she hung up. D'Ambrosio was clearly a meat-and-potatoes man, but she'd bet her bottom dollar that his cholesterol level was fine. She realized that she was unreasonably glad that she'd worn her new Donna Karan jumpsuit today. The cranberry shade suited her and the gold belt with the clasped hands accentuated her small waist. Nona knew that her waistline was her one vanity. Then she had a flash of overwhelming sadness. Erin had made that belt for her for Christmas.

Shaking her head as though to negate the reality of Erin's death, she got up and walked around her desk, rotating her shoulders. She'd spent the entire day working on the documentary and felt as though her body was a mass of knots. At three o'clock, Gary Finch, the Hudson Cable anchorman, had reviewed it with her. At the end of the session, Finch, a notorious perfectionist, smiled and said, "It's going to be great."

"Approbation from Sir Hubert is praise indeed." Nona stretched and tried to decide whether or not to call Emma Barnes in Lancaster again. She'd already tried three or four times. Admittedly, Liz was smart to suggest having Barnes appear on the program to talk about her missing daughter who had answered personal ads. Liz was bright and imaginative. But she was trying to skunk me when she discussed Barnes with Hamilton, Nona decided. She wants my job. Let her try.

She gave one last, long stretch, sat at her desk, and dialed the Lancaster number. Once more the Barnes household did not answer.

Vince arrived promptly at seven. He was wearing a well-cut gray pinstriped suit accompanied by a brown and beige tie. It's for sure no woman picks out his ties, Nona thought, remembering how fussy Matt had been about what tie went with which shirt and what suit.

The restaurant was on Broadway, a few blocks from Nona's apartment. "Let's save the serious stuff for dessert," Vince suggested. Over salads they briefly sketched their personal lives. "If you were placing a personal ad, what would you say about your-self?" he asked.

Nona reflected. "Divorced White Female, age 41, cable televi-sion producer."

He sipped his scotch. "Go on."

"Manhattan born and bred. Think anyone who lives anywhere else is mentally ill."

He laughed. She noticed that caused friendly creases in the cor-ners of his eyes.

Nona sipped her wine. "This is terrific burgundy," she com-mented. "I hope you're planning to have some when the steak comes."

"I am. Finish your ad, please."

"Barnard graduate. I didn't even leave Manhattan for college, you see. I did have a year abroad, and I do like to travel as long as I'm not gone more than three weeks."

"Your ad's getting expensive."

"I'll wind it up. Clean but not particularly tidy. You've noticed my office. Do not have green thumb. Good cook but hate fussy food. Love jazz. And oh, yes, I'm a good dancer."

"That's how you got friendly with Erin Kelley and Darcy Scott, in a dance class," D'Ambrosio commented, and then watched as pain darkened Nona's eyes. Hurriedly he added, "My ad's a little shorter. I work for the government. Divorced White Male, 43 years old, FBI agent, brought up in Waldwick, New Jersey, grad-uated from NYU. Can't dance without tripping over my own feet. Like to travel as long as it isn't Vietnam. Three years there was enough. And last, but certainly not least, I have a fifteen-year-old son, Hank, who's a swell kid."

As she had promised, the steaks were superb. Over coffee they talked about the program. "We're taping it in two weeks," Nona said. "I'd like to save you for last so people are left with a sobering warning about the potential danger of answering these ads. You're going to show the pictures of the missing girls, aren't you?"

"Yes. There's always the chance a viewer may have information about one of them."

It was biting cold when they left the restaurant. A frosty winter wind made Nona gasp. Vince took her arm as they crossed the street. He did not remove it the rest of the way to her apartment.

He accepted her invitation to come up for a nightcap. Nona remembered happily that her cleaning lady, Lola, had been in. The place would look presentable.

The seven-room apartment was in a prewar building. She could see D'Ambrosio's eyebrows raise as he took in the large foyer, the high ceilings, the long windows on Central Park West, the paintings in the living room, the massive Jacobean furniture. "Very nice," he commented.

"My folks gave it to me as is when they moved to Florida. I'm an only child, and this way when they come up to New York, my father feels comfortable. He hates hotels." She went to the bar. "What'll it be?"

She poured Sambuca for both of them, then paused. "It's only quarter past nine. Do you mind if I take a minute to phone someone?" She reached in her purse. As she looked up the Barnes's number, she explained why she was calling them.

This time the phone was picked up immediately. Nona froze as she realized the sound she was hearing was a woman screaming. A man's voice gave a distracted greeting. In shocked bewilderment he said, "Whoever this is, please get off the phone. I must call the police immediately. We've been away all day and just opened the mail. There was a package addressed to my wife."

The screams were now a shrieking crescendo. Nona motioned to Vince to pick up the portable telephone on the table beside him.

"Our daughter," the bewildered voice went on. "She's been missing for two years. That package has one of Claire's own shoes and a high-heeled satin slipper in it." He began to shout, "Who sent this? Why did they send it? Does this mean Claire is dead?"

ARCY WAS handed out of the cab by the door-
man, entered Le Cirque, and felt herself begin to unwind. She had
not realized how much energy she had put into the meeting with
Len Parker. Her head was still buzzing with the realization that he
had met Erin. Why had he denied it? Erin had walked out on him.
Certainly, she'd never dated him again. Was it simply that he
didn't want to be questioned and have to admit the lies about his
background?

Every time her mother and father were in New York they dined
at Le Cirque. It was a wonderful restaurant. Darcy found herself
wondering why she didn't come here more often. *How ever did
two such stunning people manage to produce that mousy-looking
child?* And how could one sentence remain so imbedded in memory?

The bar was to the left. Small and charming, it was not a hang-
out but a place to wait for a guest or a table. A young couple was
standing near it, chatting animatedly. A single man was at the end.
The most ordinary-looking person you'll see.

Michael Nash had not been kind to himself. Dark blond hair, a
face that was saved from being conventionally handsome by a
rather sharp chin, a long, trim body, dark blue suit with faint
pinstripes, silver and blue tie. As he looked at her with obvious
recognition and pleasure, Darcy was aware that Michael Nash's
eyes were an unusual shade, somewhere between sapphire and
midnight blue.

"Darcy Scott." It was a statement, not a question. He signaled
to the maître d' and put his hand under her elbow.

They were seated at a prime table in full view of the entrance.
Michael Nash must be a frequent and valued customer of Le
Cirque.

"A drink? Wine?"

"White wine, please. And a glass of water."

He ordered a bottle of Pellegrino with the Chardonnay, then smiled. "Now that for the moment we've taken care of the necessaries, as an old friend puts it, Darcy, it's good to meet you."

For the next half hour, she realized that he was deliberately steering the conversation away from Erin. It was only after she had begun to sip the wine and pick at a roll that he said, "Mission accomplished. I think you are finally starting to feel safe."

Darcy stared at him. "Whatever do you mean?"

"I mean that I was watching for you. I saw the way you hurried in. Everything about you suggested a high level of tension. What happened?"

"Nothing. I'd really like to talk about Erin."

"I would too. But Darcy . . ." He stopped. "Look, I can't get out of the business of doing what I do all day. I'm a psychiatrist." His smile was apologetic.

She felt herself at last begin to relax. "I'm the one who should apologize. You're absolutely right. I did feel pretty tense coming here." She told him about Len Parker.

He listened attentively, his head slightly tilted. "You'll of course report this man to the police."

"The FBI, actually."

"Vincent D'Ambrosio? As I told you when you called, he came to my office on Tuesday. Unfortunately, I could tell him very little. I met Erin for a drink several weeks ago. I had the immediate feeling that a girl like her had no need to answer personal ads. I challenged her with that and she told me about the program her friend is putting together. She mentioned you. Said her best friend was answering ads with her."

Darcy nodded, hoping that her eyes were not going to fill with tears.

"I don't usually explain that the reason I'm going this route is because of a book I'm working on, but I did tell Erin. We exchanged some stories about our various dates. I've tried to remember everything she said, but she didn't give any names and they were funny stories. Certainly, I had no hint that anyone worried her."

" 'Close encounters of the worst kind,' she used to call them."

Nash laughed. "She told me that. I asked if we could plan dinner soon, and she agreed. I was trying to wrap up my book and she was completing a necklace she had designed. I said I'd get back to her. When I tried, there was no answer. From what Vincent D'Ambrosio said, it was already too late."

"That was the night she thought she was meeting someone named Charles North. I still think that even though he didn't show up, her death has to do with a personal ad she answered."

"Thinking that, why are you answering personal ads now?"

"Because I'm going to find that man."

He looked troubled but did not comment. They studied the menu, both selecting the Dover sole. As they ate, Nash seemed to be deliberately trying to keep her mind off Erin's death. He told her about himself. "My father made his money in plastics. Literally lived out that famous line from *The Graduate.* Then bought a rather garishly ornate mansion in Bridgewater. He was a decent, fine man, and every time I wonder why three of us needed twenty-two rooms, I remember how happy he was showing them off."

He touched on his divorce. "I married the week after I graduated from college. Terrible mistake for both of us. It wasn't a financial problem, but medical school, especially when it involves the continuing study of psychoanalysis, is a long, hard road. We didn't have time for each other. By the end of four years, she'd had enough. Sheryl lives in Chicago now and has three children."

It was Darcy's turn. Carefully, she steered around giving the names of her famous parents, jumping quickly to leaving the advertising agency and setting up her budget decorating business. "Somebody once told me I'm a new version of Sanford and Son, and I guess it's true, but I love it." She thought of the room she was decorating for the recuperating sixteen-year-old.

If he noticed gaps in the background, he did not comment. The salads arrived just as a producer friend of her parents stopped at the table. "Darcy!" A warm kiss, a hug. He introduced himself to Michael Nash. "Harry Curtis." He turned back to Darcy. "You get prettier every day. I hear your parents are touring in Australia. How's it going?"

"They just got there."

"Well, give them my love." Another hug and Curtis left for his own table.

Nash's eyes did not signal curiosity. That's the way it works with shrinks, Darcy thought. They wait for you to tell them. She did not offer an explanation of what Curtis had said.

It was a pleasant dinner. Nash confessed to two passions, riding and tennis. "They're what keep me in Bridgewater." Over espresso, he returned to the subject of Erin's death. "Darcy, I don't usually offer advice to people, even free advice, but I wish you'd drop the idea of answering these ads. That FBI fellow seemed perfectly competent to me and if I'm any judge, he's not going to rest until whoever murdered Erin is paying the price."

"He told me that in so many words. I guess we all do what we have to do." She managed a smile. "The last time I spoke to Erin, she said she'd met one nice guy and wouldn't you know it, he hadn't called back. I'd bet my bottom dollar it was you."

He took her home in a cab, told the driver to wait, and walked her to the door. The wind was sharp and he turned so that he was protecting her from its full blast as she turned the key. "May I call you again?"

"I'd like that." For a moment she thought he was going to kiss her cheek, but he simply pressed her hand and went back to the waiting cab.

The wind pulled at the door, causing it to close slowly. As the lock clicked, the sound of footsteps made her turn. Through the glass she could see the figure of a man rushing up the steps. An instant sooner and he would have been in the vestibule with her. As she stared at him, her mouth too dry to scream, Len Parker pounded at the door, kicked it, then turned and ran down the block.

X
FRIDAY
March 1

G*RETA SHERIDAN* debated between getting up or trying to sleep for another hour. A gusty March wind was rattling the windowpanes and she remembered that Chris had been after her to have these windows replaced.

The early-morning light filtered through the drawn draperies. She loved a cold room for sleeping. The quilt and blankets were warm and the blue and white moire canopy gave the bed a comforting enclosed feeling.

She had been dreaming of Nan. The anniversary of her death, March thirteenth, was two weeks away. Nan had turned nineteen the day before. This year she would have been celebrating her thirty-fourth birthday.

Would have been.

Impatiently, Greta tossed back the covers, reached for her velour robe, and got up. Pulling on her slippers, she went into the hallway and down the winding staircase to the main floor. She understood why Chris was concerned. It was a large house and it was generally known that she lived alone. "You don't know how easy it is for a professional to disarm a security system," he had warned several times.

"I love this house." Every room held so many happy memories. Somehow, Greta felt that to leave this place would be to leave them as well. And, she thought with an unconscious smile, if Chris would finally settle down one of these days and give me some grandchildren, it will be a wonderful place for them to visit.

The *Times* was at the side door. As the coffee perked, Greta began to read. There was a brief item on an inside page about that girl who'd been found dead in New York last week. Copycat murder. What a horrible thought. How could there be two such evil people, the one who had snuffed out Nan's life and the one who had killed Erin Kelley? Would Erin Kelley still be alive if that program had not been aired?

And what was it that she had been trying to remember when she insisted on watching it? Nan. Nan, she thought. You told me something that I should have realized was important.

Nan, chatting about school, her classes, her friends, her dates. Nan looking forward to the summer program in France. Nan who loved to dance. "I Could Have Danced All Night." The song could have been written for her.

Erin Kelley had also been found wearing one high-heeled shoe. High heel? What was it about those two words? Impatiently, Greta opened the *Times* to the crossword puzzle.

The phone rang. It was Gregory Layton. She'd met him at the club dinner the other night. In his early sixties, he was a federal judge and lived in Kent about forty miles away. "An attractive widower," Priscilla Clayburn had whispered to her. He *was* attractive, and he was asking her to have dinner with him tonight. Greta accepted and replaced the receiver, realizing that she was looking forward to the evening.

Dorothy came in at the stroke of nine. "Hope you don't have to go out this morning, Mrs. Sheridan. That wind is mean." She was carrying the mail, including a bulky package under her arm.

She laid everything on the table and frowned. "That's a funny looking thing. I mean, no return address. I hope it's not a bomb or something."

"Probably more of that awful crank mail. Damn that program." Greta started to pull at the string on the package and had a sudden sense of panic. "It does look funny. Let me call Glenn Moore."

Police Chief Moore had just arrived in his office at headquarters. "Don't touch that package, Mrs. Sheridan," he told her crisply. "We'll be right over." He called the state police. They promised to rush a portable security surveillance unit to the Sheridan household.

At ten o'clock, handling the package with infinite caution, an officer in the bomb squad positioned it to be X-rayed.

From the living room to which she and Dorothy had been banished, Greta heard the man's relieved laughter. Dorothy at her heels, she hurried back to the kitchen.

"These won't blow up, ma'am," she was assured. "Nothing in there except a pair of mismatched shoes."

Greta saw Moore's startled expression, felt the blood drain from her face as the package was ripped open, revealing a shoe box with the sketch of an evening slipper on the cover. The lid came off. Inside, nestled together in tissue, were a high-heeled sequined slipper and a scuffed running shoe.

"Oh, Nan! Nan!" Greta did not feel Moore grab her as she fainted.

*A*T THREE O'CLOCK on Friday morning, Darcy was yanked from restless sleep by the insistent ringing of the phone. Reaching for it, she saw the time on the clock radio. Her "hello" was quick and breathless.

"Darcy." Her name was whispered. The voice sounded familiar, but she couldn't place it.

"Who is this?"

The whisper became a shout. "Don't you ever close the door in my face again! Hear me? Hear me?"

Len Parker. She slammed down the phone, pulled the covers around her. A moment later the phone began to ring again. She did not pick it up. The ringing continued. Fifteen, sixteen, seventeen rings. She knew she should take the receiver off the hook but could not bear to touch it, knowing that Parker was on the other end.

Finally it stopped. She yanked the jack from the wall, rushed into the living room, and put the answering machine on automatic pickup, then hurried back to bed, slamming the bedroom door behind her.

Had he done this to Erin? Followed her when she walked out on him? Maybe followed her to the bar where she was supposed to meet someone named Charles North? Maybe forced her into a car?

She'd call Vince D'Ambrosio in the morning.

For the next two hours she lay awake, finally falling into a sleep that once again was troubled with vague, restless dreams.

At seven-thirty, she awakened with an instant sense of fear, then remembered the reason for it. A long, hot shower relieved some

157

of the tension. She pulled on jeans, a turtleneck sweater, her favorite boots.

The answering machine showed only hangups.

Juice and coffee at the table by the window. Staring down into the lifeless garden. At eight o'clock the phone rang. Not Len Parker, please. Her "hello" was guarded.

"Darcy, I hope it's not too early to call. I just wanted to tell you how much I enjoyed being with you last night."

She exhaled, a relieved sigh. "Oh, Michael, I can't tell you how much I enjoyed being with you too."

"Something happened. What was it?"

The concern in his voice was comforting. She told him about Len Parker, the episode on the steps, the phone call.

"I blame myself that I didn't see you upstairs."

"Please don't."

"Darcy, call that FBI agent and report this Parker character, and can I implore you to stop answering those ads?"

"I'm afraid not. But I will call Vince D'Ambrosio right away."

When she said good-bye, she hung up feeling oddly consoled.

She called Vince from the office. A wide-eyed Bev stood by her desk as she spoke to another agent. Vince had flown to Lancaster. The other agent took the information. "We're working with the police department. We'll get right onto that character. Thanks, miss."

Nona phoned and told her why Vince had gone to Lancaster. "Darce, this is so scary. It's one thing if someone saw that *True Crimes* episode and was perverted enough to repeat it, but this means someone may have been doing this for a long time. Claire Barnes has been missing for two years. She and Erin were so alike. She was just about to get her first big break in a Broadway musical. Erin had just gotten her first big break with Bertolini's."

Her first big break with Bertolini's. The words rippled through Darcy's mind as she made and received phone calls, went through Connecticut and New Jersey papers for notices of estate and moving sales, made a quick trip to the rental apartment she was furnishing, and finally stopped for a sandwich and coffee at a lunch counter.

That was where she realized what had been bothering her. *Her first big break with Bertolini's.* Erin had told her she was to receive twenty thousand dollars for designing and executing the necklace. In the rush of events, she forgot about the strange message on Erin's answering machine. She'd call them as soon as she got back to the office to confirm.

Aldo Marco came to the phone. Was this a family member making inquiries?

"I'm executor of Erin Kelley's estate." The words sounded appalling to her ears.

Payment had already been made to Miss Kelley's manager, Jay Stratton. Was there a problem?

"I'm sure there isn't." So Stratton presumed to act as Erin's manager.

He was not home. The message she left was brusque. Please call her immediately about Erin's check.

Jay Stratton phoned just before five o'clock. "I'm sorry. Of course I should have gotten to you sooner. I've been away. How shall I make out the check?" He told Darcy that while he was out of town he'd thought of nothing but Erin. "That beautiful, talented girl. I firmly believe that someone knew about that jewelry, killed her for it, and then tried to make it look like a copycat murder."

You of all people knew about the jewelry. It was an effort to listen to Stratton, to respond pleasantly to his sympathetic comments. He would be out of town again for a few days. She agreed to meet him Monday evening.

For minutes after she said good-bye to him, Darcy stared

straight ahead, lost in thought, then said aloud, "After all, as you say, Mr. Stratton, two of Erin's closest friends really ought to know each other better." She sighed. She'd better get some work done before it was time to dress for her date with Box 1527.

*V*INCE FLEW to Lancaster on the earliest flight Friday morning. He had urged Claire Barnes's father not to tell anyone outside the family about the package of shoes. But when he arrived at the airport the local paper had the story in headlines. He phoned the Barnes's home and learned from the maid that Mrs. Barnes had been rushed to the hospital last night.

Lawrence Barnes was a heavy-set executive type who, Vince decided, in other circumstances would have a commanding presence. Seated at the bedside, a young woman next to him, he was anxiously looking down at his heavily sedated wife. Vince showed him his card and was followed out into the corridor.

Barnes introduced the young woman as his other daughter, Karen. "A reporter happened to be in the emergency room when we got here," Barnes said tonelessly. "He heard Emma screaming about the package and that Claire was dead."

"Where are the shoes now?"

"At home."

Karen Barnes drove him to get them. A corporate lawyer in Pittsburgh, she had never shared her parents' hope that one day Claire would suddenly show up. "There was no way, if she were alive, she would have given up the chance to be in Tommy Tune's show."

The Barnes's home was a large Colonial in an impressive neighborhood. Zoning at least an acre, Vince thought. There was a television mobile unit on the street. Karen drove quickly past it, into the driveway, and around to the back of the house. A policeman prevented the reporter from stopping her.

The living room was filled with framed family pictures, many of them showing Karen and Claire in their growing-up years. Karen picked one of them off the piano. "I took this one of Claire the last time I saw her. We were in Central Park just a few weeks before she disappeared."

Slender. Pretty. Blond. Mid-twenties. Joyous smile. You can pick 'em, Buster, Vince thought bitterly. "May I take this? I'll make copies and get the original right back to you."

The package was on the foyer table. Ordinary brown wrapper, address label you could buy anywhere, block printing. Postmarked New York City. The box had no markings except for a delicately drawn sketch of a high-heeled slipper on the lid. The mismatched shoes. One a white Bruno Magli sandal, the other a gold slingback with an open toe and narrow high heel. They were the same size, six narrow.

"You're sure this sandal is hers?"

"Yes. I have an identical pair. We bought them together that last day in New York."

"How long had your sister been responding to personal ads?"

"About six months. The police checked out anyone whose ad she had answered, at least anyone they could find."

"Did she ever place any?"

"Not that I know of."

"Where did she live in New York?"

"On West 63rd Street. An apartment in a brownstone. My

father paid the rent for nearly a year after she disappeared, then
gave it up."

"Where did you put her belongings?"

"The furniture wasn't worth shipping. Her clothes and books
and whatever are upstairs in her old room."

"I'd like to see them."

There was a cardboard file box on a shelf in the closet. "I packed
that," Karen told him. "Her address book, date book, stationery,
some mail, that sort of thing. When we reported her missing, the
New York police went through all her personal papers."

Vince lifted down the box and opened it. A date book now two
years old was on top. He skimmed through it. From January till
August the pages were filled with appointments. Claire Barnes had
not been seen after August fourth.

"What makes it hard is that Claire had her own kind of short-
hand." Karen Barnes's voice quavered. "You see where it
says 'Jim.' That meant Jim Haworth's studio, where she took
dancing lessons. See, August fifth, 'Tommy.' That meant rehear-
sal for the Tommy Tune show, *Grand Hotel.* She'd just been
hired."

Vince turned the pages back. On July fifteenth at five o'clock he
saw "Charley."

Charley!

In a noncommittal tone he pointed to the entry. "Do you know
who this one is?"

"No. Although she did mention a Charley who took her dancing once. I don't believe the police were able to locate him." Karen
Barnes's face paled. "That slipper. It's the sort of thing you'd wear
to a dance."

"Exactly. Miss Barnes, keep that name between the two of us,
please. By the way, how long had your sister lived in her apartment?"

"Just about a year. Before that she had a place in the Village."

"Where?"

"Christopher Street. At 101 Christopher Street."

*A*T QUARTER OF FIVE, Darcy handed Bev the last of the bills to be paid, and on impulse phoned the mother of the recuperating teenager. The girl was coming home at the end of next week. The painter Darcy hired, a cheerful moonlighting security guard, was already on the job. "We'll have the room all set by Wednesday," Darcy assured the woman.

Thank heaven I had the brains to bring some clothes with me this morning, she thought as she changed from her sweater and jeans to an oval-necked, long-sleeved black silk blouse, a calf-length Italian silk skirt in tones of green and gold, a matching stole. Gold chain, a narrow gold bracelet, gold earrings—the jewelry all designed by Erin. In a crazy way she felt as though she was donning Erin's coat of arms as she rode into battle.

She released her hair from the clip and brushed it loose around her face.

Bev came back just as she finished applying eyeshadow. "You look fabulous, Darcy." Bev hesitated. "I mean, it always seemed to me that you kind of tried to play down your looks and now, I mean, oh God, I'm not saying it right. I'm sorry."

"Erin pretty much said the same thing," Darcy reassured her. "She was always bullying me to use more makeup or wear some of the fancy duds my mother sends me."

Bev was wearing a skirt and sweater Darcy had seen on her frequently. "By the way, how do Erin's clothes fit?"

"Perfect. I'm so glad to get them. The tuition just jumped again and I swear, with today's prices, I was getting ready to do a Scarlett O'Hara and make a dress out of curtains."

Darcy laughed. "That's still my favorite scene in *Gone With the Wind.* Look, I know I asked you to avoid wearing Erin's things to the office, but she'd be the first to say enjoy them. So feel free."

"Are you sure?"

Darcy reached past the faithful leather jacket for her cashmere cape. "Of course I'm sure."

She was meeting Box Number 1527, David Weld, at the grill at Smith and Wollensky's at five-thirty. He'd said he'd be at the last seat at the bar, "or standing near it." Brown hair. Brown eyes. About six feet tall. Wearing a dark suit.

It was easy to pick him out.

A pleasant guy, Darcy decided fifteen minutes later as they sat across from each other at one of the small tables. Born and raised in Boston. Worked for Holden's, the department store chain. Had been coming back and forth for the last few years as they expanded into the Tri-State Area.

She judged him to be in his mid-thirties, then wondered if there was something about that age that sent unattached singles scurrying to the personal ads.

It was easy to direct the conversation. He'd gone to Northeastern. His father and grandfather had been executives with Holden's. He'd worked there from the time he was a kid. After school. Saturdays. Summer vacations. "Never occurred to me to do anything else," he confided. "Retailing runs in the family."

He had never met Erin. He'd read about her death. "That's what makes you feel funny placing these ads. I mean, all I want is to meet some nice people." Pause. *"You're nice."*

164

"Thank you."

"I'd be very pleased to have dinner with you if you can stay."
He looked hopeful but the request was made with dignity.

No ego problem here, Darcy thought. "I honestly can't, but I
bet you've met some nice people answering these ads, haven't
you?"

He smiled. "A couple of very nice ones. One of them, if you can
believe it, just started to work for Holden's in the Paramus, New
Jersey, store. She's a buyer. Same kind of job I had before I went
into the management end."

"Oh? What was that?"

"I was shoe buyer for our New England stores."

*V*INCE GOT BACK to his office at Federal Plaza at
three o'clock Friday afternoon. There was an urgent message for
him to call Police Chief Moore in Darien. From him, Vince learned
about the package that had arrived at the Sheridan home.

"You're sure they're the mates of the ones Nan Sheridan was
wearing?"

"We've compared them. We have both sets now."

"Has the press gotten hold of this?"

"Not so far. We're trying to keep it quiet, but no guarantees.
You've met Chris Sheridan. That was his first concern."

"It's mine, too," Vince said quickly. "What we now know is
that this killer started fifteen years ago, if not sooner. He has to

have a reason for sending those shoes back at this time. I want to talk to one of our psychiatrists to get his opinion. But if anyone questioned about Nan Sheridan's death also can be linked to Claire Barnes, we've got something positive to go on."

"How about Erin Kelley? Don't you include her?"

"I'm still keeping an open mind. Her death may have been connected to the missing jewelry and made to look like a copycat murder." Vince arranged to pick up the shoes the next day and hung up.

His assistant, Ernie Cizek, a new young agent from Colorado, briefed him on Darcy's call about Len Parker.

"This guy's a weirdo," Cizek said. "Works in maintenance at NYU. An electrical whiz. Can fix anything. Loner. Paranoid about money. But get this! The family is loaded. Parker's got a hefty income. A trustee banks an allowance for him. He only made one large withdrawal, some years ago. The trustee thinks he bought property. Seems to live on his maintenance salary in a cheap walkup on Ninth Avenue. Has an old station wagon. No garage. He parks it on the street."

"Police record?"

"Same sort of thing that the Scott girl complained about. Following girls home. Shouting at them. Banging on doors. He's a great one for placing personal ads. Everybody brushes him off. So far no physical attacks. Restraining orders but no convictions."

"Bring him in now."

"I've talked to his shrink. He says he's harmless."

"Sure he's harmless. Just like Peeping Toms supposedly never act out their fantasies. We both know better, don't we?"

*S*USAN'S ANNOUNCEMENT that she was plan-
ning to take the children to visit her father in Guilford, Connecticut, for the weekend was received with eager agreement by her
husband. Doug had made the date to go dancing with the divorced
real estate broker and was wondering if he should break it. He had
been late two nights this week and even though Susan had seemed
to enjoy their New York dinner on Monday night, there was
something about her attitude that he could not put his finger on.

Susan's visiting her father with the kids till Sunday gave him
two nights off. He did not offer to go with her. It would have been
an empty gesture. Susan's father had never liked him, always made
cracks about how important Doug must be that he worked so
many nights. "Funny, with all that hard work, you needed to
borrow so much from me to buy the house, Doug. I'd be glad to
go over your budget with you and see where the problem is."

Sure you would.

"Have a good time, honey," Doug told Susan when he was
leaving on Friday morning. "And give my best to your Dad."

That afternoon, while the baby slept, Susan phoned the investigative agency for a report. Calmly she took down the information
they gave her. The meeting with the woman in the SoHo bar. The
date they'd made to go dancing. The apartment in London Terrace
under the name Douglas Fields. "Carter Fields is his old buddy,"
she told the investigator. "They're two of a kind. Don't bother to
follow him again. I don't want to hear any more."

Her father lived year-round in the pre-Revolutionary house that
had been their summer home. Several heart attacks had left him

with a permanent pallor that tore at Susan's heart. But there was nothing fragile about his demeanor or voice. After dinner, Beth and Donny went next door to visit friends. Susan put Trish and the baby to bed, then fixed demitasse and brought it into the library.

She knew her father was studying her as she prepared his cup with sweetener and a lemon peel.

"Exactly when do I hear the reason for this unexpected, although most welcome, visit?"

Susan smiled. "Now, I guess. I'm going to divorce Doug."

Her father waited.

Promise not to say "I told you so," Susan prayed silently, then went on, "I've had an investigative agency following him. He has a sublet in New York under the name Douglas Fields. Calls himself a freelance illustrator. Doug does sketch very well as you know. Has plenty of dates. In the meantime, he rants on to me about how hard he works, 'all those night meetings.' Donny can see through his lies and is angry and contemptuous. He'll be better off to expect nothing from his father than to keep on hoping that it will change."

"Would you like to move in here, Susan? There's plenty of room."

She flashed him a grateful smile. "You'd go crazy in a week. No. The Scarsdale house is too large. Doug insisted we buy it to impress the people at the club. We couldn't afford it then, and I'm beginning to understand why we can't afford it now. I'll sell it, get a smaller place, put the baby in a day care center next year— there's a terrific one in town. Then I'll get a job."

"It won't be easy."

"It'll be a lot better than it is now."

"Susan, I'm trying not to say, 'I told you so,' but there it is. That fellow is a born womanizer and he's got a vicious streak. Remember your eighteenth birthday? That night he was so drunk when he brought you home that I threw him out? The next morning every window in my car was broken."

"You still can't be sure it was Doug."

"Come on, Susan. If you're going to start facing facts, face them all. And tell me this. Weren't you covering for him when he was questioned in that girl's death?"

"Nan Sheridan?"

"Of course, Nan Sheridan."

"Doug simply isn't capable—"

"Susan, what time did he pick you up the morning she died?"

"Seven o'clock. We wanted to get back to Brown for a hockey game."

"Susan, before she died I got the truth out of Grandma. You were in tears because you thought Doug had stood you up again. He got to our place after nine. At least grant me the satisfaction of telling the truth now."

The front door banged shut. Donny and Beth came in. Donny's face looked relaxed and happy. It was becoming a carbon copy of Doug's face at that age. She'd had a crush on Doug from their sophomore year in high school.

Susan felt a stab of pain. I'll never get over him completely, she acknowledged. *Doug pleading with her, "Susan, my car broke down. They're trying to accuse me. They want to blame somebody. Please say I was here at seven."*

Donny came over to kiss her. She reached back and smoothed his hair, then turned to her father. "Dad, come on. You know how confused Grandma was. Even back then she didn't know one day from another."

XI
SATURDAY
March 2

*I*T WAS 2:30 a.m. Saturday morning when he got to the place. By then his need to be there was overwhelming. When he was in the place, Charley could be his own person. No more skulking behind the other one. Able to dance in synch with Astaire, smiling down at the phantom in his arms, crooning in her ear. The wonderful solitude of the place, the draperies drawn against the unseemly gaze of a casual interloper, the bolts securing him from the outside world, the limitless sense of self, unrestrained by listeners or observers, free to roam in the delicious memories.

Nan. Claire. Janine. Marie. Sheila. Leslie. Annette. Tina. Erin. All of them smiling at him, so glad to be with him, never getting the chance to turn on him, sneer at him, look at him with contempt. In the end, when they understood, it had been so wonderfully satisfying. He regretted that he hadn't given Nan a chance to realize what was happening, to beg. Leslie and Annette had pleaded for their lives. Marie and Tina had cried.

Sometimes the girls came back to him one by one. Other times they appeared together. *Change partners and dance with me.*

By now the first two packages would have arrived. Oh, if only one could be the proverbial fly on the wall, watching the moment when they were opened, when the puzzled expression changed to comprehension.

Copycat.

They wouldn't call him that anymore. Now had Janine been next, or Marie? Janine. September twentieth, two years ago. He'd send her package now.

He went to the basement. The boxes with the shoes were such an amusing sight. Pulling on the plastic gloves he always used when he handled anything that belonged to the girls, he reached for the one behind the placecard marked "Janine." He'd send it to her family in White Plains.

His eye lingered on the last placecard. "Erin." He began to giggle. Why not send hers now? That would really put their copycat notion in the gutter. She'd told him her father was in a nursing home. He'd send them to her New York address.

But suppose no one in her apartment building was smart enough to give the package to the police? What a waste to have it gathering dust in some storeroom.

What about sending the shoes care of the morgue? After all, that was her last address in New York. How funny that would be.

First, make sure to wipe the shoes and boxes thoroughly just to make sure there were absolutely no prints on them. Get out the identification. He'd plucked their wallets from their purses, then buried the purses.

Wrap fresh tissue around the mismatched sets. Close the lids. He admired his sketches. He was getting better. The one on Erin's box was as good as any professional could do.

Brown wrapping paper, sealing tape. Address label. Any one of them could have been bought anywhere in the United States.

He addressed Janine's package first.

Now it was Erin's turn. The New York telephone book would give the address of the morgue.

Charley frowned. Suppose some dumb klutz in the mailroom

didn't open it, just gave it back to the postman. "Nobody with that name works here." Without a return address the package would go into the dead-letter office.

There was one other possibility. Would it be a mistake? No. Not really. He giggled again. This will certainly keep them guessing!

He began to print the name of the person he had chosen to receive Erin's boot and special slipper.

DARCY SCOTT . . .

*O*N SATURDAY, Darcy met Box 1143, Albert Booth, for brunch at the Victory Café. She judged him to be about forty. In their telephone conversation she'd managed to learn that his ad claimed he was a computer expert, enjoyed reading, skiing, golfing, waltzing, leisurely strolls through museums, and listening to records. He also said he had a good sense of humor.

That, Darcy decided, after Booth asked her "if meeting a box number made her feel boxed in," stretched truth to the breaking point. By the time she had finished her first cup of coffee, she also doubted just about everything else he'd claimed except computer expert. He had a soft couch-potato look that did not hint of a skier, golfer, waltzer, or walker.

His conversation consisted solely of the past, present, and future of computers. "Forty years ago a computer took two big rooms of heavy equipment to do what the one on your desk is doing now."

"I finally bought one just last year."

He looked shocked.

Over eggs Benedict, he shared his disgust with the way clever students were manipulating school records by breaking into computer systems. "They should go to jail for five years. And pay a big fine too."

Darcy was sure that desecration of the sanctuary or ark of the temple would not have been any more serious to him.

Over the last cup of coffee, he finally finished expounding his theory that future wars would be won or lost by experts able to crack enemy computers. "Change all the figures, see what I mean. You think you have two thousand nuclear warheads in Colorado. Somebody changes it to two hundred. You have armies deployed. The statistics change. Where's the Fifth Division? The Seventh? You don't know anymore. Right?"

"Right."

Booth smiled suddenly. "You're a good listener, Darcy. Not many girls are good listeners."

It was the opening she needed. "I've just started to answer personal ads. You certainly meet a variety of people. What are most of them like?"

"Most of them are pretty boring." Albert leaned across the table. "Listen, you want to know who I took out just two weeks ago?"

"Who?"

"That girl who was murdered. Erin Kelley."

Darcy hoped she would not overreact. "What was *she* like?"

"Pretty girl. Nice. She was worried about something."

Darcy gripped her coffee cup. "Did she tell you what was worrying her?"

"She sure did. She told me she was finishing some necklace and it was her first really big job and as soon as she was paid she was going to look for a new apartment."

"Any reason?"

"She said the superintendent was always brushing against her when she passed him and making excuses to be in her apartment. Looking for a water leak, a heat blockage, that kind of thing. She said she supposed he was harmless, but it was kind of creepy to walk into her bedroom and find him there. I guess it had just happened again the day before I met her."

"Don't you think you ought to let the police know about this?"

"No way. I work for IBM. They don't want any of their employees ever to be mentioned in the papers unless they're getting married or buried. I tell the police and they start checking on me. Right? But I wonder. Do you think I ought to drop them an anonymous note?"

*T*HE VAST RESOURCES of the FBI swung into high gear for the search for the retail outlet where the high-heeled evening slipper that had been returned to the home of Claire Barnes and the one found on Erin Kelley's body had been purchased. In the case of Nan Sheridan, fifteen years ago the police had traced the slipper to a shoe outlet on Route 1 in Connecticut. No one then had had any memory of who had bought it.

The Claire Barnes slipper was expensive, a Charles Jourdan, sold in fine department stores all over the country. Two thousand pairs, to be exact. Impossible to trace. Erin Kelley's was a Salvatore Ferragamo, a current model.

Agents and NYPD detectives began to fan through department stores, shoe salons, discount outlets.

. . .

Len Parker was brought in for questioning. He began immediately to rant about how rude Darcy had been to him. "I just wanted to apologize. I knew I'd been mean. Maybe she did have a dinner date. I followed her and she wasn't lying. I waited outside in the cold while she ate in that fancy restaurant."

"You just stood there?"

"Yes."

"And then?"

"She got right in a cab with some guy. I took one too. Got out down the block. The guy walked her to the door and left. I ran up. After all I went through to apologize, she slammed the door in my face."

"How about Erin Kelley? Did you follow her?"

"Why should I? She walked out on me. Maybe that was my fault. I was in a bad mood when I saw her. I told her all women were rotten gold diggers."

"Then why didn't you admit that to Darcy Scott? When she asked you, you denied meeting Erin."

"Because I knew I'd end up here."

"You live on Ninth Avenue and Forty-eighth Street?"

"Yes."

"Your trustee at the bank thinks you have another residence. You withdrew a large sum of money five or six years ago."

"It was my money to spend as I please."

"Did you buy another residence?"

"Prove it."

On Saturday afternoon when he was finished with Len Parker, Vince D'Ambrosio drove to 101 Christopher Street and rang the bell. Gus Boxer, his face set in surly lines, came to the door. He was wearing a long-sleeved undershirt. Tattered suspenders held up shapeless trousers. He acted unimpressed by the FBI badge. "I'm off duty. What do ye want?"

"I want to talk to you, Gus. Your place or headquarters? And drop the righteous indignation. I have your file on my desk, Mr. Hoffman."

Boxer's eyes darted nervously. "Come on in. And keep your voice down."

"I wasn't aware I'd raised it."

Boxer led the way to his ground-floor apartment. As Vince had expected from the way the man dressed, the apartment was a further extension of his personality. Shabby, stained upholstery. Remnants of a once-beige rug. A rickety table piled with porn magazines.

Vince riffled through them. "Quite a collection you have here."

"Any law against it?"

Vince slapped down the magazines. "Listen, Hoffman, we've never gotten anything on you, but your name has an unhealthy way of coming up on the computer. Ten years ago you were the super of an apartment where a twenty-year-old girl was found dead in the basement."

"I had nothing to do with that."

"She'd filed a complaint with the management that she found you in her apartment going through her closet."

"I was looking for a water leak. There was a waterpipe in the wall behind that closet."

"That's the same story you gave Erin Kelley two weeks ago, isn't it?"

"Who said that?"

"She told someone that she was going to move as soon as possible because she'd found you in her bedroom."

"I was—"

"Looking for a water leak. I know. Now let's talk about Claire Barnes. How many times did you drop in on her unexpectedly when she lived here?"

"Never."

When he left Boxer, Vince went directly to his office, arriving there just in time to get a call from Hank. Was it okay if he didn't get in until eight or so? There was a basketball game at school and some of the gang were going out for pizza afterward.

A great kid, Vince told himself again as he assured Hank that was fine. Worth all the years of trying to make a go of his marriage to Alice. Well at least she was happy now. The pampered wife of a guy whose wallet was as fat as his waistline. And he? I'd like to meet someone, Vince admitted to himself, then realized that Nona Roberts's face was suddenly filling his mind.

His assistant Ernie told him there'd been a break. A detective from the Midtown North Precinct had picked up Petey Potters, the derelict who lived on the pier where Erin Kelley's body was found. They were bringing Petey into the precinct for questioning. Vince turned and ran for the elevators.

Petey was having trouble with his vision. Seeing double. That happened sometimes after he'd had a coupla bottles of dago red. That meant that instead of three cops he was seeing three sets of twin cops. Nobody's eyes were friendly.

Petey thought about the dead girl. How cold she'd felt when he'd lifted the necklace.

What was the cop saying? "Petey, there are fingerprints on Erin Kelley's throat. We're going to compare them with yours."

Through a haze, Petey thought of one of his friends who'd happened to stab a guy. He was in prison for five years now and the guy he stabbed had hardly been scratched. Petey had never been in trouble with the cops. Never. He wouldn't hurt a fly.

He told them that. He could tell they didn't believe him.

"Look," he volunteered in a burst of confidence. "I found that girl. I didn't have enough money to buy even a cuppa coffee." Tears formed in his eyes at the memory of how thirsty he'd been. "I could tell the necklace was real gold. It had a long chain with lots of fancy coins attached. Figured if I didn't take it, the first guy who found her would. Including some cops I've heard about." He was sorry he'd added that.

"What'd you do with the necklace, Petey?"

"Sold it for twenty-five bucks to that big dude who works Seventh Avenue around Central Park South."

"Buy-and-Sell Bert," one of the cops remarked. "We'll pick him up."

"When did you find the body, Petey?" Vince asked.

"When I woke up late morning." Petey squinted. His eyes took on a crafty expression. Everything was coming into focus. "But real early, I mean when it was still pitch dark, I heard a car drive onto the pier, pass my place, and stop. I figured it might be a drug deal so I stayed inside. Honest."

"Even when you knew it was driving away?" one of the detectives asked. "You didn't even peek?"

"Well, when I was sure it was going . . ."

"Did you get a look at it, Petey?"

They believed him. He knew it. If he could only tell them something else to make them feel like he was trying to cooperate. Petey forced the alcoholic haze to retreat for a split second from his brain. All the days of standing with a bottle of sudsy water and a squeegee at the Fifty-sixth Street exit of the West Side Highway rushed through his mind. He'd had plenty of chance to know what the backs of cars looked like.

Again he could see the taillights of the car disappearing off the pier. Something about the rear window. "It was a station wagon," he said with a triumphant wheeze. "On Birdie's grave, it was a station wagon."

As the haze rushed back, Petey had to force himself not to cackle. Birdie was probably still alive.

*D*ARCY AND NONA had planned to have dinner together on Saturday night. Other friends were calling, inviting her to join them, but Darcy was in no mood yet to see anyone.

They arranged to meet at Jimmy Neary's Restaurant on East Fifty-seventh Street. Darcy arrived first. Jimmy had saved the left back corner table for them. "A damn shame," he said as he greeted Darcy. "Erin was one of the prettiest lasses ever to walk through this door, God rest her." He patted Darcy's hand. "You were a grand friend to her. And don't think I don't know it. Sometimes when she'd come in for a quick bite, I'd sit with her for the moment. I told her to watch her step answering those crazy ads."

Darcy smiled. "I'm surprised she told you about them, Jimmy. She'd have known you wouldn't approve."

"Be sure I didn't. She reached in her jacket pocket for a handkerchief last month and pulled out one that she'd torn from a magazine. It fell to the floor and when I picked it up, it caught my eye. I said to her, 'Erin Kelley, I hope you're not into that foolishness.'"

"That's what I'm afraid of," Darcy told him. "Erin was a fabulous jewelry designer but not much of a record keeper. The FBI is trying to trace anyone Erin wrote to or met, but I'm sure the list isn't complete." Darcy decided against saying that she was also answering personal ads. "Do you remember what that ad said?"

Neary's brow furrowed in thought. "No, but I got a fair glance at it, and I will. Something about singing or—ah, it'll come. Look, here's Nona and she has someone with her."

Vince followed Nona to the table. "I'm only going to stop by for a minute," he told Darcy. "I don't want to interfere with your dinner, but I was trying to reach you, phoned Nona, and found out you were here.''

"It's fine, and I wish you'd stay." Darcy noticed that Nona's eyes had a brightness she had never seen in them before. "You got the message about Erin's telling one of her dates that she'd found the superintendent in her apartment again?"

"I saw Boxer today." Vince raised an eyebrow. *"Again?"*

"Erin told me he pulled that last year, but she always dismissed him as being harmless. Apparently as of two weeks ago she changed her mind."

"We're following up on him as well as other people. I'd like to hear about the guy from last night."

"He was a nice guy . . ."

Liz came to take their orders. She gave Darcy a quick, sympathetic smile. She always took such good care of us, Darcy thought. She had told Erin that growing up in Ireland she'd been a redhead too.

Dubonnet for Darcy and Nona. A beer for Vince.

Darcy and Nona decided on the red snapper. Nona said crisply to Vince, "You've got to eat sometime."

He ordered the corned beef and cabbage.

Vince got back to Darcy's other date. "I want to know about everybody you met. You've already seen two who admitted knowing Erin. Please let me decide on who is or isn't important."

She told him about David Weld. "He's an executive from Boston with the Holden chain. I gather he's been back and forth to New York for the last few years as they opened new stores." She felt as though she could read Vince D'Ambrosio's mind. *Back and forth to New York for the last two years.* Darcy said, "The one thing that did strike me is that he's been a shoe buyer."

"Shoe buyer! What's this guy's name?" Vince made a note in his book. "David Weld, Box 1527. Believe me, we'll check him out. Darcy, Nona told you about the shoes that were returned to the parents of the girl from Lancaster?"

"Yes."

He hesitated, glanced around, and saw that the people at the next table were absorbed in their own conversation. "We're trying to keep this one quiet. Another pair of mismatched shoes were delivered yesterday. They were the mates of the ones Nan Sheridan was found wearing fifteen years ago."

Darcy gripped the table. "Then Erin's death may not be a copy-cat crime."

"We just don't know. We're digging to see if anyone who knew Claire Barnes also knew Nan Sheridan."

"And Erin?" Nona asked.

"That would of course clinch the fact we have another Ted Bundy who's been getting away with serial murders for years." Vince put down his fork. "I've got to tell it to you straight. A lot of people who answer these ads turn out to be a far different cry from the way they describe themselves. All the young women our computer targeted as being possible serial-killer victims are in your age bracket, in your intelligence bracket, in your looks bracket. In other words, our killer may date fifty girls and then one turns him on. I know I can't dissuade you from answering these ads. Frankly, you've turned up some mighty interesting people for us to investigate. Nevertheless, you're not trained to be a decoy. You're a thoroughly nice, vulnerable young woman who doesn't have the ability to protect herself if she suddenly finds that she's painted into a corner."

"I don't intend to let myself get painted into a corner."

Vince had a quick coffee and left. He explained that his son, Hank, was coming in on a train from Long Island and he wanted to be in the apartment when he arrived.

Nona's eyes followed him as he stopped to pay the check. "Did you notice his tie?" she asked. "Today it was a blue and black check with a brown tweed jacket."

"So? Surely that doesn't bother you."

"No, I like it. Vince D'Ambrosio is so determined to find whoever killed these girls that I swear he blocks out anything unimportant. I happened to call the Barnes home in Lancaster just after they opened the package with the shoes and I tell you, hearing them broke my heart. Today I called Nan Sheridan's brother to ask him to be on the program. I could hear that same pain in his voice. Oh, Darcy, please God, be careful."

XII
SUNDAY
March 3

ON SUNDAY MORNING at nine o'clock, Michael Nash phoned. "I've been thinking about you, even worrying about you. How's it going?"

She had slept reasonably well. "Okay, I guess."

"Up to a drive to Bridgewater, New Jersey, and an early dinner?" He did not wait for her to answer. "In case you haven't looked out the window, it's a beautiful day. Really feels like spring. My housekeeper is a great cook and has to be treated for frustration if I don't bring company home at least once over the weekend."

Somehow, she had dreaded this day. If they didn't have other plans, she and Erin had often met for brunch on Sundays and spent the afternoon at Lincoln Center or in a museum. "That sounds fine." They arranged that he'd pick her up at eleven-thirty.

"And don't get all gussied up. In fact, if you like to ride, wear a pair of jeans. I've got a couple of darn good horses."

"I love to ride."

· · ·

His car was a two-seater Mercedes. "Very fancy," Darcy said.

Nash was wearing a turtleneck sport shirt, jeans, a herringbone jacket. The other night at dinner, she'd had the impression of how kind his eyes were. Today they were still kind, but there was something else. Maybe, she told herself, just the look a guy got when he was interested in a woman. Darcy realized that the thought pleased her.

The drive was pleasant. As they progressed south on Route 287, the suburbs disappeared. Houses that could be glimpsed from the road were now farther and farther apart. Nash talked with affectionate warmth about his parents. "To paraphrase that old commercial, 'My father made his money the old-fashioned way, he earned it.' He was just starting to hit it big when I was born. For ten years we moved every year, one house larger than the other, until he bought the present place when I was eleven. As I told you, my tastes are somewhat simpler, but God he was so proud the day we moved in. Carried my mother over the threshold."

Somehow it was easy to talk with Michael Nash about her famous parents and the Bel-Air mansion. "I always felt like a changeling there, as though the princess daughter of the royal couple must be living in a cottage and I was an impostor in her place." *How ever did two such stunning people manage to produce that mousy-looking child?*

Erin was the only one who knew about that. Now Darcy found herself telling Michael Nash. Then she added, "Hey, this is Sunday. You're off duty, doctor. Be careful, you've got a way of being too good a listener."

He glanced at her. "And when you grew up, you never looked in the mirror and realized what an outrageous statement that was?"

"Should I have?"

"I would say so." He was steering the car off the highway,

187

through the quaint town, along a country road. "The fence starts the property."

It was a full minute before they turned into the gate. "My God, how many acres do you have?"

"Four hundred."

At the Le Cirque dinner he had said the house was too ornate. Darcy silently agreed but nevertheless decided that it was an imposing and substantial mansion. The trees and plants were still bare of leaves and flowers, but the evergreens that edged the long driveway were full and luxuriant. "If you decide you've enjoyed yourself and come back next month, the grounds will be worth the trip," Nash commented.

Mrs. Hughes, the housekeeper, had prepared a light lunch. Sandwiches quartered with the crusts cut off—chicken, ham and cheese —then cookies, coffee. She looked approvingly at Darcy, severely at Michael. "I hope this is enough, miss. Doctor said that since you'll be having an early dinner I mustn't overdo now."

"It's perfect," Darcy told her sincerely. They ate in the breakfast room off the kitchen. Michael then gave her a quick tour of the house.

"Interior-decorator picture perfect," he said. "Don't you agree? Antiques that cost a fortune. I suspect half of them are fakes. Someday I'll change everything, but for now it just isn't worth the effort. Unless I'm having guests I live in the study. Here we are."

"Now this is a comfortable room," Darcy said with real pleasure. "Warm. Lived-in. Wonderful view. Good lighting. It's the kind of look I try to give a place when I refurbish."

"You really haven't told me much about your job. I want to hear, but how about that ride now? John has the horses ready."

Darcy had begun riding when she was three. It was one of the few activities she had not shared with Erin. "She was afraid of horses," Darcy told Michael as she swung onto the coal-black mare.

"Then riding won't be memory lane for you today. That's good."

The air, fresh and clean, seemed to at last cleanse the scent of funeral flowers from her nostrils. They cantered across Michael's property, slowed the horses to a walk as they went across town, joined other riders whom he introduced as his neighbors.

At six o'clock, they had dinner in the small dining room. The temperature had dropped. A fire was blazing, the white wine chilling, a decanter of red wine on the sideboard. John Hughes, now in uniform, served the beautifully prepared meal. Crabmeat cocktail. Veal medallions. Tiny asparagus. Roast potatoes. Green salad with pepper cheese. Sherbet. Espresso.

Darcy sighed as she sipped the coffee. "I can't thank you enough. If I'd been home by myself all day, it would have been pretty rough."

"If I'd been here alone all day, it would have been pretty boring."

She could not help overhearing Mrs. Hughes comment to her husband as they were leaving, "Now there is one lovely girl. I hope Doctor brings her back."

XIII
MONDAY
March 4

*O*N MONDAY EVENING, Jay Stratton met Mer-
rill Ashton in the Oak Bar of the Plaza. The bracelet, a band of
diamonds in a charming Victorian setting, won Ashton's instant
approval. "Frances is just going to love that," he enthused. "I'm
sure glad you convinced me to order it for her."

"I knew you'd be pleased. Your wife is a very pretty woman.
That bracelet will look lovely on her arm. As I told you, I want
you to have it appraised when you get home. If the jeweler tells
you it's worth one cent less than forty thousand dollars, the deal
is off. In fact, he'll undoubtedly tell you that you drove a hard
bargain. But the fact is that I'm hoping that next Christmas you'll
think of another piece for Frances. A diamond necklace? Diamond
earrings? We'll see."

"So this is your loss leader for me?" Ashton chuckled as he
reached for his checkbook. "That's good business."

Jay felt the peculiar thrill that came with taking risks.
Any decent jeweler would tell Ashton that at fifty thousand the
bracelet would still be a bargain. Tomorrow he had a lunch date

with Enid Armstrong. He couldn't wait to get his hands on her ring.

Thank you, Erin, he thought as he accepted the check.

Ashton invited Jay to have a quick bite before he left for the airport. He was taking a 9:30 plane home to Winston-Salem. Stratton explained that he was meeting a client at seven. He did not add that Darcy Scott was hardly the kind of client he wanted. He had a check in his pocket for seventeen thousand five hundred dollars; the twenty thousand from Bertolini less his commission.

Effusive good-byes. "Give my very best to Frances. I know how happy you'll make her."

Stratton did not notice another man quietly leave a nearby table and follow Merrill Ashton into the lobby.

"If I may have a word with you, sir."

Ashton accepted the card that was offered to him. *Nigel Bruce, Lloyd's of London.*

"I don't understand," Ashton sputtered.

"Sir, if Mr. Stratton comes out, I don't want to be observed. Would you mind if we step into the jewelry shop right over there? One of our experts will meet us. We'd like to have a look at the jewelry you just purchased." The investigator took pity on Ashton's bewildered expression. "It's routine."

"Routine! Are you suggesting that the bracelet I just bought was stolen?"

"I'm not suggesting anything, sir."

"The hell you're not. Well, if there's anything funny about this bracelet, I want to know right now. That check isn't certified. I can have payment stopped in the morning."

*T*HE INVESTIGATIVE REPORTER for the *New York Post* had done his job well. Somehow he managed to learn that a package had been delivered to Nan Sheridan's home and that it contained the mates of the mismatched shoes she'd been wearing when her body was found. Nan Sheridan's picture; Erin's picture; Claire Barnes's picture. Splashed side by side on the front page. SERIAL KILLER ON THE LOOSE.

Darcy read the paper in a cab on the way to the Plaza.

"Here we are, miss."

"What? Oh, all right. Thank you."

She was glad that she had had wall-to-wall appointments that day. Once again, she had brought clothes to the office. This time she changed into the red wool Rodeo Drive ensemble. As she got out of the cab, she remembered that she'd worn this outfit the last time she spoke to Erin. If only I'd seen her just once more, she thought.

It was ten of seven, a bit early for her meeting with Jay Stratton. Darcy decided to pop into the Oak Room. Fred, the maître d' of the restaurant, was an old friend. Ever since she could remember, when she and her parents had come to New York they had stayed at the Plaza.

Something Michael Nash had said yesterday was gnawing at her. Hadn't he been suggesting that she was still harboring a child's resentment at a careless, even cruel remark that had no present validity? She found herself looking forward to the next time she saw Nash. I suppose it's like getting a free consultation, but I'd like to ask him about it, she acknowledged as a beaming Fred rushed to greet her.

. . .

194

Promptly at seven she went next door to the bar. Jay Stratton was at a corner table. The only other time she had met him had been at Erin's apartment. Her first impression had been distinctly unfavorable. He'd been angry about the missing Bertolini necklace, then after it was found switched to a display of anxiety over the missing pouch of diamonds. He'd been infinitely more concerned about the necklace than about the fact that Erin was missing. Tonight it was like being with a different person. He was really trying to turn on the charm. Somehow, she was sure she'd seen the real Jay Stratton the first time.

She asked him where he had met Erin.

"Don't laugh. She happened to answer a personal ad I placed. I knew her casually and called her. One of those serendipity things. Bertolini had asked me about resetting those jewels and when I read Erin's letter I remembered that wonderful piece she did that won the N.W. Ayer award. And so we got together. It was strictly business, although she did ask me to escort her to a benefit. A client had given her the tickets. We danced the night away."

Why had he felt it necessary to add "strictly business"? Darcy wondered. And would it have been strictly business for Erin? Only six months ago Erin had said almost wistfully, "You know, Darce, I'm at the point where I'd really like to meet some nice guy and fall madly in love."

The Jay Stratton who was sitting across the table, attentive, handsome, able to understand Erin's talent, might well have fit the bill.

"What ad of yours did she answer?"

Stratton shrugged. "Frankly, I place so many of them I forget." He smiled. "You look shocked, Darcy. I'll explain to you what I explained to Erin. I will marry a very rich woman someday. I haven't met her yet, but be assured I will. I meet many women through these ads. It is not very difficult to persuade older women, ever so gently, to relieve their loneliness by treating themselves to a particularly beautiful piece of jewelry or by resetting their own rings, necklaces, or bracelets. They're happy. I'm happy."

"Why are you telling me this?" Darcy asked. "I hope it's not your way of letting me down easily. I didn't think of tonight as a date. For me, it's 'strictly business.' "

Stratton shook his head. "God forbid I should be so presumptuous. I'm telling you exactly what I told Erin after she explained to me her purpose in answering the ads. Your producer friend's documentary, isn't it?"

"Yes."

"What I'm trying to say and probably not doing it very well is that there was no romantic spark between Erin and me. The next point I'd like to make is to profoundly apologize for my behavior the first time we met. Bertolini is a valued client of mine. I'd never worked with Erin before. I didn't know her well enough to be totally sure that she wouldn't go away on a whim and forget the deadline for delivery. Believe me, I've had very uncomfortable moments of communing with myself and realizing the impression I must have made on you when you were heartsick with worry about your missing friend and I was talking client deadlines."

A wonderful speech, Darcy thought. I should warn him I've lived most of my life with two of the best actors in this country. She wondered if it would be appropriate to burst into applause. Instead she said, "You do have the check for the necklace?"

"Yes. I didn't know how to make it out. Do you think 'Estate of Erin Kelley' will be appropriate?"

Estate of Erin Kelley. All the years Erin had cheerfully done without the things that most of their friends considered essential. So proud that she could keep her father in a private nursing home. Just on the threshold of major success. Swallowing over a lump in her throat, Darcy said, "That will do."

She looked down at the check. Seventeen thousand five hundred dollars made out to the Estate of Erin Kelley, drawn on Chase Manhattan Bank, and signed by Jay Charles Stratton.

XIV
TUESDAY
March 5

ON *TUESDAY MORNING* when Agent D'Ambrosio entered Sheridan Galleries, he took a quick look around before he was ushered upstairs to Chris Sheridan's office. The furniture reminded him of the contents of Nona Roberts's living room. Funny. One of the things that had always been on his list was to take courses in art and antique furniture. The Bureau's Art Theft program had only whetted his appetite in that area.

In the meantime, Vince thought as he followed a secretary down the corridor, I live with Alice's mistakes. At the time of the divorce he'd gotten tired of expecting a fair shake from her. "Take what you want if it's so important to you," he'd offered.

She'd certainly taken him at his word.

Sheridan was on the phone. He smiled and waved Vince to a seat. Without appearing to be paying attention, Vince took in the conversation. Something about a collection being wildly overvalued.

Sheridan was saying, "Tell Lord Kilman that they may promise him that amount but they can't deliver. We'll be happy to set reasonable opening bids. The market isn't as strong as it was a few years ago, but is he prepared to wait it out another three to five years? Otherwise, I think if he looks carefully at our estimates he'll realize that many of the pieces he acquired fairly recently will still turn him a handsome profit."

Confident. Knowledgeable. Innate warmth. That was the way Vince had sized up Chris Sheridan last week when he'd gone to Darien. At that time, Sheridan had been wearing a sports shirt and windbreaker. Today he was dressed in a charcoal gray suit, white shirt, red and gray tie, very much the executive.

Chris hung up and reached across the desk to shake hands. Vince apologized for giving him such short notice and got right to the point. "When I saw you last week, I was pretty sure that Erin Kelley's death was a copycat murder because of the *True Crimes* program about your sister. I'm not sure about that anymore." He told him about Claire Barnes and the package that had been returned to her home.

Chris listened attentively. "Another one."

It seemed to Vince that all the residual pain of his sister's murder was in those two words.

"Is there anything I can do to help?" Chris asked.

"I don't know," Vince said frankly. "Whoever killed your sister must have known her. The matching shoe size can't be a coincidence. We have three possibilities. The same murderer has continued to kill young women all through these years. The same murderer stopped killing and started again several years ago. The third possibility is that Nan's murderer confided his modus operandi to someone else who decided to take over. The last one is the least likely."

"Then you're going to try to connect someone whom Nan knew to someone these other women knew?"

"Exactly. Although in Erin Kelley's case, because of the missing diamonds, there is still a possibility that we have a different culprit. That's why we're planning to explore both avenues. The reason I'm here is that I'm going to try to link one person with Nan, Erin Kelley, and Claire Barnes."

"Someone who knew my sister fifteen years ago and recently met those girls through personal ads?"

"You've got it. Darcy Scott was Erin Kelley's closest friend. They'd been answering the ads only because a television producer friend is doing a documentary and asked them to take part in the research. Darcy was out of town for a month. She gave Erin a sample of the letter she was sending, and some photographs. We know Erin answered some of those ads for both of them. Darcy Scott is hoping that whoever killed Erin will contact her."

Chris frowned. "You mean, you're allowing another young woman to be set up as a possible victim?"

Vince raised his hand as though to wave away the suggestion. "You don't know Darcy Scott. I'm not allowing anything. It's what she's determined to do. The one thing I have to grant her is she's already met some pretty interesting characters and come up with information that might be helpful."

"I still think it's a lousy idea," Chris said flatly.

"So do I and now that we've established that, here's how I hope you can help. The faster we get this guy, the less chance Darcy Scott or some other young woman might get hurt. We're going to Brown to get a roster of everyone who was in the student body or on the faculty when your sister was there. We'll check those names against anyone we know Erin met or Darcy meets on these dates. I also think it would be a good idea if, besides the school yearbooks that we can get ourselves, you dig out any snapshots, albums, whatever, of your sister's friends or acquaintances. You've got to understand that not everybody who answers a personal ad uses his own name. I want Darcy Scott to look over Nan's pictures to see if she can spot anyone she meets along the way."

"Of course we've got endless snapshots of Nan," Chris said slowly. "Ten years ago, after my father died, I managed to persuade my mother to pack up most of them and put them in the attic. Mother admitted that Nan's room was getting to be a shrine."

"Good for you," Vince said. "You must have been pretty persuasive."

Chris smiled quickly. "I pointed out that it was one of the brightest rooms in the house and would be great for a visiting grandchild someday. The problem is, as my mother frequently reminds me, I haven't delivered." The smile disappeared. "I can't get up to Connecticut until the weekend. I'll bring everything down on Sunday."

Vince stood up. "I appreciate this. I know how tough this has been on your mother, but if it turns out that we find the guy who was responsible for your sister's death, believe me, in the long run it will give her a lot of peace."

As he turned to go, his beeper sounded. "Do you mind if I call my office?"

Sheridan handed him the phone, watched as D'Ambrosio's forehead furrowed. "How is Darcy?"

Chris Sheridan felt a cold wave of apprehension. He didn't know this girl but experienced a sudden unreasoning fear for her. He had never told anyone that when Nan went for a jog the morning after their birthday party, he had heard her go out. Still half asleep, he'd started to get up. Some instinct was urging him to follow her. He'd shrugged it off and gone back to sleep.

Vince hung up the phone and turned back to Chris. "Is there any way you could possibly get those pictures immediately? The White Plains police phoned. The father of Janine Wetzl, another one of the missing girls, just received the sort of package your mother and the Barnes family got. Her own shoe and a high-heeled white satin slipper." He slapped his hand on the table. "And while one agent was taking that call, Darcy Scott phoned. She had just opened a package that came in the morning mail. The mates of the shoes found on Erin Kelley's body were sent to her."

Chris knew that the frustrated anger he saw on Agent D'Ambrosio's face mirrored his own expression. "Why the hell is he doing this?" Chris blurted. "To prove the girls are dead? To taunt? What makes him tick?"

"When I know that, I'll know who he is," Vince said quietly. "And now, do you mind if I use your phone again? I have to call Darcy Scott."

*F*ROM THE MOMENT Darcy saw the package, she'd known. The mailman arrived just as she was leaving for work. He'd handed her the package and the letters and magazines and junk mail. Afterward, Darcy remembered that he'd looked puzzled when she did not respond to his greeting.

Like an automaton she'd walked stiffly upstairs to her apartment and laid the package on the table by the window. Deliberately keeping her gloves on, she opened it, unknotting the twine and slitting the sealing tape at the flaps.

The sketch of the slipper on the lid. Remove the lid. Separate the tissue. Look down at Erin's boot and a pink and silver slipper nestled together.

The slipper is so pretty, she thought. It would have gone beautifully with the dress Erin was buried in.

She did not have to look up Vince D'Ambrosio's number, her brain produced it effortlessly. He was not there but they promised to locate him. "Can you wait for him?"

"Yes."

He called a few minutes later, was at the apartment within half an hour. "This is rough for you."

"I touched the heel of the slipper with my glove," she confessed. "I simply had to know if it was Erin's size. It was."

Vince looked at her compassionately. "Maybe you should take it easy today."

Darcy shook her head. "That would be the worst thing in the world for me to do." She attempted a smile. "I've got a big project scheduled, and then, guess what? I have a date tonight."

*W*HEN VINCE left with the package, Darcy went directly to the newly purchased hotel on West Twenty-third Street. Small, a total of thirty guest rooms, rundown, badly in need of paint, it still had tremendous possibilities. The owners, a couple in their late thirties, explained that the cost of basic repairs would leave very little for refurbishing. They were delighted with her suggestion that they decorate in the style of an English country inn. "I can get plenty of sofas and upholstered chairs and lamps and tables in very good condition at private sales," she'd told them. "We can give this place a lot of charm. Look at the Algonquin. The most intimate bar in Manhattan and you'd be hard put to find a chair that isn't threadbare."

She walked through the rooms with them, making notes on their various sizes and shapes, and marking what furniture was usable. The day passed quickly. She had intended to go home and change for her date, but then decided against it. When Doug Fields called to reconfirm, he'd told her that he dressed casually. "Slacks and a sweater are pretty much a uniform for me."

They were meeting at six at the Twenty-third Street Bar and Grill. Darcy got there exactly on time. Doug Fields was fifteen minutes late. He burst into the bar, clearly irritated and filled with apologies. "I swear I've never seen this block so messed up. So many cars, you'd swear it was an assembly line in Detroit. I'm so sorry, Darcy. I never keep people waiting. It's a thing with me."

"It really doesn't matter." He's good-looking, Darcy thought. Attractive. Why had he found it necessary to immediately insist that he never kept people waiting?

Over a glass of wine, she listened to him on two levels. He was amusing, self-confident, well-spoken. Extremely likable. He'd been raised in Virginia, went to the University there, dropped out of law school. "I'd have made a lousy lawyer. Don't have enough of the 'go for the jugular.' "

Go for the jugular. Darcy thought of the bruises on Erin's throat.

"Switched to art school. Pointed out to my father that instead of cracking the books, I was doing caricatures of the profs. It was a good decision. I love illustrating and do well at it."

"There's an old saying, 'If you want to be happy for a year, win the lottery. If you want to be happy for life, love what you do.' " Darcy hoped she sounded relaxed. This was the kind of guy Erin would have enjoyed meeting, the kind who after a date or two she would have trusted. An artist? The sketch? Was everybody suspect?

The inevitable question came. "Why would a pretty girl like you need to answer personal ads?"

This time the question was easy to parry. "Why would a good-looking, successful guy like you need to place personal ads?"

"That's easy," he said promptly. "I was married for eight years and now I'm not. I'm not interested in getting serious. You get introduced to somebody at a friend's house, take her out a few times, and bingo, everybody's looking at the two of you waiting for the big announcement. This way, I meet a lot of nice women. Lay the cards on the table just like this and see if it clicks. Tell me, how many dates from ads have you had this week?"

"You're the first one."

"Last week, then. Starting with Monday."

Monday I was standing over Erin's casket, Darcy thought. Tuesday I was watching that casket being lowered. Wednesday I was home watching the reenactment of Nan Sheridan's murder. Thursday she had met Len Parker. Friday, David Weld, the mild-mannered, rather shy man who described himself as a department store executive and claimed not to have known Erin. Saturday, Albert Booth, a computer analyst who was enthralled with the wonders of desktop publishing and who knew Erin was frightened of her superintendent.

"Oh, come on, admit you had dates last week," Doug urged. "I called you Wednesday and you weren't free until tonight."

Startled, Darcy realized that a number of times recently, someone had to repeat a question. "I'm sorry. Yes, I did go out a couple of times last week."

"And had fun?"

She thought of Len Parker pounding on the door. "You could call it that."

He laughed. "That speaks volumes. I've met some winners too. Now you've gotten my life history, how about telling me about yourself?"

She gave a carefully edited version.

Doug raised one eyebrow. "I sense a lot of omissions but maybe when you get to know me a bit better, you'll fill me in."

She refused a second glass of wine. "I really have to be going."

He did not argue. "Actually, I do too. When am I going to see you again, Darcy? Tomorrow night? Let's make it dinner."

"I really am busy."

"Thursday?"

"I'm working on a job that's going to tie me up. Will you call in a few days?"

"Yes. And if you keep turning me down, I promise I won't persist. But I hope you don't."

He really is nice, Darcy thought, or else he's a heck of a good actor.

Doug put her in a cab, then quickly waved one down for himself. In the apartment, he tore off the sweater and slacks and rushed into the suit he'd worn to the office. At quarter of eight he was on the train to Scarsdale. At quarter of nine he was reading a bedtime story to Trish while Susan broiled a steak for him. She certainly understood how maddening these late meetings were. "You work too hard, Doug, dear," she had said soothingly when he stamped into the house, ranting about missing the earlier train by a hairbreadth.

*T*HROUGH HOURS of intense questioning, Jay Stratton remained calm. His only explanation for the diamonds in the bracelet that he had sold to Merrill Ashton was that it must have been a ghastly error. Erin Kelley had been commissioned to create settings for a number of fine diamonds. Stratton claimed that somehow he had made a mistake and inadvertently substituted other fine stones for some of the ones that were meant to be in the diamond pouch he had given Kelley. That was not to say that those others were not of equal value. Take a look at his various insurance policies.

A search warrant revealed no other missing diamonds in his apartment or in his safety deposit box. He was booked on suspicion of receiving stolen goods and bail was set. Disdainfully, he strode from the precinct with his lawyer.

Vince had shared the interrogation with detectives from the Sixth Precinct. They all knew he was guilty, but as Vince said, "There goes one of the most convincing con men I've ever come across and believe me, I've run into a lot of them."

The crazy thing, Vince thought as he left for his office, is that Darcy Scott ends up being a witness *for* Stratton. She'd opened the safe for him and would swear that the pouch wasn't there. And of course the big question was, would Stratton have had the nerve to claim those diamonds were missing unless he knew that Erin Kelley would never show up to say what happened to them?

In the office, Vince snapped out orders. "I want to know everything, and I mean *everything*, about Jay Stratton. Jay Charles Stratton."

XV
WEDNESDAY
March 6

CHRIS SHERIDAN studied Darcy Scott, liking what he saw. She was wearing a leather jacket belted at the waist, tan slacks that disappeared into scuffed but fine leather boots, a knotted silk scarf that accentuated the hollow in the nape of her neck. Her brown hair, darted with blond highlights, was soft and loose around her face. Hazel eyes, soft brown flecked with green, were framed by dark lashes. Charcoal brows accentuated her porcelain complexion. He judged her to be in her late twenties.

She reminds me of Nan. The realization shocked him. But they don't look alike, he thought. Nan had been the typical Nordic beauty with her pink and white skin, vivid blue eyes, hair the color of daffodils. Then where was the resemblance? It was in the absolute grace with which Darcy moved. Nan had walked like that, as though if music began to play, she would glide into a dance step.

Darcy was aware of Chris Sheridan's scrutiny. She had been making some observations of her own. She liked his strong features, the slight bump on the bridge of his nose, probably the result of a break. The width of his shoulders and an overall impression of disciplined fitness suggested athletic prowess.

A few years ago, her mother and father had both had plastic surgery. "A nip here, a tuck there," her mother had said, laughing. "Don't look so disapproving, darling Darcy. Remember, our looks are an important part of our stock in trade."

How totally irrelevant to remember that now, Darcy thought. Was she simply trying to escape the delayed shock of opening the package with Erin's boot and the dancing slipper? She'd been composed all day yesterday, then woke up this morning at four o'clock to find her face and pillow wet with tears. She bit her lip at the memory, but could not prevent new tears from welling in her eyes. "I'm sorry," she said quickly, and tried to sound brisk. "It was good of you to go to Connecticut for the pictures last night. Vince D'Ambrosio told me you had to change your plans."

"They weren't important." Chris sensed that Darcy Scott wanted him to ignore her distress. "There's an awful lot of stuff," he said matter-of-factly. "I have it laid out on a table in the conference room. My suggestion is that you take a look at it. If you want to bring everything home or to your office, I can have it delivered. If you want part of it, we can arrange that too. I know most of the people in the pictures. Some, of course, I don't. Anyhow, let's take a look."

They went downstairs. Darcy realized that in the fifteen minutes she'd been in Chris Sheridan's office, the crowd inspecting the items for the next auction had increased substantially. She loved auctions. Growing up she had regularly gone to them with the dealer representing her parents. They never could go themselves. If either one of them was known to be interested in acquiring a painting or antique, the price shot up instantly. It was hearing her mother and father recite the history of their acquisitions that made her uncomfortable.

She was walking next to Sheridan toward the rear of the building when she spotted a cylinder writing desk and darted over to it. "Is this really a Roentgen?"

Chris ran his hand over the mahogany surface. "Yes, it is. You know your antiques. Are you in the business?"

Darcy thought of the Roentgen in the library of the Bel-Air house. Her mother loved to tell the story of how Marie Antoinette had sent it to Vienna as a gift to her mother, the Empress, which was why it had escaped being sold during the French Revolution. This one had obviously been shipped out of France as well.

"Are you in the business?" Chris repeated.

"Oh, I'm sorry." Darcy smiled, thinking of the hotel she was refurbishing with garage sale trappings. "In a way you could say that."

Chris raised his eyebrows but did not ask for an explanation. "Down this way." A wide foyer led to a double-doored room. Inside, a protective cloth covered a Georgian banquet table. Albums, yearbooks, framed pictures, snapshots, and carousels of slides were neatly placed rowlike on the table.

"Don't forget, these were all taken somewhere between fifteen and eighteen years ago," Sheridan warned.

"I know." Darcy considered the mass of material. "How much do you use this room?"

"Not that often."

"Then would it be possible to leave everything here and let me come in and out? The thing is, when I'm in the office I'm always busy. My apartment isn't large, and anyhow I'm not there very much."

Chris knew it was none of his business but could not stop himself. "Agent D'Ambrosio told me you were answering personal ads." He watched the withdrawal in Darcy Scott's expression.

"Erin didn't want to answer those ads," Darcy said. "I persuaded her. The only way I can possibly atone for that is to try to help find her killer. Is it all right if I come back and forth? I promise I won't bother you or your staff."

Chris realized what Vince D'Ambrosio had meant when he said that Darcy Scott was going to do what she wanted about the personal ads. "You won't be any bother. One of the secretaries is always here by eight. The cleaning staff is around until ten at night. I'll leave word for them to let you in. Better yet, let me give you a key."

Darcy smiled. "I promise not to make off with a Sèvres. Is it okay if I stay for a while now? I have a few hours free."

"Of course. And remember, I know many of those people. Try me if you want a name."

At three-thirty Sheridan returned, followed by a maid carrying a tea tray. "I thought you might need a break. I'll join you if I may."

"That would be fine." Darcy realized she had a vague headache and remembered she had skipped lunch. She accepted a cup of tea, poured a few drops of milk from the delicate Limoges pitcher, and tried not to look too anxious as she reached for a sugar cookie. She waited until the maid left, then commented, "I know how hard it must have been for you to put all this together. Memory Lane is pretty shattering."

"My mother did most of it. She surprises me. She fainted when that package of shoes arrived, but now, whatever she can do to track down Nan's killer and to stop him from harming anyone else is all she cares about."

"And you?"

"Nan was six minutes older than I. She never let me forget it. Called me 'little brother.' She was outgoing. I was shy. We kind of balanced each other. Long ago I gave up the hope of seeing her killer in court. Now that hope is within reach again." He looked at the stack of pictures she had separated. "Anyone you know?"

Darcy shook her head. "Not so far."

· · ·

At quarter of five, she poked her head in his office. "I'm running along now."

Chris jumped up. "Here's the key. I meant to give it to you when I came down."

Darcy pocketed it. "I'll probably come back early in the morning."

Chris could not resist. "Have you got one of those dates now? I'm sorry. I have no right to ask. I'm only concerned because I think it's so dangerous."

This time he was glad to see Darcy Scott did not stiffen. She simply said, "I'll be fine," and with a half-wave left him.

He stared after her, remembering the one time he had gone hunting. The doe had been drinking water from a stream. Sensing danger, it had lifted its head, listening, poised for flight. An instant later it sank to the ground. He had not joined in the exultant cheers the others in the party accorded the marksman. His instinct had been to shout a warning to the deer. That same instinct was crying out to him now.

*H*OW'S THE PROGRAM GOING?" Vince asked Nona as he tried to find a comfortable spot on the green love seat in her office.

"It is and it isn't." Nona sighed. Wearily, she ran a hand

through her hair. "The hardest thing is to find a balance. When you wrote and asked me to include a segment about the possible dangers of answering those ads, I had no idea what the next week would bring. I still think my original concept is right. I want to give an overall picture and then end with a warning." She smiled at him. "I'm glad you called and suggested pasta."

It had been a long day. At four-thirty, Vince had had a brainstorm. He'd had a list made of the dates the eight young women had disappeared and ordered researchers to start collecting personal ads from New York area newspapers and magazines that had appeared three months previous to those dates.

A sense of accomplishment at the new possible lead had made him realize that he was gut-level tired. The thought of going back to the apartment and finding some food in the neglected refrigerator had been depressing. Instead, almost inadvertently, he'd reached for the phone and dialed Nona.

Now it was seven o'clock. He'd just arrived at her office and Nona was ready to pack it in.

The phone rang. Nona raised her eyes to heaven, reached for it, and identified herself. Vince watched as her expression changed.

"You're right, Matt. Always a safe bet that you'll find me here. What can I do for you?" She listened. "Matt, get it straight. I'm not in the market to buy you out. Not today. Not tomorrow. If you'll remember, last year when we had a buyer you didn't think it was enough. The usual. Now I can wait. You can wait. What the heck is the rush? Does Jeanie need braces or something?"

Nona laughed as she hung up. "That was the man I promised to love, honor, and cherish all the days of my life. Trouble is, he forgot to remember."

"It's been known to happen."

They went to Pasta Lovers on West Fifty-eighth Street. "I duck in here a lot when I'm by myself," Nona told him. "Wait till you taste the pasta. It would drive anyone's blues away."

A glass of red wine. The salad. Warm bread. "It's the connection," Vince heard himself saying. "There's got to be a connection between one man and all those girls."

"I thought you were convinced that except for Nan Sheridan the connection is the personal ads."

"It is. But don't you see? He can't just *happen* to have the right-sized slipper for each one of them. Granted, he could have bought the slippers after he killed the girls, but he certainly had the one he left on Nan Sheridan's foot with him when he attacked her. This type of killer usually follows a pattern."

"So you're talking about someone who met these girls, somehow managed to learn their shoe size without any of them getting bad vibes, and then was able to get them in a situation where they disappeared without a trace."

"You've got it." Over linguine with clam sauce, he told her about his plan to analyze personal ads that had been placed in the New York area in the three months before each of the women disappeared, to see if the same one showed up. "And of course that could be another dead end," he acknowledged. "For all we know, the same guy is placing a dozen different ads."

They both ordered decaf cappuccino. Nona began talking about the documentary. "I still haven't settled on a psychiatrist," she said. "I certainly don't want to get one of those professional show-biz experts who pop up whenever you turn the dial."

Vince told her about Michael Nash. "Very articulate guy. Writing a book about personal ads. He'd met Erin."

"Darcy told me about him. A very good idea, Agent D'Ambrosio."

Vince took Nona home in a cab, and had it wait while he saw her inside her building. "I have a hunch we're both pretty beat," he said in answer to her suggestion of a nightcap. "But please give me a raincheck."

"You've got it." Nona grinned. "I am tired, and anyhow, my

cleaning woman hasn't been around since last Friday. I don't think you're ready for the real me."

It was all Vince could do to remember that he was technically on the job. That did not stop him from wondering how it would feel to hold Nona Roberts in his arms.

Back at his apartment, there was a message on his answering machine. Ernie, his assistant. "No emergency, but I thought you'd be interested in hearing this, Vince. We have the roster of students from Brown for the time Nan Sheridan was there. Guess who was a returning student and in some of her classes? None other than our friend the jeweler, Jay Stratton."

*D*ARCY'S five-thirty date was to meet Box 4307, Cal Griffin, in the bar at Tavern on the Green. He's not in his early thirties, was her first impression. Griffin was closer to fifty. A beefy man who combed his hair across the top of his head to conceal his bald spot, he was expensively and conservatively dressed. He was from Milwaukee, but, as he explained, got into New York regularly.

A suggestive wink followed. Don't get him wrong, he was a happily married man, but when he came in on business it would sure be good to have a friend. Another wink. Believe you me, he knew how to treat a woman. What show haven't you seen? He knew how to get house seats. What's your favorite restaurant? Lutèce? Expensive, but worth every penny.

Darcy managed to ask him the last time he'd been in New York.

Too long. Last month he'd taken the wife and kids—great teenagers but you know teenagers—skiing in Vail. They had a house there. They were building a bigger place. Money's no object. Anyhow, the kids brought their friends and it was bedlam. That rock and roll stuff. Drive you crazy, wouldn't it? They had a great stereo system in the house.

Darcy had ordered a Perrier. Halfway through it, she made a business of glancing at her watch. "My boss was real mad at me for leaving," she said. "I'm going to have to cut this short."

"Forget him," Griffin ordered. "You and I are going to have a nice night."

They were sitting at a banquette. A beefy arm went around her. A moist kiss was planted on her ear.

Darcy did not want to make a scene. "Oh, my God," she said, pointing to a nearby table where a man was sitting alone, his back to them. "That's my husband. I've got to get out of here."

The arm disappeared from around her waist. Griffin looked shaken. "I don't want trouble."

"I'll just slip away," Darcy whispered.

On the way home in the cab, she tried not to laugh out loud. Well, one thing's for sure—it's not that one.

The phone was ringing as she turned her key in the lock. It was Doug Fields. "Hi, Darcy. Why are you so unforgettable? I know you said you were busy tonight, but my plans changed and I decided to take a chance. How about a hamburger at P. J. Clarke's or something?"

Darcy realized that she had forgotten to tell Vince D'Ambrosio about Doug Fields. A nice guy. Attractive. An illustrator. The kind Erin might easily have been interested in. "That sounds great," she answered. "What time?"

*H*OW STUPID does Doug think I am? Susan wondered as she sat at the kitchen table with Donny and went over his geometry homework. The guidance counseler had phoned her this afternoon. Was there a problem at home? Donny, always a good student, was slipping in all his subjects. He seemed distracted and depressed.

"Well, that's it," she said cheerfully. "As *my* geometry teacher used to say, 'It shows what you can do, Miss Frawley, when you put your mind to it.' "

Donny smiled and gathered up his books. "Mom . . ." He hesitated.

"Donny, you've always been able to talk to me. What is it?"

He looked around.

"The little kids are in bed. Beth is taking one of her thirty-minute showers. We can talk," Susan assured him.

"And Dad is in one of his meetings," Donny said bitterly.

He suspects, Susan thought. There was no use trying to protect him. This was as good a time as any to be straight with him. "Donny, Dad isn't in a meeting."

"You know?" Relief flooded the troubled face.

"Yes, I do. But how did you find out?"

He looked down. "Patrick Driscoll, one of the guys on the team, was in New York Friday night when we were visiting Grandpa. Dad was in a restaurant with some woman. They were holding hands and kissing. Patrick said it was gross. His mother wants to tell you. His dad won't let her."

"Donny, I'm planning to divorce your father. It's not something I want, but living like this isn't great for any of us. This way we won't always be waiting for him to come home, always putting up with his lies. I hope he makes it his business to see you kids, but I can't guarantee it. I'm sorry. I'm terribly, terribly sorry." She realized she was crying.

Donny patted her shoulder. "Mom, he doesn't deserve you. I promise I'll help with the other kids. I swear I'll do a better job than he did with us."

Donny may look like Doug, but thank God, Susan thought, he's got enough of my genes in him that he'll never act like his father. She kissed Donny's cheek. "Let's keep this between us for now. Okay."

Susan went to bed at eleven o'clock. Doug was still not home. She turned on the late news and watched horrified as the anchorman updated the story of the missing young women and the packages of mismatched shoes that were being returned to their families.

The announcer was saying, "Although the FBI refuses to comment, inside sources tell us that the latest shoes to be returned are the mates of the ones Erin Kelley was wearing when her body was found. If true, she is probably linked to the disappearance of two young women originally from Lancaster and White Plains, who had been living in Manhattan, and the long-unsolved murder of Nan Sheridan."

Nan Sheridan. Erin Kelley.

"Oh my God," Susan moaned. Her hands clenched in fists, she stared at the screen.

Pictures of Claire Barnes, Erin Kelley, Janine Wetzl and Nan Sheridan were flashed on the screen.

The announcer was saying, "The trail of death seems to have begun on that cold March morning, fifteen years ago next week, when Nan Sheridan was strangled on the jogging path near her home."

Susan felt her own throat close. Fifteen years ago she had lied for Doug when he was questioned about Nan's death. If she hadn't, would these other young women not have disappeared? That night almost two weeks ago when the announcement came about Erin Kelley's death, Doug had had a nightmare. Called out *Erin* in his sleep.

"... The FBI is cooperating with the New York Police Department in an attempt to trace the evening shoes back to the purchaser. The file on Nan Sheridan's death has been reopened ..."

Suppose they questioned Doug again? Suppose they question *me*, Susan thought. Did she have a duty to tell the police she had lied fifteen years ago?

Donny. Beth. Trish. Conner. What would their lives be like if they grew up as the children of a serial killer?

The police commissioner of New York was being interviewed. "We believe we're dealing with a vicious serial killer."

Vicious.

"What shall I do?" Susan whispered to herself. Her father's words rang in her ears. "Vicious *streak* ..."

Two years ago when she challenged him about his relationship with the *au pair,* his face had contorted with rage. The fear she had experienced at that moment swept through her again. As the news ended, Susan finally faced the fact she had never allowed herself to consider. "I thought he was going to hurt me that night."

*S*HALL WE DANCE? *Shall we dance? Shall we dance? On a bright cloud of music shall we fly? ... Shall we still be together with our arms around each other, shall we dance? Shall we dance? Shall we dance?*

Charley laughed aloud at the sheer exultation of the music. Whirling and stepping in synch with Yul Brynner, he stamped his foot, twisted, twirled an imaginary Darcy in his arms. They'd dance to this next week! Then Astaire! What joy! What joy! It was only seven days away: Nan's fifteenth anniversary!

On the clear understanding that this kind of thing can happen, shall we dance? Shall we dance? Shall we dance?

The music stopped. He reached for the remote control and snapped off the video. If only he could spend the night. But that would be foolish. Do what he had come to do.

The basement stairs creaked and he frowned. Must take care of that. Annette had fled down these stairs. Listening to the frantic tapping of the heels on the bare wood had enthralled him. If Darcy tried to escape him that same way, he didn't want a creaking noise to interfere with the sound of her slippers on their futile flight.

Darcy. How hard it had been to sit across the table from her. He had wanted to say "Come with me" and bring her here. Like the Phantom of the Opera inviting his beloved to the netherworld.

The shoe boxes. Five of them now. Marie and Sheila and Leslie and Annette and Tina. Suddenly he realized he wanted to send them all back at once. Be finished with it. And then there would be only one.

Only Darcy's package would be here next week. Maybe he'd never return it.

He opened the latch of the freezer, lifted the heavy door, and stared down into the empty space. Awaiting a new ice maiden, Charley thought. This one he wouldn't give back.

XVI
THURSDAY
March 7

"*H*OW WELL DID you know Nan Sheridan?" Vince snapped. He and a detective from the Midtown North precinct were taking turns questioning Jay Stratton.

Stratton remained unruffled. "She was a student at Brown when I was there."

"You dropped out of Brown and came back the year she was a sophomore?"

"That's right. I wasn't much of a student my freshman year. My uncle, who was my guardian, thought it would do me a lot of good to mature a bit. I went into the Peace Corps for two years."

"I repeat: How well did you know Nan Sheridan?"

How well indeed, Stratton thought. Lovely Nan. *To dance with her was to feel a will-o'-the-wisp in your arms.*

D'Ambrosio's eyes narrowed. He had seen something in Stratton's face. "You haven't answered me."

Stratton shrugged. "There's no answer to give. Certainly I remember her. I was there when the whole student body was talking endlessly about the tragedy."

"Were you invited to her birthday party?"

"No, I was not. Nan Sheridan and I happened to be in several classes together. Period."

"Let's talk about Erin Kelley. You were in an awfully big hurry to report those missing diamonds to the insurance company."

"As Miss Scott can certainly verify, my first response when I spoke with her was irritation. I really didn't know Erin well. It was her work I knew. When she didn't keep the appointment to turn over the necklace to Bertolini, I convinced myself that she simply lost track of time. The moment I met Darcy Scott I realized how foolish that was. Her terrible concern made me see the situation clearly."

"Do you often mix up valuable gemstones?"

"Certainly not."

Vince tried another tack. "You didn't know Nan Sheridan well, but did you know anyone who had a crush on her? Besides you, of course," he added deliberately.

XVII
FRIDAY
March 8

*O*N *FRIDAY AFTERNOON,* Darcy went to the West Side apartment where she'd redecorated the room for Lisa, the recuperating teenager. She brought with her plants for the windowsill, some throw pillows, a porcelain vanity set that she'd picked up at a house sale. And Erin's much-loved poster.

The large pieces were already in; the pewter and brass bed, the dresser, the night table, the rocker. The Indian rug that had been in Erin's living room was perfect in this space. Candy-striped wallpaper gave the room a feeling of movement. Almost like a carousel, Darcy thought. The tieback curtains and spread were the same candy stripe as the paper. A starched white cotton dust ruffle picked up the glistening white of the ceiling and trim.

Carefully, Darcy positioned the poster. It depicted an Egret painting, one of his early, lesser known works: a young dancer soaring through the air, her arms extended, her toes pointed. He'd called it, "Loves Music, Loves to Dance."

She drove picture hooks into the wall, thinking of all the dance classes she and Erin had taken. "Why jog in the freezing rain when you can get just as much exercise dancing?" Erin would ask. "There's an old slogan, 'To put a little fun in your life, try dancing.' "

Darcy stepped back to be sure the poster was hanging straight. It was. Then what was gnawing at her? *The personal ads.* But why now? Shrugging, she closed her toolbox.

She went directly to Sheridan Galleries. So far, all the poring over the pictures had proven useless. She had come across Jay Stratton's picture, but Vince D'Ambrosio had already picked his name from the student roster. Yesterday, Chris Sheridan had pointed out that she probably had a better chance of winning the lottery than of having a familiar face jump out at her.

She'd been afraid that he might have regretted his decision to let her use his conference room, but that wasn't the case. "You look wiped out," he'd said to her late yesterday afternoon. "I understand you've been here since eight o'clock this morning."

"I was able to rearrange some appointments. This seems more important."

Last night had been Box 3823, Owen Larkin, an internist from New York Hospital. He'd been pretty full of himself. "Trouble with being an unattached doctor is that all the nurses keep offering to have you over for a home-cooked meal." He was from Tulsa and hated New York. "The minute I finish my residency I'm on my way back to God's country. You can keep these crowded cities."

Casually, she'd brought up Erin's name. His tone confidential, he'd told her, "I didn't meet her, but one of my friends at the hospital who answers these ads did. Just once. He's keeping his fingers crossed that she didn't keep records. The last thing he needs is to be questioned in a murder investigation."

"When did he see her?"

"Early February."

"I wonder if I've ever met him."

"Not unless you met him around that time. He'd broken up with his girlfriend and they got back together."

"What's his name?"

"Brad Whalen. Say, is this some kind of inquisition? Let's talk about you and me."

Brad Whalen. Another name for Vince D'Ambrosio to check out.

Chris was standing at his office window when he saw the cab pull up and Darcy get out of it. He shoved his hands in his pockets. It was windy and he watched as Darcy closed the door of the cab and turned to the building. She pulled her jacket around her neck and bent forward slightly as she crossed the sidewalk.

Yesterday had been busy. He had some important Japanese clients examining the silver from the von Wallens estate to be auctioned next week. He'd spent the better part of the afternoon with them.

Mrs. Vail, the housekeeper for the gallery, had made sure that morning coffee, a light lunch, and tea were brought to Darcy Scott. "That poor girl is going to ruin her eyes, Mr. Sheridan," Vail had fussed.

At four-thirty, Chris had gone to the conference room. He'd realized what a blunder he'd made when he suggested the task was hopeless. He hadn't meant it to come out like that. It was just that when you analyzed it, the chances of Darcy Scott's meeting someone who had known Nan, and recognizing him in a picture fifteen years old, were, to say the least, very slim.

Yesterday she'd asked him if Nan had ever dated anyone named Charles North.

Not to his knowledge. When he came to Darien, Vince D'Ambrosio had asked him and his mother the same question.

230

Chris realized that he wanted to go downstairs now and talk to Darcy. He wondered if she would get the feeling again that he was anxious to be rid of her.

The phone rang. He let his secretary pick it up. A moment later she buzzed through. "It's your mother, Chris."

Greta came directly to the point. "Chris, you know that business about someone named Charles. As long as we had to get all those pictures down, I decided to go through the rest of Nan's things. No use leaving the job to you someday. I reread her letters. There's one from the September before . . . before we lost her. She'd just started the fall semester. She wrote about dancing with a fellow named Charley who teased her about wearing Capezios.

"Here's exactly the way she put it: 'Can you believe that a guy in my generation thinks girls should wear spike heels?' "

"*I* WAS FINISHED with my patients at three o'clock and thought it would be a lot easier to come over and talk with you than discuss this on the phone." Michael Nash shifted slightly, trying to find a comfortable position on the green love seat in Nona's office. He could not help analyzing why an obviously bright and outgoing person like Nona Roberts would submit her visitors to this torturous object.

"Doctor, I'm sorry." Nona yanked files from the one comfortable chair next to her desk. "Please."

Nash moved willingly.

"I really should get rid of that thing," Nona apologized. "It's

just I never get around to it. There's always something more interesting to do than fool around with arranging furniture." Her smile
was guilty. "But for heaven's sake, don't tell Darcy that."

He returned the smile. "In my profession, I'm sworn to secrecy.
Now, how can I help you?"

A really attractive man, Nona thought. Late thirties. A maturity
that probably comes with the territory of being a psychiatrist.
Darcy had told her about the visit to his place in New Jersey.
Don't marry for money, as Nona's old aunts used to say, but it's
just as easy to love a rich man as a poor one. Not, God knows,
that Darcy needed to marry money. Her folks had been making
millions since before she was born. But Nona had always sensed
a loneliness in Darcy, a little girl lost. Without Erin, that was
bound to get worse. It would be wonderful if she met the right
guy now.

She realized that Dr. Michael Nash was looking at her with an
amused expression. "Will I pass?" he asked.

"Absolutely." She fished for the documentary file. "Darcy probably told you why she and Erin got into answering personal ads."

Nash nodded.

"We've got the program pretty much together, but I want to
have a psychiatrist do an overall viewpoint about the kind of
people who place or answer ads and what motivates them. Maybe
it would be possible to give some hints as to what kind of behavior
should raise warning signals. Am I saying it right?"

"You're saying it very explicitly. I gather that the FBI agent will
concentrate on the serial killer aspect."

Nona felt herself tense. "Yes."

"Ms. Roberts, Nona, if I may, I wish you could see the expression on your face right now. You and Darcy are alike. You must
stop torturing yourselves. You are no more responsible for Erin
Kelley's death than the mother who takes her child for a walk and
sees it crushed by an out-of-control car. Some things must be
considered acts of fate. Grieve for your friend. Do anything you

can to alert others that there is a madman out there. But don't try to play God."

Nona tried to keep her voice steady. "I wish I could hear that about five times a day. If it's bad for me, it's ten times worse for Darcy. I hope you've told her that."

Michael Nash's smile reached his eyes. "My housekeeper has called three times this week with suggested menus if I'll only bring Darcy back. She's going to drive to Wellesley to see Erin's father on Sunday, but she will have dinner with me on Saturday."

"Good! And now how about the program. We tape next Wednesday. It will be aired Thursday night."

"I usually shy away from this sort of thing. Too many of my colleagues rush to be on television panels or in the witness box at criminal trials. But maybe I can contribute something here. Count me in."

"Terrific." They stood up together. Nona waved her hand at the desks in the open area outside her office. "I understand you're writing a book about personal ads. If you need any more research, most of the uncommitted people out there have been playing the game."

"Thanks, but my own file is pretty thick. I'll be turning my book in by the end of the month."

Nona watched Nash's long, easy stride as he made his way to the elevator. She closed the door of her office and dialed Darcy's apartment.

When the answering machine came on, she said, "I know you're not home yet, but I had to tell you. I just met Michael Nash and he's a doll."

*D*OUG'S WARNING ANTENNA was signaling him. When he phoned Susan this morning, saying he didn't want to wake her up by calling when he knew he couldn't get home last night, she'd been warm and pleasant.

"That was sweet of you, Doug. I did get to bed early."

The warning signal had come after he'd hung up and realized that she didn't ask him if he'd be on time tonight. Up till a couple of weeks ago, she'd always pulled that martyred, anxious routine. "Doug, those people have to realize you have a family. It's not fair to expect you to stay for meetings night after night."

She'd seemed pretty happy when she'd met him for dinner in New York. Maybe he should call back and suggest she meet him again tonight.

Or maybe he'd better get home early, make a fuss over the kids. They had been away last weekend.

If Susan ever got mad, really mad, especially with the way the personal ad murders were getting played up and all the interest in Nan . . . !

Doug's office was on the forty-fourth floor of the World Trade Center. Unseeingly, he stared down at Lady Liberty.

It was time to play the role of devoted husband and father.

Something else. He'd better stop using the apartment for a while. His clothes. His sketches. The ads. When he got a chance next week, he'd bring them up to the cottage.

Maybe he'd better think about leaving the station wagon there too.

*W*AS IT POSSIBLE? Darcy blinked and reached for the magnifying glass. This five-by-seven snapshot of Nan Sheridan and her friends on the beach. The maintenance man in the background. Did he look familiar or was she crazy?

She did not hear Chris Sheridan come in. His quiet greeting, "I don't want to interrupt you, Darcy," made her jump.

Chris rushed to apologize. "I knocked. You didn't hear me. I'm terribly sorry."

Darcy rubbed her eyes. "You shouldn't have to knock. It's your place. I guess I'm getting jumpy."

He looked at the magnifying glass in her hand. "Do you think you've come across something?"

"I can't be sure. It's just this guy . . ." She pointed to the figure behind the cluster of girls, "looks a little like someone I know. Do you remember where this picture was taken?"

Chris studied it. "On Belle Island. That's a few miles from Darien. One of Nan's best friends has a summer home there."

"May I take this?"

"Of course." Concerned, Chris watched as Darcy slipped the snapshot into her carrying case and began to stack the pictures she had perused into orderly piles. Her movements were slow, almost mechanical, as though she were terribly tired.

"Darcy, do you have one of your dates tonight?"

She nodded.

"Drinks, dinner?"

"I try to keep them to a glass of wine. By then, I think I can get a handle on whether or not they either met Erin or sound funny if they deny knowing her."

"You don't drive off with them or go to their homes?"

"Lord, no."

"That's good. You look as though you wouldn't have much strength to fight back if someone made a pass at you." Chris hesitated. "Believe it or not, I'm not here to ask questions about something that isn't my business. I just wanted you to know that my mother came across a letter from Nan, written six months before she died. In it she refers to a Charley who thought girls ought to wear spike heels."

Darcy looked up at him. "Have you told Vince D'Ambrosio?"

"Not yet. I will, of course. But I'm wondering if it would be a good idea for you to talk to my mother. It was digging out all these pictures that made her go through Nan's letters. No one had asked her to do that. I just think that if there is anything my mother knows, it might come to the surface faster if she talks to another woman who understands the kind of pain she's been living with all these years."

Nan was six minutes older than I. She never let me forget it. She was outgoing. I was shy.

Chris Sheridan and his mother had probably come to terms with Nan Sheridan's death, Darcy thought. The *True Crimes* program, Erin's murder, the returned shoes, and now me. They've been forced to rip open whatever scars had healed. For them as well as me, there'll be no peace until this is over.

The distress in Chris Sheridan's face for the moment robbed it of the aura of sophistication and executive confidence that had been so noticeable a few days ago.

"I'd like to meet your mother," Darcy said. "She lives in Darien, doesn't she?"

"Yes. I'll drive you."

"I'm going up to Wellesley early Sunday morning to visit Erin Kelley's father. If it's all right, I'll stop late Sunday afternoon on my way home."

"Sounds like a long day for you. Tomorrow wouldn't be better?"

Darcy thought it was ridiculous at her age to blush. "I have plans for tomorrow."

She got up to go. Robert Kruse was meeting her at Mickey Mantle's at five-thirty. As of now, no one else had called. She had run out of personal ad dates.

Next week she'd start writing to the ads Erin had circled.

*L*EN PARKER had been angry at work. A maintenance man at NYU, there was nothing he couldn't fix. Not that he'd studied much. It was just the feel of wires in his hands, the feel of a lock and key, doorjambs, switches. He was supposed to do only routine maintenance, but often when he saw something wrong, he'd fix it without talking about it. It was the one thing that gave him peace.

But today, his thoughts had been confused. He'd yelled at his trustee for hinting that he might have a house somewhere. Whose business? Whose?

His family? What about them? His brothers and sisters. Never even invited him to visit. Glad to wash their hands of him.

That girl, Darcy. Maybe he'd been mean to her, but she didn't realize how cold it had been standing waiting outside that fancy restaurant to apologize to her.

He'd told Mr. Doran, the trustee, about that. Mr. Doran said, "Lenny, if you'd only understand that you have enough money to eat in Le Cirque or anywhere else every night of your life."

Mr. Doran just didn't understand.

Lenny could remember his mother yelling at his father all the time. "You'll put your children in the streets with your crazy investments." Lenny used to cower in bed. He hated to think of being out in the cold.

Was that when he started going outside in his pajamas so he'd be used to it when it really happened? No one knew he did that. By the time his father made all that money, he was used to being in the cold.

It was hard to remember. He got so confused. Sometimes he imagined things that didn't happen.

Like Erin Kelley. He'd looked up her address. She'd told him she lived in Greenwich Village and there she was: Erin Kelley, 101 Christopher Street.

One night he'd followed her, hadn't he?

Was he wrong?

Was it just a dream that she went to that bar and he stood outside? She sat and had something. He didn't know what it was. Wine? Club soda? What difference? He'd tried to decide whether or not to go in and join her.

Then she'd come out. He'd been about to go up and talk to her when the station wagon pulled up.

He couldn't remember if he'd gotten a look at the driver. Sometimes he dreamed about a face.

Erin got in.

That was the night they say she disappeared.

The thing was that Lenny wasn't sure if he'd just dreamed that. And if he told that to the cops, would they try to say he was crazy and make him go back to the place where they locked him up?

XVIII
SATURDAY
March 9

AT NOON on Saturday, FBI agents Vince D'Ambrosio and Ernie Cizek sat in a dark-gray Chrysler across the street from the entrance to 101 Christopher Street.

"There he goes," Vince said. "All dressed up for his day off."

Gus Boxer was exiting from the building. He was wearing a red and black check lumber jacket over loose-fitting dark brown polyester pants, heavy laced boots, a black cap with a rim that half-covered his face.

"You call that dressed up?" Ernie exclaimed. "In that getup I thought he was paying off a bet."

"You just never saw him in his underwear and suspenders. Let's go." Vince opened the driver's door.

They had checked with the building managers. Boxer was off from noon every other Saturday till Monday morning. In his absence, a substitute super, José Rodriguez, handled complaints and did minor repairs.

Rodriguez answered their ring. A sturdy man in his mid-thirties with a direct manner, Vince wondered why the management didn't keep him full-time. He and Ernie showed their Bureau credentials. "We're going from apartment to apartment questioning the tenants about Erin Kelley. A number of them were not in the last time we went through."

Vince did not add that today he was going to get very specific about what the tenants thought of Gus Boxer.

On the fourth floor, he hit gold. An eighty-year-old woman answered the door, taking care not to remove the security chain. Vince showed his badge. Rodriguez explained, "It's all right, Miss Durkin. They just want to ask a few questions. I'll stay right here where you can see me."

"Can't hear," the old woman yelled.

"I just want to . . ."

Rodriguez touched D'Ambrosio's arm. "She can hear better than you or me," he whispered. "Come on, Miss Durkin, you liked Erin Kelley. Remember how she always asked you if you needed anything from the store and how she'd take you to church sometimes? You want the cops to get the guy who did that to her, don't you?"

The door opened the length of the chain. "Ask your questions." Miss Durkin looked severely at Vince. "And don't shout. It gives me a headache."

For the next fifteen minutes, the two agents got an earful of what a native New York octogenarian thought of how the city was being run. "I've lived here all my life," Miss Durkin informed them crisply, her wavy gray hair bobbing as she spoke. "We never used to lock our doors. Why would you? Who'd bother you? But now, all this crime and no one doing a thing about it. Disgusting. I tell you, they should ship all those drug dealers to the ends of the earth and let them sail off."

"I agree with you, Miss Durkin," Vince said wearily. "Now about Erin Kelley."

The old woman's face saddened. "A sweeter girl you'd never find. I'd like to get my hands on whoever did that to her. Now a few years ago, I happened to be sitting at the window looking at that apartment building across the street. A woman was murdered. They came around asking questions but May and I—she lives next door—decided to keep our mouths shut. We saw it. We know who did it. But that woman was no better than she ought to be, and there was good reason."

"You witnessed a murder and didn't tell the police?" Ernie asked incredulously.

She snapped her lips closed. "If I said that, I didn't say it the way I meant. What I meant was, I have my suspicions and so does May. But that's as far as it goes."

Suspicions! She saw that murder, Vince thought. He also knew that no one would ever get her or her friend May to testify. With an inward sigh, he said, "Miss Durkin, you sit by the window. I have a feeling you're a good observer. Did you see Erin Kelley leave with anyone that evening?"

"No. She left alone."

"Was she carrying anything?"

"Only her shoulder bag."

"Was it large?"

"Erin always carried a large shoulder bag. She often carried jewelry and didn't want anything that could be yanked from her hand."

"Then it was generally known she carried jewelry?"

"I guess so. Everyone knew she was a designer. From the street, you could see her sitting at her worktable."

"Did she date much?"

"She dated. But I wouldn't say much. Of course, she might have been meeting people outside. That's the way young people do it now. In my day, a young man picked you up at your home or you didn't set foot out the door. It was better then."

"I'm inclined to agree." They were still standing in the hall. "Miss Durkin, I wonder if we might just step inside for a moment. I don't want to be overheard."

"Your feet aren't muddy, are they?"

"No, ma'am."

"I'll wait right here, Miss Durkin," Rodriguez promised.

The apartment had the same layout as the one where Erin Kelley had lived. It was meticulously neat. Overstuffed horsehair furniture protected with antimacassars, standing lamps with elaborate silk shades, polished end tables, framed family pictures of bewhiskered men and severe women. Vince was carried back to the memory of his grandmother's parlor in Jackson Heights.

They were not invited to sit down.

"Miss Durkin, tell me, what do you think of Gus Boxer?"

A ladylike snort. "That one! Believe me, this is one of the few apartments he doesn't barge into looking for one of his famous water leaks. And this is the one that has it. I don't like that man. I don't know why the management keeps him on. Goes around in those disgusting clothes. Surly. The only thing I can figure is that they get him cheap. Just a week before she disappeared, I heard Erin Kelley tell him that if she found him in her apartment again, she'd call the police."

"Erin told him that?"

"You bet she did. And she was right."

"Was Gus Boxer aware of the amount of jewelry Erin Kelley handled?"

"Gus Boxer is aware of everything that goes on in this place."

"Miss Durkin, you've been very helpful. Is there anything else you can think of to tell us?"

She hesitated. "For a few weeks before Erin disappeared, from time to time a young fellow used to hang out across the street. Always when it was getting dark so you couldn't see him clearly. Now I don't know what he was up to. But that Tuesday night that Erin left here for the last time, I could make out that she was alone and carrying that big shoulder bag. My glasses had fogged up and

I'm not sure if it was that same fellow across the street, but I think it was, and when Erin started walking down the block, he went in the same direction."

"You didn't see him clearly that night, but you saw him other times. What did he look like, Miss Durkin?"

"Beanpole. Collar up. Hands in his pockets, kind of hugging his arms against his body. Thin face. Dark, messy hair."

Len Parker, Vince thought. He glanced at Ernie, who obviously had the same idea.

"*I'VE BEEN* looking forward to this." Darcy leaned back in the passenger seat of the Mercedes and smiled at Michael. "It's been quite a week."

"So I gathered," he said drily. "It was all I could do to catch you in at home or at your office."

"I know. I'm sorry."

"Don't be sorry about anything. It's a great day for a ride, isn't it?"

They were on Route 202 nearing Bridgewater. "I never knew very much about New Jersey," Darcy commented.

"Except comedians' jokes. Everyone judges it by that turnpike strip with all the refineries. Believe it or not, it has a longer coastline than most other states on the eastern seaboard and has among the highest number of horses per capita in the nation."

"So there!" Darcy laughed.

"So there. Who knows? With my missionary zeal, maybe I'll make you a convert."

Mrs. Hughes was bathed in smiles. "Oh, Miss Scott, I've been planning the nicest dinner since Doctor said you were coming."

"How nice of you."

"The guest room at the head of the stairs is all ready. You can just freshen up there after your ride."

"Great."

If anything, the day was even more perfect than last Sunday. Cool. Sunny. A hint of spring in the air. Darcy managed to give herself completely to the enjoyment of the canter.

When they stopped to let the horses rest, Michael said, "I don't have to ask if you're having a good time. It shows."

The late afternoon turned sharply cooler. A fire had been laid in Michael's study. The draft from the chimney was brisk, causing the flames to leap up.

Michael poured wine for her, made an old-fashioned for himself, sat beside her on the comfortable leather couch, stretched his feet on the coffee table. His arm went around the back of the sofa. "Do you know," he said, "I've spent more time this week thinking about what you told me. It's terrible that a chance remark can hurt a child so much. But Darcy, can you honestly say that sometimes you don't look in the mirror and see the fairest of all?"

"I certainly do not." Darcy hesitated. "God forbid I should angle for a free consultation, but I've been meaning to talk to you about that. No, never mind."

His hand ruffled her hair. "What? Shoot. Spit it out."

She looked directly at him, concentrating on the kindness in his eyes. "Michael, I get the feeling that you understand how devastating that remark was for me, but that you think I've been—how can I put this—subconsciously blaming my mother and father all these years."

Michael whistled. "Hey, you'd put me out of business. Most people take a year of therapy before they come to that kind of conclusion."

"You haven't answered me."

He kissed her cheek. "And I don't intend to. Come on, I think Mrs. Hughes has the fatted calf on the table."

They got back to her apartment at ten o'clock. He parked the car and walked her to the door. "This time I don't leave until I make sure you're safely inside. I wish you'd let me drive you to Wellesley tomorrow. That's a heck of a long round-trip for one day."

"I don't mind it. And I have to make a stop on the way back."

"More garage sales?"

She did not want to talk about the Nan Sheridan pictures. "Something like that. Another fishing expedition."

He put his hands on her shoulders, tilted up her face, brought his lips down to hers. His kiss was warm but brief. "Darcy, call me when you get home tomorrow night. I just want to be sure you're safe."

"I will. Thank you."

She stood inside the door until the car disappeared down the block. Then, humming, she ran up the stairs.

*H*ANK WAS COMING in early Saturday evening. We have so little time together, Vince fretted as he opened the door to his apartment. When they were married, he and Alice had been living in Great Neck. There hadn't been much point in his commuting after they split up, so when they sold the house he'd taken this apartment at Second Avenue and Nineteenth Street. The Gramercy Park area. Not Gramercy Park, of course. Not on his salary.

But he liked his apartment. On the ninth floor, his windows offered a typical midtown view. To the right a peek of the Park with its elegant brownstones, straight down the murderous traffic on Second Avenue, across the street a blend of residential and office buildings with storefront restaurants, delis, Korean produce markets, a video store.

He had two bedrooms, two baths, a fair-sized living room, a dinette, a minuscule kitchen. The second bedroom was for Hank, but he'd put bookshelves and a desk in it and it also served as a study.

The living room and dinette were furnished in Alice-in-Mistakeville decor. The year before they broke up, she'd gone pastel modern in the living room. Pale peach and white sectional, pale peach carpet, peach and teal no-arms easy chair. Glass tables. Lamps that looked like bones in a desert. She'd wished that stuff on him, taking all the traditional furniture that he liked. One of these days, when he got around to it, Vince was going to get rid of everything and buy good old-fashioned, comfortable furniture. He was sick of feeling as though he'd stumbled into Barbie's Dream House.

Hank hadn't arrived yet. Vince stripped, stood under a hot shower, pulled on underwear, a sweater, chinos, and loafers. He opened a beer, stretched out on the sectional, and reviewed the case.

This was one baffling investigation. Look under any rock and you'll find a new clue.

Boxer. Erin had threatened to go to the police about him. Yesterday, Darcy Scott had called saying she thought she had a picture of Nan Sheridan at Belle Island with a maintenance man in the background who might have been Boxer. They'd picked up the picture and were checking it out.

Miss Durkin had seen someone who sure as blazes sounded like that looney, Len Parker, hanging around Christopher Street, and she thought he had followed Erin Kelley the night she disappeared.

There was a direct connection between that con man Jay Stratton and Nan Sheridan. A direct connection between Jay Stratton and Erin Kelley.

Vince heard the turn of a key in the latch. Hank bounded in. "Hi Dad." Dropped his overnight bag. Quick hug.

Vince felt the tousled hair brush his cheek. He always had to check himself from showing the fierce love he felt for his son. The kid would be embarrassed. "Hi, pal. How's it going?"

"Great. I think. I aced the chemistry."

"You studied hard enough."

Hank took off his school jacket, flung it into space. "Boy, it's great to have midterms over." He took long steps into the kitchen and opened the refrigerator door. "Dad, it looks as though you could use Meals-on-Wheels."

"I know. It's been quite a week." Inspiration seized Vince. "I found a terrific new pasta restaurant the other night. It's on West Fifty-eighth Street. We can take in a movie after."

"Great." Hank stretched. "Oh boy, it's good to be here. Mom and Blubber are sore at each other."

It's none of my business, Vince thought, but couldn't help himself. "Why?"

"She wants a Rolex for her birthday. A sixteen, five Rolex."

"Sixteen thousand five hundred dollars? And I thought she was expensive when I was married to her."

Hank laughed. "I love Mom, but you know her. She thinks big. What's going on with the serial murder case?"

The phone rang. Vince frowned. Not again on Hank's night, he thought, observing that Hank's reaction was to look interested. "Maybe there's been a break," Hank said as Vince picked up the phone.

It was Nona Roberts. "Vince, I hate to call you at home, but you did give your number. I was out on location all day and stopped by the office just now. There's a message from Dr. Nash. His editor doesn't want him talking about personal ads now when his own book is scheduled for fall publication. Have you any other ideas about a shrink who might be particularly tuned in to this subject?"

"I deal with a few who are members of AAPL. That's an organization of shrinks who are specialists in psychiatry and law. I'll try and get one of them for you by Monday."

"Thanks a lot. Again, forgive me for bothering you. I'm off to Pasta Lovers for another bowl of that spaghetti."

"If you get there first, ask for a table for three. Hank and I are just leaving." Vince realized he sounded presumptuous. "Unless, of course, you're with your own friends." Or *friend,* he thought.

"I'm by myself. That sounds great. See you there." The phone clicked in his ear.

Vince looked at Hank. "Is that okay with you, Chief?" he asked. "Or would you have preferred just the two of us?"

Hank reached for the jacket that had landed on the armless easy chair. "Not at all. It's my duty to check out your dates."

XIX
SUNDAY
March 10

*D*ARCY LEFT for Massachusetts at seven o'clock Sunday morning. How many times had she and Erin driven up together to see Billy, she wondered as she steered the car onto the East River Drive. Sharing the driving, stopping midway for carry-out coffee at McDonald's, always deciding they really ought to get around to buying a thermos like the one they had had in college.

The last time they'd agreed on that, Erin had laughed. "Poor Billy will be dead and buried before we ever get that thermos."

Now it was Erin who was dead and buried.

Darcy drove straight through and got to Wellesley at eleven-thirty. She stopped at St. Paul's and rang the doorbell of the rectory. The monsignor who had celebrated Erin's funeral mass was there. She had coffee with him. "I left word at the nursing home," she told him, "but I wanted you to know as well. If Billy needs anything, if he starts sinking, or if he becomes conscious and aware, please send for me."

"He's not going to become aware anymore," the monsignor said quietly. "I think that's a special mercy for him."

She attended the noon mass and thought of the eulogy less than two weeks ago. "Who can forget the sight of that little girl pushing her father's wheelchair into this church?"

She went to the cemetery. The ground had not yet settled over Erin's grave. The dark brown soil was still uneven; a glaze of frost over it shimmered in the slanting rays of the weak March sun. Darcy knelt, removed her glove, and placed her hand on the grave. "Erin. Erin."

From there she went to the nursing home and sat by Billy's bed for an hour. He did not open his eyes, but she held his hand and kept up a steady stream of small talk. "Bertolini's is crazy about the necklace Erin designed. They want her to do a lot more work for them."

She talked about her own business. "Honestly, Billy, if you saw Erin and me rummaging through attics looking for goodies, you'd think we were crazy. She has a great eye and has picked out some furniture that I would have missed."

As she left, she leaned over and kissed his forehead. "God bless, Billy."

There was a faint pressure on her hand. He does know I'm here, she thought. "I'll be back soon," she promised.

Her car was a Buick station wagon with a cellular built-in phone. The traffic was slow heading south, and at five o'clock she called the Sheridan home in Darien. Chris answered. "I'm running later than I expected," she explained. "I don't want to interfere with your mother's plans—or your plans, for that matter."

"No plans," he assured her. "Just come along."

She pulled into the Sheridan property at quarter of six. It was almost dark, but outside lights illuminated the handsome Tudor mansion. The long driveway had a roundabout at the main entrance. Darcy parked just past the bend.

It was obvious that Chris Sheridan had been watching for her. The front door opened and he came out to greet her. "You made good time at that," he said. "It's nice to see you, Darcy."

He was wearing an oxford cloth shirt, corduroy pants, and loafers. As he extended his hand to assist her from the car, she was again aware of the breadth of his shoulders. She was also glad to see that he was not in a jacket and tie. On the way down it had occurred to her that she was arriving at dinnertime and her own corduroy pants and wool sweater might not be suitable garb.

The interior of the house had the charming combination of lived-in comfort and exquisite taste. Persian carpets were scattered in the high-ceilinged foyer. A Waterford chandelier and matching sconces enhanced the magnificent carving on the curving staircase. Paintings Darcy longed to study covered the stairway wall.

"Like most people, my mother uses the den more than any other room," Chris told her. "Through here."

Darcy glanced at the living room as they passed. Chris noticed and said, "The whole house is done in American antiques. Anywhere from early Colonial to Greek Revival. My grandmother was hooked on antiques and I guess we learned by osmosis."

Greta Sheridan was sitting in a comfortable armchair by the fireplace. *The New York Times* was scattered around her. The Sunday magazine section was open to the puzzle page and she was studying a crossword dictionary. She got up gracefully. "You must be Darcy Scott." She took Darcy's hand. "I'm so sorry about your friend."

Darcy nodded. What a beautiful woman, she thought. Many of the film stars who were her mother's intimates would enjoy Greta Sheridan's high cheekbones, patrician features, slender frame. She was wearing pale blue wool slacks, a matching cowl neck sweater, diamond earrings, and a diamond pin in the shape of a horseshoe.

To the manner born, Darcy thought.

Chris poured sherry. A platter of cheese and crackers was on the coffee table. He poked at the fire. "By the end of the day, you know it's still March."

Greta Sheridan asked about the trip. "You have more courage than I to go up in the morning to Massachusetts and back a few hours later."

"I'm in the car a lot."

"Darcy, we've known each other for five days," Chris commented. "Will you please tell me exactly what you do?" He turned to Greta. "The first time I took Darcy through the main floor of the gallery, she spotted the Roentgen writing desk out of the corner of her eye. Then she told me she was 'sort of in the business.' "

Darcy laughed. "You won't believe, but here goes."

Greta Sheridan was fascinated. "What a sensational idea. If you're interested, I'll be a scout for you. You'd be amazed at the wonderful furnishings people discard or sell for next to nothing in this area."

At six-thirty, Chris said, "I'm the chef. I hope you're not a vegetarian, Darcy. We're having steaks, baked potato, salad. Gourmet delight time."

"I'm not a vegetarian. It sounds wonderful."

When he had left, Greta Sheridan began to talk about her daughter and the reenactment of her murder on the *True Crimes* television series. "When I received that letter telling me a dancing girl was going to die in New York in Nan's honor, I thought I would go mad. There's nothing worse than not being able to prevent a tragedy you know is going to happen."

"Except to feel you had a hand in causing it," Darcy said. "I know that the only way I can make up to Erin for urging her to answer those cursed ads is to stop her killer from hurting anyone else. You obviously feel the same way. I understand how it must be tearing you apart to go through Nan's letters and pictures, and I'm grateful."

"I've found some others. They're here." Greta pointed to a stack of small albums on the raised hearth. "These were on a high shelf of the library and missed getting put away." She reached for the top one. Darcy pulled up a chair beside her and together they bent over it. "Nan got interested in photography that last year," Greta said. "We gave her a Canon for Christmas, so these were all taken between late December and early March."

The salad days, Darcy thought. She had albums like this of the Mount Holyoke crowd. The only difference was Mount Holyoke was a women's college. In these pictures there were as many guys as coeds. They began to go through them.

Chris appeared in the doorway. "Five-minute warning."

"You're a good cook," Darcy said approvingly as she ate the last bite of steak.

They began talking about Nan's reference to someone named Charley who had liked girls to wear spike heels. "That's what I was trying to remember," Greta said. "On the program and in the newspapers they were talking about high-heeled slippers. It was the letter from Nan about spike heels that was gnawing at me. Unfortunately, it really hasn't helped much, has it?"

"Not yet," Chris said.

Chris carried a tray with coffee into the study.

"You make a marvelous butler," his mother said affectionately.

"Since you refuse to have live-in help, I've had to learn."

Darcy thought of the Bel-Air mansion with its permanent staff of three live-ins.

When she finished the coffee, she got up to go. "I hate to break this up, but it will be over an hour before I get home and if I relax too much, I'll end up falling asleep at the wheel." She hesitated. "Can I just look at that first book again?"

In that first album, on the next to the last page, there was a group scene. "The tall fellow in the school sweater," Darcy said. "The one with his face turned from the camera. There's something about him." She shrugged. "I just have a feeling I may have met him somewhere."

Greta and Chris Sheridan studied the picture. "I can pick out some of the kids," Greta said, "but not that one. How about you, Chris?"

"No. But look, Janet is in it. She was one of Nan's big buddies," he explained to Darcy. "She lives in Westport." He turned to his mother. "She loves to visit you. Why not ask her to drop in soon?"

"She's so busy with the children. I could drive down there."

As Darcy said good-bye, Greta Sheridan smiled and said, "Darcy, I've been studying you all night. Except for the color of your hair, has anyone ever told you that you have a striking resemblance to Barbara Thorne?"

"Never," Darcy said honestly. It was not the moment to say that Barbara Thorne was her mother. She smiled back. "But I have to tell you, Mrs. Sheridan, that's a very nice thing to say."

Chris walked her to the car. "You're not too tired to drive?"

"Oh no. You should see the long treks I take when I'm out on one of my hunts for furniture."

"We really are in the same business."

"Yes, but you take the high road . . ."

"Will you be coming to the gallery tomorrow?"

"I'll be there. Good night, Chris."

. . .

Greta Sheridan was waiting at the door. "She's a lovely girl, Chris. Lovely."

Chris shrugged. "I think so too." He remembered how Darcy had blushed when he'd asked her about coming up yesterday.

"But don't start matchmaking, Mother. I've got a hunch she's taken."

*O*VER THE WEEKEND Doug had been everything any woman could ask of a devoted husband and father. Even knowing his behavior was all a sham, Susan managed to assuage her fear that Doug might be a serial killer.

He went to Donny's basketball practice, then got together a scrimmage in the outdoor court with the kids who could stay. He took everyone out to Burger King for lunch. "Nothing like health food," he'd joked.

The place was full of young families. This is the sort of togetherness we've been lacking, Susan thought. But now it's too late. She looked across the table at Donny, who had hardly said a word.

Back home, Doug played with the baby, helping him build a castle of interlocking blocks. "Let's put the little prince inside." Conner squealed with delight.

He took Trish for a ride on her scooter. "We can beat anyone on the block, can't we, toots?"

258

He had a friendly father-daughter conversation with Beth. "My little girl is getting prettier every day. I'm going to have to build a fence around this house to keep away all the boys who'll be coming after you."

While she was getting dinner, he nuzzled Susan's neck. "We should go dancing some night, honey. Remember how we used to dance in college?"

Like a cold wind, that ended the fantasy that maybe she had been ridiculous in suspecting him of anything stronger than womanizing. *Dancing shoes found on dead bodies.*

Later, in bed, Doug reached for her. "Susan, have I ever told you how much I love you?"

"Many times, but one stands out in my mind." *When I lied for you after Nan Sheridan died.*

Doug pulled up on one elbow, stared down at her in the dark. "Now when was that?" he asked teasingly.

Don't let him know what you're thinking. "The day we were married, of course." She laughed nervously. "Oh, Doug, no. Please, I'm really tired." She could not bear his touch. She realized she was afraid of him.

"Susan, what the hell is the matter with you? You're trembling."

Sunday was more of the same. Family togetherness. But Susan could spot the wary expression in Doug's eyes, the lines of worry around his mouth. *Do I have an obligation to report my suspicions to the police? And if I admit that I lied for him fifteen years ago, could I go to prison too? And if that happened, what would become of the children? And if he suspected I was going to tell the police that I lied for him about the morning Nan died, how would he try to stop me?*

XX

MONDAY
March 11

ON MONDAY MORNING, Vince called Nona. "I've got a shrink for your program. Dr. Martin Weiss. A nice guy. Sensible. A member of AAPL and very knowledgeable. He says it straight and he's willing to do the show. Want to take down his number?"

"Absolutely." Nona repeated it, then added, "I like Hank, Vince. He's terrific."

"He wants to know if you'd like to see him pitch when baseball starts."

"I'll bring the Cracker Jacks."

Nona phoned Dr. Weiss. He agreed to come to the studio at four o'clock on Wednesday. "We tape at five. It will be aired Thursday night at eight."

*D*ARCY SPENT a good part of Monday in the warehouse tagging furniture for the hotel. At four o'clock she arrived at Sheridan Galleries. An auction was taking place. She saw Chris standing on the side of the first row, his back to her. She slipped down the corridor to the conference room. Many of the snapshots were dated. She wanted to find others in that same time frame. Maybe she'd come across another picture of the student who had seemed vaguely familiar.

At six-thirty she was still at it. Chris came in. She looked up, smiling. "The bidding out there sounded hot and heavy. Was it a good day?"

"Very. No one told me you were here. I noticed the light was on."

"I'm glad you did. Chris, does this fellow look like the one I pointed out yesterday?"

He studied it. "Yes, it does. My mother left a message a few minutes ago. She saw Janet today. That guy was one of the many questioned in Nan's death. He had a crush on her, I gather. His name was Doug Fox." At Darcy's shocked expression he asked, "You know him then?"

"As Doug Fields. Through a personal ad."

"*H*ONEY, THEY CALLED an emergency meeting. I can't talk, but a company we've recommended to our biggest client is going under."

Somehow Susan got through the evening. She gave the baby and Trish a bath and helped Donny and Beth with their homework.

At last she was able to turn out the lights and go to bed. For hours she lay sleepless. He'd managed to stay home for a weekend. Now he was on the loose again. And if he was responsible for the deaths of those girls, she was equally guilty.

It would be so easy if she could only run away. Bundle the kids in the car and drive as far as they could go.

But it didn't work like that.

The next afternoon when she'd seen Trish off on the school bus and put Conner down for his nap, Susan picked up the phone and asked information for the number of the FBI headquarters in Manhattan.

She dialed and waited. A voice said, "Federal Bureau of Investigation."

It was not too late to disconnect. Susan shut her eyes, forced her voice above a whisper. "I want to talk to someone about the dancing-shoe murders. I may have some information."

*O*N *MONDAY EVENING,* Darcy met Nona for dinner at Neary's and filled her in about Doug Fox. "Vince was out when I tried to reach him," she said. "I left word with his assistant." She broke off a piece of roll and lightly buttered it. "Nona, Doug Fox, or Doug Fields as he introduced himself to me, is exactly the kind of guy Erin would have enjoyed and trusted. He's good-looking, bright, artistic, and he's got one of those boyish faces that would appeal to a nurturer like Erin."

Nona looked grave. "It's pretty scary that he was questioned in Nan Sheridan's death. You'd better not see him again. Of course, Vince did say that a lot of guys don't give their right names when they answer these ads."

"But how many others were questioned in Nan Sheridan's death?"

"Just don't get your hopes up. So far, it isn't really more of a lead than the fact that Jay Stratton also went to Brown or that Erin's superintendent worked near Nan Sheridan's home fifteen years ago."

"I just want it to be over," Darcy sighed.

"Let's not talk about it anymore. You've been eating and breathing it. How's work going?"

"Oh, I've been neglecting it, of course. But I did have a nice call today about a room I did for a sixteen-year-old girl who had a terrible accident. I used some of Erin's things to furnish it. The mother wanted me to know that her daughter Lisa came home from the hospital Saturday and loves the room. And you know what the mother said really got Lisa excited?"

"What?"

"Remember the poster Erin had on the wall opposite her bed? The one of the Egret painting?"

"Sure I do. 'Loves Music, Loves to Dance.' "

They hadn't noticed that Jimmy Neary had come up to their table. *"That's it,"* he said vehemently. "By heaven, that's it. That's the way the ad began that fell out of Erin's pocket, right here on this very spot."

XXI
TUESDAY
March 12

*S*USAN HIRED a babysitter on Tuesday and took
the train down to New York. Vince had asked her to come in. "I
can understand how difficult this is for you, Mrs. Fox," he'd said
carefully. He did not tell her that they already had a connection
to her husband. "We'll do everything to keep our investigation
from the media, but the more we know, the easier that will be."

At eleven o'clock, Susan was in FBI headquarters. "You can
contact the Harkness Agency," she told Vince. "They've been
trailing Doug. I would like to think he's just a philanderer, but if
it's more than that, I can't let it go on."

Vince saw the agony in the face of the pretty young woman
opposite him. "No, you can't let it go on," he said quietly. "However, it's a long jump from knowing your husband is playing
around to thinking that he might be a serial killer. How did you
make that jump?"

"I was only twenty and I was so in love with him." It was as
though Susan was talking to herself.

"How long ago was that?"

"Fifteen years."

Vince kept his face impassive. "What happened at that time, Mrs. Fox?"

Her eyes fixed somewhere on the wall behind him, Susan told Vince about lying for Doug when Nan Sheridan died and how Doug had called out Erin's name in his sleep the night her body was discovered.

When she was finished, Vince said, "The Harkness Agency knows where his apartment is?"

"Yes." After she revealed everything she knew or suspected, Susan felt a vast weariness. Now all she had to do was live with herself for the rest of her life.

"Mrs. Fox, this is one of the hardest things you'll ever have to do. We need to check with the Harkness Agency. The fact that they were following your husband could be of great value. Can you act normally with him for the next day or two? Don't forget, our investigation may clear him."

"It isn't hard to keep up appearances with my husband. Most of the time he doesn't notice me except to complain."

When she left, Vince called in Ernie. "We have our first big break and I don't want to blow it. This is what we'll do. . . ."

*O*N TUESDAY AFTERNOON, Jay Charles Stratton was booked for grand theft. The NYPD detectives, in conjunction with the Lloyd's of London security staff, had found the jeweler who fenced some of his stolen diamonds. The rest of the gems that were listed as being in the missing pouch were traced to a private safe deposit box rented under the name Jay Charles.

*I*T HAD BEEN a long meeting and the tension in the office all day was brutal. How do you explain to your best clients that a company's accountants pulled the wool over your eyes? That sort of thing wasn't supposed to happen anymore.

Doug called home several times and was surprised to hear the babysitter pick up the phone. Something was definitely up. He'd make it his business to get home tonight. It wasn't that hard to straighten Susan out. His confidence oozed away. She wasn't beginning to suspect . . . Or was she?

*O*N TUESDAY EVENING, Darcy went straight home from work. All she wanted to do was heat a can of soup and go to bed early. The tension of the last two weeks was catching up with her. She knew it.

At eight o'clock Michael phoned. "I've heard tired voices, but yours just might win first prize."

"I'm sure it would."

"You've been driving yourself too hard, Darcy."

"Don't worry. I intend to come straight home from the office for the rest of the week."

"That's a good idea. Darcy, I'll be out of town for a few days, but keep Saturday for me, won't you? Or Sunday? Or better still, both days?"

Darcy laughed. "Let's plan on Saturday. Have fun."

"It isn't fun. It's a psychiatric convention. I've been asked to fill in for a friend who's had to cancel. You want to know what it's like to have four hundred shrinks in one room at the same time?"

"I can't imagine."

XXII
WEDNESDAY
March 13

*D*DAY, NONA thought as she slipped off her cape and tossed it on the love seat. It was not quite eight A.M. She was grateful to see that Connie was already there and the coffee brewing.

Connie followed her in. "It's going to be a great program, Nona." She was carrying freshly washed mugs.

"I think Cecil B. DeMille did one of his epics faster than I handled this one," Nona said wryly.

"You've been doing all your regular shows while putting this together," Connie pointed out.

"I suppose. Let's be sure to reconfirm all the guests by phone. You did send them a follow-up letter?"

"Of course." Connie looked astonished that she'd ask.

Nona grinned. "I'm sorry. It's just that Hamilton has been such a pain about this program, and Liz is determined to take the credit for what's good in it and leave me holding the bag if there are any snafus . . ."

"I know."

"Sometimes I wonder who runs this office, Connie, you or me. There's only one area where I wish we weren't alike."

Connie waited.

"I wish you talked to plants. You're like me. You never even see them." She pointed to the plant on the windowsill. "That poor thing is gasping. Pour something liquid on it, will you?"

*L*EN PARKER WAS tired Wednesday morning. Yesterday he hadn't been able to stop thinking about Darcy Scott. When he left work he'd hung around her apartment building and seen her step out of a cab around six-thirty or seven. He'd waited until ten, but she hadn't come out. He really wanted to talk to her. Other times he was mad at her for being so mean to him. There was something he had thought about the other day that had been important, but now it was gone. He wondered if he'd remember again.

He put on his maintenance uniform. Nice thing about wearing a uniform, it didn't cost you anything for work clothes.

*V*INCE'S SECRETARY had taken a message from Darcy Scott before he got to the office on Wednesday morning. She'd be out all day on different jobs but wanted him to know that Erin had probably answered an ad that began *"Loves Music, Loves to Dance."* That certainly sounded like the kind of ad those missing girls would have answered too, Vince thought.

Following up on the personal ads was a grueling job. Anyone who didn't want his real identity known could fake a few ID's, open a checking account, and rent a private box where magazines and newspapers could forward the responses to the nameless ads. No home address to trace. The people who ran those private box services were in the business of offering secrecy to their clients.

It was going to be a long haul. But this ad had a ring to it. He got on the phone to the researchers. They were closing in on Doug Fox, also known as Doug Fields. The Harkness Agency's file on him was an FBI investigator's dream.

Fields had been subletting the apartment for two years, starting just about the time Claire Barnes disappeared.

Joe Pabst, the Harkness man, had sat near Fox in the SoHo restaurant. It was clear he had met the woman through a personal ad.

He'd made a date to take her dancing.

He had a station wagon.

Pabst was sure that Fox had some sort of hideout. He'd overheard him telling the real estate broker in SoHo that he had a retreat he'd love to have her visit.

He was passing himself off as an illustrator. The super of the London Terrace building had been in and out of Fields's apartment and said that there were sketches lying around that were really good.

And he had been questioned in Nan Sheridan's death.

But it was all circumstantial, Vince reminded himself. Did Fox place ads, or answer them, or both? Would it be better to tap his London Terrace phone for a while, see what that turned up?

Should they bring him in for questioning? It was a tough one to call.

Well, at least Darcy Scott was already alerted to the possibility that Fox was the one. She wouldn't let herself get painted into a corner by him.

And wouldn't it be a bonus if it turned out that Fox had placed the ad they knew Erin Kelley had been carrying around? *"Loves Music, Loves to Dance."*

At noon, Vince got a VICAP alert from headquarters in Quantico. Calls had come in from police departments all over the country. Vermont. Washington, D.C. Ohio. Georgia. California. Five more packages of mismatched shoes had been returned. All of them contained a shoe or boot and a high-heeled slipper. All of them were sent to families of the young women who had turned up in the VICAP file, the young women who had lived in New York and been reported missing in the last two years.

At three-thirty, Vince was ready to leave his office for Hudson Cable Network. His secretary stopped him as he passed her desk and handed him the phone. "Mr. Charles North. He says it's important."

Vince felt his eyebrows go up. Don't tell me that stuffy ambulance chaser is starting to cooperate, he thought. "D'Ambrosio," he said crisply.

"Mr. D'Ambrosio, I have been doing a great deal of thinking."

Vince waited.

"There is only one possible explanation I can come up with to account for how my plans may have fallen on the wrong ears."

Vince felt a stir of interest.

"When I came to New York in early February to make final living arrangements, I attended a benefit at the Plaza as the guest of my senior partner. The 21st Century Playwrights' Festival Benefit. It was quite a glittery crowd. Helen Hayes, Tony Randall, Martin Charnin, Lee Grant, Lucille Lortel. I was introduced to a great many people during the cocktail hour. The senior partner at my firm was anxious that I become known. I spoke to a group of four or five people right before dinner was announced. One of them asked me for my card, but I can't think of his name."

"What did he look like?"

"You're speaking to someone with a very poor memory for both faces and names, which I am sure must be puzzling to someone in your profession. I'm vague about him. About six feet. Late thirties or early forties. Late thirties, I would think. Well-spoken."

"Do you think that if we got a roster of the people who attended that benefit it might stir your memory?"

"I don't know. It might."

"Okay, Mr. North. I'm grateful for this. We'll get the list and perhaps you can ask your senior partner if he recognizes the names of any of the people you spent time with."

North sounded alarmed. "And how would I explain the need for that information?"

The faint stirring of gratitude that Vince had felt for the man's attempt to be helpful disappeared. "Mr. North," he snapped, "you're a lawyer. You should be used to getting information without giving it." He hung up and yelled for Ernie. "I need the guest list for the 21st Century Playwrights' Benefit at the Plaza in early February," he said. "Shouldn't be hard to get. You know where I'll be."

*I*T *WAS MARCH* thirteenth, Nan's anniversary. Yesterday had been their thirty-fourth birthday.

Long ago Chris had started to celebrate his on the twenty-fourth, Greta's birthday. It was easier for both of them. His mother had phoned yesterday before he left for work. "Chris, I thank my stars every day that I have you. Happy birthday, dear."

This morning he'd phoned her. "The tough day, Mother."

"I guess it always will be. Are you sure you want to be on that program?"

"Want to? No. But I think if it does anything to help solve this case, it's worth it. Maybe someone watching it will remember something about Nan."

"I hope so." Greta sighed. Her tone changed. "How's Darcy? Chris, she is so dear."

"I think this whole business is wearing her down."

"Will she be on the program as well?"

"No. And she doesn't want to watch it being taped."

It was a quiet day at the gallery. Chris had a chance to catch up on paperwork. He'd left instructions that if Darcy came in he was to be notified. But there was no sign of her. Maybe she wasn't well. At two he phoned her office. Her secretary said she was working on some outside job all day and then planned to go directly home.

At three-thirty, Chris was hailing a cab to go to Hudson Cable.

Let's get this over with, he thought grimly.

*T*HE GUESTS for the program gathered in the greenroom. Nona introduced them. The Corras, a couple in their mid-forties. They'd separated. Each had placed a personal ad. They'd answered each other's ad. That had been the catalyst that brought them back together.

The Daleys, a serious-looking couple in their fifties. Neither had ever married. They'd both been embarrassed about placing and answering ads. They'd met three years ago. "It was good from the very beginning," Mrs. Daley said. "I've always been much too reticent. I was able to put on paper what I couldn't say to anyone." She was a research scientist. He was a college professor.

Adrian Greenfield, the vivacious divorcée in her late forties. "I'm having more fun," she told the others. "Actually, they made a printing error. They were supposed to say that I was well-liked. Instead, they put down that I was wealthy. I swear, you need a U-Haul for the mail I've gotten."

Wayne Harsh, the shy president of a toy manufacturing company. In his late twenties. Every mother's dream of the kind of guy her daughter will bring home, Vince decided. Harsh was enjoying his dates. In his ad he'd written that it frustrated him to see the toys he manufactured being enjoyed by kids all over the world while he is childless. Anxious to meet sweet, bright woman in her twenties who wants a nice guy who'll be home on time and won't drop his laundry on the floor.

The lovebirds, the Cairones. They fell in love on their first personal ad date. At the end of the evening he had gone over to the piano at the bar where they met and played "Get Me to the Church on Time." They were married a month later.

"Until they came along, I was worried that we didn't have any young couples," Nona had confided to Vince when he arrived. "Those two make you believe in romance."

Vince saw the psychiatrist, Dr. Martin Weiss, come in and got up to greet him.

Weiss was a man in his late sixties with a strong face, a good head of silver hair, penetrating blue eyes. They went over to the coffeepot.

"Thank you for doing this on short notice, Doctor," Vince said.

"Hello, Vince."

Vince turned as Chris came up to them. He remembered that this was the anniversary of Nan Sheridan's death. "Not the best day for you," he said.

*A*T *QUARTER OF FIVE,* Darcy leaned back in the cab, her eyes closed. At least today she'd made up for lost time. The painters would start next Monday at the hotel. This morning she'd brought down a brochure from the Pelham Hotel in London. "This is an absolutely elegant and intimate hotel. It's like your place in the sense that the rooms aren't large, the reception area is small, the parlor off it is perfect for receiving visitors. Notice the little bar in the corner. You can have the same thing. And study the rooms. We're not going to be nearly that grand, of course, but we can give it the effect."

It was obvious they were delighted.

Now, Darcy thought, I've got to get in touch with the window designer at Wilston's. She'd been shocked to realize that when a window display was taken down, the fabrics were often sold for peanuts. Yards and yards of top-quality goods.

She shook her head, trying to dislodge a nagging headache. I don't know whether I'm getting a bug or if I just ache, but it's another early night for me. The cab was pulling up to her building.

In the apartment her answering machine was blinking. Bev had left a message. "Darcy, you got the craziest call about twenty minutes ago. Call me right away."

Quickly, Darcy dialed her office. "Bev, what's the message?"

"It was some woman. Spoke real low. I could hardly hear her. She wanted to know where she could get in touch with you. I didn't want to give your home number so I said I'd give you a message. She said she was in the bar the night Erin disappeared, afraid to admit it because her date wasn't her husband. She saw Erin meet someone who was coming in just as Erin was leaving. They walked away together. She got a good look at him."

"How can I get back to her?"

"You can't. She wouldn't leave her name. She wants you to meet her at that bar. It's Eddie's Aurora on West Fourth Street off Washington Square. She said to come alone and sit at the bar. She'll be there by six unless she can't get away. Don't wait any longer than that. She'll call tomorrow if you don't get together tonight."

"Thanks, Bev."

"Listen, Darcy, I'm going to stay late. I have an exam to study for and there's no peace and quiet in my apartment with my roommate's friends always hanging around. Call me back, won't you? I'd just like to know that you're okay."

"I'll be fine. But yes, I'll call you back."

Darcy forgot that she was tired. It was five of five. She had just time to freshen her face, brush her hair, and change from her dusty jeans to a skirt and sweater. Oh, Erin, she thought. Maybe it's ending.

*N*ONA WATCHED THE CREDITS roll as the guests chatted quietly, still on-camera but off-mike. "Amen," she said as the screen went dark. She jumped up and ran down the steps to the set. "You were wonderful," she said. "Every one of you. I can't thank you enough."

A relaxed smile from some of the participants. Chris, Vince, and Dr. Weiss got up together.

"I'm glad it's over," Chris said.

"Understandable," Martin Weiss said. "From what I've heard toʊay, both you and your mother have shown remarkable strength through all this."

"You do what you have to do, Doctor."

Nona came up to them. "The others are leaving, but I wish you people would come back to my office for a cocktail. You've certainly earned it."

"Oh, I don't think . . ." Weiss shook his head, then hesitated. "I must check in with my office. If I can do it from there?"

"Of course."

Chris debated. He realized how low he was feeling. Darcy's secretary had said she was going straight home. He wondered if he could talk her into a quick dinner. "Can I get on line for the phone too?"

"Dial away."

The beeper went off on Vince's belt. "I hope you have a lot of phones around here, Nona."

Vince dialed from the secretary's desk and received a message to call Ernie at the 21st Century Playwrights' Festival office. When he reached him, Ernie was brimming with news.

"I've got the guest list. Guess who was there that night?"

"Who?"

"Erin Kelley and Jay Stratton."

"Holy smoke." He thought of the description North had given him of the man who had taken his card. Tall. Late thirties or early forties. Well-spoken. But Erin Kelley! That afternoon in Kelley's apartment Darcy had selected a pink and silver dress for Erin to be buried in. Darcy had told him Erin bought it to wear *to a benefit.* Then when he'd picked up the package of shoes that had been mailed to Darcy's apartment, she'd said that the evening slipper in the package went better with Erin's pink and silver dress than the ones Erin had bought herself. He suddenly knew why the shoes went so well with it. Her killer had been at the benefit and seen her wearing that dress.

"Meet me in Nona Roberts's office," he told Ernie. "We might as well go downtown together."

In the office Dr. Weiss seemed more relaxed. "No problems. I was concerned that one patient might need to see me tonight. Ms. Roberts, I'm going to take advantage of your kindness. My youngest son is a communications major and will be graduating from college in June. How does he get a foothold in this business?"

Chris Sheridan had moved the phone from Nona's desk to the windowsill. Absently, he fingered the dusty plant. Darcy wasn't home. When he'd called her office, her secretary had been evasive. Something about expecting to hear from her later. "A very important meeting had come up."

His intuition was pounding at him. Something was wrong.

He knew it.

*D*ARCY WASN'T SUPPOSED to wait any longer than six o'clock. She stayed until six-thirty, then decided to give up for tonight. Obviously the woman who called hadn't been able to meet her. She paid for the Perrier and left.

She stepped out onto the street. The wind had stirred up again and seemed to cut through her body. I hope I can get a cab, she said to herself.

"Darcy. I'm so glad I caught you. Your secretary said you'd be here. Hop in."

"Oh, you're a lifesaver. What luck."

Len Parker huddled in a doorway across the street and watched the vanishing taillights. It was just like last time when Erin Kelley came out and someone called her from that station wagon.

Suppose this was the same person who had killed Erin Kelley? Should he call that FBI agent? His name was D'Ambrosio. Len had his card.

Would they think he was crazy?

Erin Kelley had walked out on him and Darcy Scott had refused to have dinner with him.

But he'd been mean to them.

Maybe he should call.

He'd spent a lot of money on cabs following Darcy Scott these last couple of days.

And the phone call would only cost a quarter.

*C*HRIS TURNED FROM the window. He had to ask. Vince D'Ambrosio had just come back into the room. "Do you know if Darcy is answering another one of those damn ads tonight?" he demanded.

Vince saw the concern on Sheridan's face and ignored the belligerent tone. He knew it was not directed at him. "I understood from Nona that Darcy was planning an early night."

"She was." The smile vanished from Nona's face. "When I called her office, her secretary said she was going straight home from that hotel she's redoing."

"Well, something changed her mind," Chris retorted. "Her secretary sounds very mysterious."

"What's her office number?" Vince grabbed the phone. When Bev answered, he identified himself. "I'm concerned about Miss Scott's plans. If you know what they are, I want to hear them."

"I'd really rather let her get back to you—" Bev began, but was interrupted.

"Listen, miss, I have no intention of interfering with her private life, but if this has to do with a personal ad, I want to know. We're getting very close to solving this case but no one is in custody."

"Well, promise not to interfere—"

"Where is Darcy Scott?"

Bev told him. Vince gave her Nona's number. "Ask Miss Scott to call me immediately when you hear from her." He hung up. "She's meeting a woman who claims she saw Erin Kelley leave Eddie's Aurora in the Village the night she disappeared, and can describe the man she met outside. This woman hasn't come forward because she was with a guy who wasn't her husband."

"Do you believe it?" Nona asked.

"I don't like the sound of it. But if Darcy meets her in that bar, it should be okay. What time is it?"

"Six-thirty," Dr. Weiss said.

"Then Darcy should be phoning her office any minute. She was only supposed to wait until six for that caller to show up."

"Didn't the same thing happen to Erin Kelley?" Chris demanded. "As I understand it, she went to Eddie's Aurora, was stood up, left, and disappeared."

Vince felt the skin on the back of his neck start to crawl. "I'll phone there." When he reached the bar, he fired rapid questions, listened, then slammed down the receiver. "The bartender says a young woman answering Darcy's description walked out a few minutes ago. Nobody showed up to meet her."

Chris swore under his breath. The moment when he'd found Nan's body fifteen years ago today filled his mind with sickening clarity.

An escort from reception tapped on the half-open door. "Mr. Cizek from the FBI says you're expecting him," she told Nona.

Nona nodded. "Show him in."

Cizek was pulling the thick guest list for the Playwrights' gala from a bulging manila envelope as he came through the door. It was stuck. When he tried to yank it out, the clip fell off and the pages scattered. Nona and Dr. Weiss helped to retrieve them.

Chris was clenching and unclenching his fists, Vince noticed. "We have two strong suspects," he told Chris, "and we have a tail on both of them."

Dr. Weiss was examining one of the pages he picked up. As though he was thinking aloud he commented, "I'd have thought he was too busy with his personal ads to go to parties."

Vince looked up quickly. "Who are you talking about?"

Weiss seemed embarrassed. "Dr. Michael Nash. Forgive me. That was an unprofessional comment."

"Nothing is unprofessional at this point," Vince said sharply. "It could be very important that Dr. Nash was at the benefit. You sound as if you don't like him. Why?"

All eyes were on Martin Weiss. He seemed to be debating with himself, then said slowly, "This must go no farther than this room.

One of Nash's former patients, who now consults with me, noticed him in a restaurant with a young woman she knew. The next time she saw that young woman she teased her about it."

Vince felt his nerves tingling the way they always did when he sensed a break in the case. "Go on, Doctor."

Weiss looked uncomfortable. "My patient's young friend said that she had met the man when she answered his personal ad and wasn't surprised to learn that he had lied about his name and background. She felt distinctly uneasy with him."

Vince sensed that Dr. Weiss was deliberately choosing his words. "Doctor," he said, "you know what we're up against. You've got to level with me. What is your candid opinion of Dr. Michael Nash?"

"I consider it unethical for him to do research for a professional book under false pretenses," Weiss said cautiously.

"You're hedging," Vince told him. "If you were on the witness stand, how would you describe him?"

Weiss looked away. "Loner," he said flatly. "Repressed. Pleasant on the surface but basically antisocial. Probably has deep-rooted problems that began to manifest themselves in childhood. However, he's a natural dissembler and could fool most professionals."

Chris felt blood pounding in his temples. "Has Darcy been seeing this guy?"

"Yes," Nona whispered.

"Doctor," Vince continued rapidly, "I want to get in touch with that young woman immediately and find out what ad he placed."

"My patient brought it in to show me," Weiss said. "I have it in my office."

"Would you remember if it began '*Loves Music, Loves to Dance*'?" Vince asked.

As Weiss said, "Why yes, that's right," Vince's beeper went off. He grabbed the phone, dialed, and barked his name. Nona, Chris, Dr. Weiss, and Ernie waited in absolute silence as they saw the lines on Vince D'Ambrosio's forehead deepen. Still holding the receiver he told them, "That Len Parker looney just phoned in. He was following Darcy. She came out of that bar and got into the same station wagon Erin Kelley drove off in the night she disappeared." He paused, then said tersely, "It's a black Mercedes registered to Dr. Michael Nash of Bridgewater, New Jersey."

"Y*OU HAVE* a different car."

"I mostly use this one in the country."

"You got back early from the convention."

"The speaker I was to replace felt well enough to come after all."

"I see. Michael, you're sweet, but I think I'd just as soon go home tonight."

"What'd you have for dinner last night?"

Darcy smiled. "A can of soup."

"You lean your head back and rest. Sleep if you can. Mrs. Hughes is going to have a fire blazing, a terrific dinner, and then you can sleep all the way home." He reached over and gently stroked her hair. "Doctor's orders, Darcy. You know I like taking care of you."

"It's nice to be taken care of. Oh!" She reached for the car phone. "Is it all right if I call my secretary? I promised to check in with her."

He placed his hand over hers and squeezed it. "I'm afraid it will have to wait until we get to the house. The phone is broken. Now you just relax."

Darcy knew Bev would be there at least a few more hours. She closed her eyes and began to drift off. She was asleep by the time they went through the Lincoln Tunnel.

"WE'LL HAVE NASH'S apartment checked," Vince said. "But he'd never take her there or to his office. The doorman would see them."

"Darcy told me his place in Bridgewater is a four-hundred-acre estate. She's been there a couple of times." Nona was gripping the sides of the desk to steady herself.

"Then if he suggested going there with him tonight, she wouldn't be suspicious." Vince felt growing anger at himself.

Ernie returned from the next office. "I've checked surveillance. Doug Fox is home in Scarsdale. Jay Stratton is at the Park Lane with some old broad."

"That lets them out." It makes sense, Vince thought furiously. Nash left word on Erin's answering machine to call him at his apartment the night he drove off with her. I never thought to check that out. He leaves a phony message with Darcy's secretary and probably acts as though the secretary told him where to find Darcy. We know Darcy trusts him. Sure, she gets into his car. And if that weirdo Parker hadn't been trailing her, she'd have vanished into thin air too.

290

"How are we going to find Darcy?" Chris asked desperately. Agonizing fear that made it hard to breathe was crushing his chest. He knew that sometime in this past week, he had fallen hard for Darcy Scott.

Vince was on the line snapping orders to headquarters. "Alert the Bridgewater police," he was saying. "Have them meet us there."

"Be careful, Vince," Ernie warned. "We have absolutely no proof of anything, and the only witness is certifiably nuts."

Chris spun on him. "*You* be careful." He felt Weiss grip his arm.

"Get directions to Nash's place," Vince was saying. "And have a chopper at the Thirtieth Street pad in ten minutes."

Five minutes later, they were in a patrol car, lights flashing, sirens screaming, racing down Ninth Avenue. Vince was in the front seat with the driver, Nona, Chris, and Ernie Cizek in the back. Chris had flatly declared that he was going with Vince. Nona had looked at Vince, her eyes begging.

Vince did not share the chilling information received from the Bridgewater police. Nash's estate had a number of outer buildings scattered over the four hundred acres, including some in wooded areas. A search could take a long time.

And every minute we lose, the clock is running out for Darcy, he thought.

"**W**E'RE HERE, sweetheart."

Darcy stirred. "I did fall asleep, didn't I?" She yawned. "Forgive me for being such boring company."

"I was glad you were sleeping. Rest heals the spirit as well as the body."

Darcy looked out. "Where are we?"

"Only ten miles from the house. I have a little retreat where I get my writing done and I forgot my manuscript the other day. You don't mind if we stop for it? As a matter of fact, we can have a glass of sherry here."

"As long as we don't stay too long. I do want to get home early, Michael."

"You will. I promise. Come on in. Sorry it's so dark."

His hand was under her arm. "How did you ever find this place?" Darcy asked as he opened the door.

"Pure luck. I know it doesn't look like much outside, but the interior is quite nice."

He pushed the door open and reached for the light switch. Beneath it, Darcy noticed a button marked "Panic."

She looked around the large room. "Oh, this is handsome," she said, taking in the seating area by the fireplace, the open kitchen, the polished floors. Then she noticed the big-screen television and elaborate stereo speakers. "That's magnificent equipment. Isn't it wasted in a writing retreat?"

"No, it isn't." He was removing her coat. Darcy shivered even though the room was comfortably warm. There was a bottle of wine in a silver holder on the coffee table by the sofa.

"Does Mrs. Hughes take care of this place?"

"No. She doesn't know it exists." He walked the length of the room and switched on the stereo.

The opening bars of "Till There Was You" sounded from the wall speakers.

"Come here, Darcy." He poured sherry into a glass and handed it to her. "On a cold night this tastes wonderful, doesn't it?"

He was smiling at her affectionately. Then what was wrong? Why did she suddenly sense something different? His voice seemed slightly blurred, almost as though he'd been drinking. His eyes. That was it. There was something about his eyes.

Her instinct was to run for the door, but that was ridiculous. She searched frantically for something to say. Her eyes rested on the staircase. "How many rooms do you have upstairs?" To her own ears the question sounded abrupt.

He didn't seem to notice. "Just a smallish bedroom and bath. This is one of those really old-fashioned cottages."

The smile was still there, but his eyes were changing, the pupils widening. *Where were his computer and printer and books and all the usual trappings of a writer?*

Darcy felt perspiration form on her forehead. What was the matter with her? Was she going crazy suspecting . . . what? It was just nerves. This was Michael.

Holding his sherry, he settled in the large chair opposite the sofa and stretched out his legs. His eyes never left her face.

"Let me look around." She walked aimlessly through the room, pausing as though to examine one of the few pieces of bric-a-brac, running her hand over the countertop that separated the kitchen area from the rest of the room. "What beautiful cabinets."

"I had them made, but I installed them myself."

"You did!"

His voice was genial but a hard edge came into it. "I told you my father was a self-made man. He wanted me to be able to turn my hand to anything."

"He did a good job teaching you." There was no way she could stand here any longer. She turned, walked toward the sofa, and stepped on something solid that was almost covered by the fringe of the rug in the seating area.

Ignoring it, Darcy sat down quickly. Her knees were shaking so much she felt as though they would buckle under her. *What was the matter? Why was she so afraid?*

This was Michael, kind, considerate Michael. She did not want to think about Erin now, but Erin's face was looming in her mind. She took a quick sip of sherry to relieve the dryness in her mouth.

The music stopped. Michael looked annoyed, got up and went to the stereo. From the shelf above it, he took a pile of cassettes and began to examine them. "I didn't realize that tape was so close to the end."

It was as though he was talking to himself. Darcy gripped the stem of the glass. Now her hands were trembling. A few drops of sherry spilled on the floor. She grabbed the cocktail napkin and bent to pat it dry.

As she began to straighten up, she noticed that something was actually caught in the fringe of the rug, something that glinted in the light from the lamp beside the sofa. That's what she must have stepped on. It was probably a button. She reached for it. The tips of her thumb and index finger slipped into hollow space and met. It wasn't a button, it was a ring. Darcy picked it up and stared unbelieving.

A gold *E* on an onyx background in an oval setting. *Erin's ring.*

Erin had been in this house. Erin had answered Michael Nash's personal ad.

Sheer horror washed over Darcy. Michael had lied when he claimed he'd only met Erin once for a drink at the Pierre.

The stereo suddenly started to blare. "Sorry," Michael said. His back was still to her.

"Change Partners and Dance." He was humming the opening bars with the orchestra as he lowered the volume and turned to her.

Help me, Darcy prayed. Help me. He must not see the ring. He was staring at her. She clasped her hands together, managed to slip the ring on her finger as Michael came to her, his arms outstretched.

"We've never danced together, Darcy. I'm good, and I know you are."

Erin's body had been found with a dancing slipper on her foot. Had she danced with him here in this room? Had she died in this room?

Darcy leaned back on the sofa. "I didn't think you cared about dancing, Michael. When I talked about the classes Nona and Erin and I took together, I didn't think you were very interested."

He dropped his arms, reached for his glass of sherry. He perched on the chair this time, so much on the edge that it seemed as though his legs, planted on the floor, were preventing him from falling.

Almost as though any moment he might spring at her.

"I love dancing," he said. "I didn't think it would be healthy for you to be thinking about the fun you had taking those classes with Erin."

Darcy tilted her head as though considering his answer. "You don't stop riding in cars because someone you cared about was in an automobile accident, do you?" She did not wait for a response, but tried to change the subject. She examined the stem of the glass. "Lovely glassware," she commented.

"I bought a set of these in Vienna," he said. "I swear they make the sherry taste even better."

She smiled with him. Now he sounded like the Michael she knew. The strange look in his eye vanished for an instant. *Keep him like that, her intuition warned. Talk to him. Make him talk to you.*

"Michael." She made her voice hesitant, confidential. "Can I ask you something?"

"Of course." He looked interested.

"The other day, I think you were suggesting that I've been making my parents pay for that remark that hurt me so much when I was a kid. Can I possibly be that selfish?"

*D*URING THE TWENTY-MINUTE helicopter ride, no one spoke. His mind racing, Vince had gone over every detail of the investigation. Michael Nash. I sat in his office, thinking he sounded like one of the few shrinks who makes sense. Was this a wild-goose chase? What was to say that someone with Nash's money hadn't some sort of retreat in Connecticut or upstate New York?

Maybe he did, but with all his property, the odds were that he would bring his victims here. Over the whir of the propeller Vince could hear in his head the names of serial killers who buried their victims in the attics or basements of their own homes.

The chopper circled over the country road. "There!" Vince pointed to the right where twin high beams were gleaming upward, making paths through the darkness. "The Bridgewater police said they'd park right outside Nash's place. Put it down."

The mansion was outwardly tranquil. There were lights shining from several windows on the main floor. Vince insisted that Nona stay outside with the pilot. Ernie and Chris at his heels, he ran from the side lawn up the long driveway and rang the bell. "Leave the talking to me."

A woman answered, using the intercom. "Who is it?"

Vince clenched his teeth. If Nash was in there, they were giving him plenty of warning. "FBI agent Vincent D'Ambrosio, ma'am. I must speak to Dr. Nash."

A moment later the door opened slightly. The security chain was still in place. "May I see your identification, sir?" The courteous tone of a trained servant, this time a man.

Vince passed it through.

"Hurry them," Chris urged.

The security chain was released, the door opened. Housekeeping couple, Vince thought. They had that look. He asked them to identify themselves.

"We're John and Irma Hughes. We work for Dr. Nash."

"Is he here?"

"Yes, he is," Mrs. Hughes answered. "He's been in all evening. He's completing his book and doesn't wish to be disturbed."

*D*ARCY, YOU REALLY have great introspection," Michael said. "I told you that last week. You're feeling a little guilty about your attitude toward your parents, aren't you?"

"I think I am." Darcy could see that his pupils were closer to normal size. The blue-gray color was visible in his eyes.

The next song on the tape began to play. "Red Roses for a Blue Lady." Michael's right foot began to move in synch with the music.

"*Should* I feel guilty?" she asked quickly.

297

"**W**HERE IS DR. NASH'S room?" Vince demanded. "I'll take responsibility for disturbing him."

"He always locks the door when he wants privacy, and won't answer. He's very firm about not being interrupted when he's in his room. We haven't even seen him since we got home from shopping late this afternoon, but his car is in the driveway."

Chris had had enough. "He's not upstairs. He's driving around in a station wagon doing God knows what." Chris started for the staircase. "Where the hell is his room?"

Mrs. Hughes looked pleadingly at her husband, then led them up the stairs. Her repeated knocking brought no response.

"Have you a key?" Vince demanded.

"Doctor has forbidden me to use it when he leaves his door locked."

"Get it."

As Vince had expected, the massive bedroom was empty. "Mrs. Hughes, we have a witness who saw Darcy Scott get into the doctor's station wagon tonight. We believe she is in imminent danger. Does Dr. Nash have a studio or a cottage on this property or some other place he might have taken her?"

"You must be mistaken," the woman protested. "He's brought Miss Scott here twice. They're great friends."

"Mrs. Hughes, you haven't answered my question."

"On this estate there are barns and a stable and some storage facilities. There's no other building where he'd bring a young lady. He also has an apartment and office in New York."

Her husband was nodding in agreement. Vince could see they were telling the truth.

"Sir," Mrs. Hughes said timidly, "we've worked for Dr. Nash for fourteen years. If Miss Scott is with him, I can assure you you have nothing to worry about. Dr. Nash wouldn't hurt a fly."

*H*OW *LONG HAD* they been talking? Darcy didn't know. The music was soft in the background. "Begin the Beguine" was playing. How often had she seen her mother and father dance to this music?

"Mother and Daddy were the ones who really taught me to dance," she told Nash. "Sometimes they'd just put on records and fox-trot or waltz. They're really good."

His eyes were still kind. They were the eyes she'd seen the other times she'd been with him. As long as he didn't suspect that she knew about him, maybe he would leave with her, take her to the house for dinner. I've got to make him want to keep talking to me.

Mother had always said, "Darcy, you have a real talent for acting. Why do you keep resisting it?"

If I have it, let me prove it now, she prayed.

All her life she'd heard her mother and father discussing how a scene should be played. She must have learned something.

I can't let him see how scared I am, Darcy thought. Channel my nervousness into the performance. How would her mother play this scene, a woman trapped in the home of a serial killer? Mother would stop thinking about Erin's ring on her finger and do exactly what Darcy was trying to pull off. She'd play it as though Michael Nash was a psychiatrist and she was a patient confiding in him.

What was Michael saying?

"Have you noticed, Darcy, that when you let yourself talk about your parents you become animated? I think you enjoyed your childhood much more than you realized."

People always clustered around them. Remember the time the crowd was so great that she lost her mother's hand?

"Tell me, Darcy, what are you thinking? Say it. Let it out."

"I was so frightened. I couldn't see them. I knew that moment that I hated . . ."

"What did you hate?"

"The crowds. Being torn from them . . ."

"It wasn't their fault."

"If they weren't so famous . . ."

"You've resented that fame . . ."

"No." It was working. His voice was his own. I don't want to talk about this, she thought, but I must. I've got to be honest with him. It's my only chance. Mother. Daddy. Help me. Be here for me. "They're so far away." She didn't know she'd said it aloud.

"Who are?"

"My mother and father."

"You mean now?"

"Yes. They're touring in Australia with their play."

"You sound so forlorn, frightened even. Are you frightened, Darcy?"

Don't let him think that. "No, I'm just sorry that I won't see them for six months."

"Do you think the time you were separated from them that day was the first time you felt abandoned?"

She wanted to shout, "I feel abandoned now." Instead, she turned her mind to the past. "Yes."

"You hesitated. Why?"

"There was another time, when I was six. I was in the hospital and they didn't think I was going to live . . ." She tried not to look at him. She was so afraid the eyes would become empty and dark again.

She was reminded of the character in "One Thousand and One Nights" who had told stories to stay alive.

*C*HRIS WAS ENGULFED with a sense of helplessness. Darcy had been in this house a few days ago with the man who had killed Nan and Erin Kelley and all those other girls, and she was going to be his next victim.

They were in the kitchen, where Vince had an open line on one phone to the Bureau, a second one to the state police. More copters were on the way.

Nona was standing near Vince, looking as though she was about to pass out. The Hugheses, their expressions bewildered and frightened, were sitting, shoulders touching, at the long refectory table. A local cop was talking to them, questioning them about Nash's activities. Ernie Cizek was in the chopper, which was flying low over the grounds. Chris could hear the sound of the engine through the closed window. They were looking for Michael Nash's black Mercedes station wagon. Local squad cars were fanning out across the property checking the outer buildings.

Grimly, Chris remembered how lucky he'd been when he bought a Mercedes station wagon last year. The salesman had talked him into having the Lojack system installed. "It's built right into the wiring," he'd explained. "If your car is ever stolen, it can be located within minutes. You phone in your Lojack code number to the police, it's fed into a computer, and a transmitter activates the system in your vehicle. Many police cars are equipped to follow the signal."

Chris had owned the station wagon only one week before it was stolen outside the gallery with a one hundred thousand dollar painting in the back. He'd dashed back inside his office for his briefcase, and when he came out the car was gone. He'd phoned to report the theft, and within fifteen minutes the station wagon had been traced and recovered.

If only Nash had picked up Darcy in a stolen car that could be traced.

"Oh my God!" Chris ran across the room and grabbed Mrs. Hughes's arm. "Does Nash keep his personal files here or in New York?"

She looked startled. "Here. In a room off the library."

"I want to see them."

Vince said, "Hold it," into the phone. "What have you got, Chris?"

Chris didn't answer. "How long has the doctor owned the station wagon?"

"About six months," John Hughes replied. "He trades in regularly."

"Then I'll bet he has it."

The files were contained in a row of handsome mahogany cabinets. Mrs. Hughes knew where the key was hidden.

The Mercedes file was easy to find. Chris grabbed it. His exultant cry brought the others running. From the folder he pulled the Lojack pamphlet. The code number for Nash's black Mercedes was listed.

The Bridgewater cop realized what Chris had found. "Give me that," he said. "I'll phone it in. Our squad cars have the system."

"*Y*OU WERE IN the hospital, Darcy." Michael's voice was calm.

Her mouth was so dry. She wanted a glass of water, but she didn't dare distract him. "Yes, I had spinal meningitis. I remember feeling so sick. I thought I was going to die. My parents were at the bedside. I heard the doctor say he didn't think I'd make it."

"How did your mother and father react?"

"They were hugging each other. My father said, 'Barbara, we have each other.' "

"And that hurt you, didn't it?"

"I knew they didn't need me," she whispered.

"Oh, Darcy, don't you know that when you think you're going to lose someone you love, the instinctive reaction is to look for someone or something to hang on to? They were trying to cope, or more accurately, preparing to cope. Believe it or not, that's healthy. And ever since then, you've been trying to shut them out, haven't you?"

Had she? Always resisting the clothes her mother bought for her, the gifts they showered on her, scorning their lifestyle, something they'd worked all their lives to achieve. Even her job. Was that one-upmanship to prove something? "No, it isn't."

"What isn't?"

"My job. I really do love what I do."

"Love what I do." Michael repeated the words slowly, in cadence. A new song had begun on the tape. "Save the Last Dance for Me." He stood up. "And I love to dance. *Now*, Darcy. But first I have a present for you."

Horrified, she watched as he got up and reached behind the chair. He turned to her, a shoe box in his hand. "I bought you pretty slippers to dance in, Darcy."

He knelt in front of the sofa and pulled off her boots. Every instinct warned Darcy not to protest. She dug her nails into her palms to keep from screaming. Erin's ring had turned and she could feel the impression of the raised *E* against her skin.

Michael was opening the shoe box and parting the tissue. He took one shoe out and held it up for her to admire. It was an open-toed, high-heeled satin slipper. Gossamer ankle straps were almost transparent bands of gold and silver. Michael took Darcy's right foot in his hand and eased it into the shoe, double-knotting the long straps. He reached into the box, removed the other slipper, and caressed her ankle as he guided her foot along the insole.

When she had both shoes on, he looked up and smiled. "Do you feel like Cinderella?" he asked.

She could not answer.

"*T*HE RADAR INDICATES the wagon is parked about ten miles away in a northwest direction," the Bridgewater cop said tersely as the squad car raced down the country road. Vince, Chris, and Nona were with him.

"The signal's getting stronger," he said a few minutes later. "We're getting closer."

"Until we're there, we're not close enough," Chris exploded. "Can't you go faster?"

They rounded a curve. The driver slammed on the brakes. The squad car skidded, then straightened. "Oh hell!"

"What's the matter?" Vince snapped.

"They're digging up the road down here. We can't get through. And the damn detour will waste time."

*M*USIC FILLED THE ROOM but could not drown out his maniacal laugh. Darcy's footsteps were flying in synch with his. "I don't often do a Viennese waltz," he shouted, "but tonight it was what I planned for you." Twirling, bobbing, turning. Darcy's hair flew around her face. She was gasping but he seemed not to notice.

The waltz ended. He did not remove his arms from around her. His eyes were glittering, dark, empty holes again.

"Can't Get Started with You." Easily, he slipped into a graceful fox trot. Effortlessly, she followed him. He was holding her tightly, crushing her. She couldn't breathe. Is this what he did to the others? Got them to trust him. Brought them to this desolate house. Where were their bodies? Buried around here somewhere?

What chance did she have to get away from him? He'd catch her before she could get to the door. When they came in, she'd noticed the panic button. Was it hooked up to a security system? Knowing that someone was on the way, he might not kill her.

Now there was a growing urgency about Michael. His arm was like steel as he glided and stepped in perfect time to the music. "Do you want to know my secret?" he whispered. "This isn't my house. It's Charley's house."

305

"Charley?"

Backstep. Glide. Turn.

"Yes, that's my real name. Edward and Janice Nash were my aunt and uncle. They adopted me when I was a year old and changed my name from Charley to Michael."

He was staring down at her. Darcy could not bear to look into those eyes.

Backstep. Sidestep. Glide.

"What happened to your real parents?"

"My father killed my mother. They electrocuted him. Whenever my uncle was mad at me, he said I was getting just like him. My aunt was nice to me when I was little, but then she stopped loving me. She said they'd been crazy to adopt me. She said bad blood shows."

A new song. Frank Sinatra crooning, "Hey there, Cutes, put on your dancing boots and come dance with me."

Step. Step. Glide.

"I'm glad you're telling me this, Michael. It helps to talk, doesn't it?"

"I want you to call me Charley."

"All right." She tried not to sound tentative. He mustn't see her fear.

"Don't you want to know what happened to my mother and father? I mean, the people who raised me?"

"Yes, I do." Darcy thought of how tired her legs were. She was not used to the spike heels. She felt as though the tight ankle straps were cutting off her circulation.

Sidestep. Turn.

Sinatra urged, "Romance with me on a crowded floor . . ."

"When I was twenty-one, they were in a boating accident. The boat blew up."

"I'm sorry."

"I'm not. I rigged the boat. I *am* just like my real father. You're getting tired, Darcy."

"No. No. I'm fine. I enjoy dancing with you." Stay calm . . . stay calm.

"You can rest soon. Were you surprised when you got Erin's shoes back?"

"Yes, very surprised."

"She was so pretty. She liked me. On our date I told her about my book and she talked about the program and about how you and she were answering personal ads. That was really funny. I'd already decided you'd be next after her."

Next after her.

"Why did you choose us?"

"And while the rhythm pings, what coo-coo things I'll be saying," Sinatra sang.

"You both answered the special ad. All the girls I brought here did. But Erin wrote to one of my other ads too, the one I showed the FBI agent."

"You're very clever, Charley."

"Do you like the spike heels I bought for Erin? They match her dress."

"I know they do."

"I was at the Playwrights' Benefit too. I recognized Erin from the picture she sent me and I looked up her name on the seating list to make sure I was right. She was sitting four tables away. It was fate that I already had a date to meet her the very next night."

Step. Step. Glide. Turn.

"How did you know Erin's shoe size? My size?"

"It was so easy. I bought Erin's shoes in different sizes. I wanted just that pair for her. Remember last week when you had a pebble in your boot and I helped you take it out? I saw your size then."

"And the others?"

"Girls like to be flattered. I'd say, 'You have such pretty feet. What size are you?' Sometimes I bought shoes specially. Other times I'd take them from the ones I already had."

"The real Charles North didn't place any personal ads, did he?"

"No. I met him at that benefit too. He kept talking about himself and I asked him for his business card. I never use my own name when I call people who answer the special ad. You made it easy. You called me."

Yes, she had called him.

"You say Erin liked you when you met her the first time. Weren't you afraid she'd recognize your voice when you called and said you were Charles North?"

"I phoned from Penn Station, where there's a lot of noise. I told her I was running to catch a train to Philadelphia. I lowered my voice and spoke faster than usual. Just like this afternoon when I talked to your secretary." The timbre of his voice changed, became high-pitched. "Don't I sound like a woman now?"

"Suppose I hadn't been able to go to that bar tonight? What would you have done?"

"You told me you didn't have any plans for this evening. I knew you'd do anything to find the man Erin met the night she disappeared. And I was right."

"Yes, Charley, you were right."

He nuzzled her neck.

Step. Step. Glide.

"I'm so glad you both answered my special ad. You know what it is, don't you? It begins, *'Loves Music, Loves to Dance.'* "

"Because what is dancing but making love set to music playing?" Sinatra continued.

"That's one of my favorite songs," Michael whispered. He twirled her, never relaxing his grip on her hand. When he drew her back in, his tone became confidential, even regretful. "It was Nan's fault that I started killing girls."

"Nan Sheridan?" Chris Sheridan's face filled Darcy's mind. The sadness in his eyes when he talked about his sister. The authority and presence he had in the gallery. The way his staff obviously loved him. His mother. The easy relationship between them. She

308

could hear him saying, "I hope you're not a vegetarian, Darcy. Gourmet delight time."

His concern that she was answering these ads. How right he'd been. I wish I'd had a chance to get to know you, Chris. I wish I'd had a chance to tell my mother and father I loved them.

"Yes, Nan Sheridan. After I graduated from Stanford, I spent a year in Boston before I started med school. I used to drive down to Brown a lot. That's where I met Nan. She was a wonderful dancer. You're good, but she was wonderful."

The familiar opening bars of "Good Night, Sweetheart."

No, Darcy thought. No.

Backstep. Sidestep. Glide.

"Michael, something else I meant to ask you about my mother," she began.

He pushed her head down on his shoulder. "I told you to call me Charley. Don't talk anymore," he said firmly. "We'll just dance."

"Time will heal your sorrow," floated through the room. Darcy didn't recognize the singer's voice.

"Good night, sweetheart, good night." The last notes faded into the air.

Michael dropped his arms and smiled at Darcy. "It's time," he said in a friendly voice, although his expression was blankly terrifying. "I'll give you to the count of ten to try to get away. Isn't that fair?"

*T*HEY WERE BACK on the road. "The signal is coming from the left. Wait a minute, we're going too far," the Bridgewater cop said. "There must be a side road here some-where." The wheels screeched as they made a U-turn.

The sense of impending disaster had grown in Chris to the explosive point. He opened the car window. "There, for God's sake, *there's* a driveway."

The squad car ground to a halt, backed up, turned sharply right, raced along the rutted ground.

*D*ARCY SLIPPED AND slid on the polished floor. The high-heeled slippers were her enemies as she ran for the door. She took a precious instant to stop and try to yank the shoes off, but she couldn't. The double knots on the straps were too tight.

"One," Charley called from behind her.

She reached the door and tugged at the bolt. It did not release. She twisted the knob. It did not turn.

"Two. Three. Four. Five. Six. I'm counting, Darcy."

The panic button. She jammed her finger against it.

Hahahahahahaha. . . . A hollow, mocking laugh echoed

through the room. Hahahaha. . . . The sound was coming from the panic button.

With a shriek, Darcy jumped back. Now Charley was laughing too.

"Seven. Eight. Nine . . ."

She turned, saw the stairway, began to run to it.

"Ten!"

Charley was rushing toward her, his hands outstretched, his fingers bent, his thumbs rigid.

"No! No!" Darcy tried to reach the staircase, skidded. Her ankle turned. Sharp, stabbing pain. Moaning, she hobbled onto the first step and felt herself pulled back.

She didn't know she was screaming.

*T*HERE'S THE MERCEDES," Vince cried. The squad car slammed to a stop behind it.

He sprang out of the car, Chris and the cop with him. "Stay back," Vince shouted to Nona.

"Listen." Chris held up his hand. "Someone's screaming. It's Darcy." He and Vince threw themselves against the thick oak door. It didn't budge.

The cop pulled out his gun and pumped six bullets into the lock.

This time when Chris and Vince attacked the door, it opened.

*D*ARCY TRIED TO kick Charley with the sharp stiletto heels. He spun her around, seeming not to feel the heels stabbing at his legs. His hands were around her neck. She tried to claw them away. Erin, Erin, is this the way it was for you? She couldn't scream anymore. She opened her mouth, frantic to gulp in air, and could find none. Were those moans coming from her? She tried to keep fighting but couldn't raise her arms again.

Vaguely, she heard loud staccato sounds. Was someone trying to help her? It's . . . too . . . late . . . she thought as she felt herself fall into darkness.

Chris got through the doorway first. Darcy was dangling like a rag doll, her arms drooping at her sides, her legs buckled under her. Long, powerful fingers were squeezing her throat. Her screams had stopped.

With a cry of rage, Chris flew across the room and tackled Nash, who sagged and fell, pulling Darcy with him. His hands convulsed, then tightened their grip around her neck.

Vince threw himself next to Nash, snapped his arm around Nash's neck, forcing his head back. The Bridgewater cop grabbed Nash's thrashing feet.

Charley's hands seemed to have a life of their own. Chris could not pry his fingers loose from Darcy's throat. Nash seemed to be possessed of superhuman strength and impervious to pain. Desperately Chris sank his teeth into the right hand of the man who was snuffing out Darcy's life.

With a howl of pain Charley yanked back his right hand and relaxed the left one.

Vince and the cop twisted his arms behind him and snapped handcuffs on his wrists as Chris grabbed Darcy.

Nona had been watching from the doorway. Now she rushed into the house and dropped to her knees at Darcy's feet. Darcy's eyes were not focusing. There were ugly red bruises on her slender throat.

Chris covered Darcy's mouth with his own, pinched her nostrils closed, forced breath into her lungs.

Vince looked at Darcy's staring eyes and began to pound her chest.

The Bridgewater cop was guarding Michael Nash, who was handcuffed to the banister. Nash began to recite in a singsong voice, "Eeney, meeney, miney, mo, Catch a dancer by the toe . . ."

She's not responding, Nona thought frantically. She grasped Darcy's ankles and for the first time realized Darcy was wearing dancing slippers. I can't stand it, Nona thought, I can't stand it. Almost unaware of what she was doing, Nona began to struggle with the knots on the ankle straps.

"One little piggy went to market. One little piggy stayed home. Sing it again, Mama. I have ten piggy toes."

We may be too late, Vince thought furiously as he searched for some response from Darcy, but if we are, you lousy bastard, you'd better not think that spouting nursery rhymes now will help you prove insanity.

Chris raised his head as he gulped in air and for a split second stared at Darcy's face. The same look as Nan when he found her that morning. The bruised throat. The blue-white tone to her skin. *No! I won't let it happen. Darcy, breathe.*

Nona, weeping now, had finally untied one of the ankle straps. She pushed it back and began to pull the high-heeled slipper from Darcy's foot.

She felt something. Was she wrong? No.

"Her foot is moving!" she cried. "She's trying to get it out of the shoe."

At the same instant, Vince saw a pulse begin to beat in Darcy's throat and Chris heard a long, drawn-out sigh come from her lips.

XXIII
THURSDAY
March 14

*T*HE NEXT MORNING, Vince phoned Susan. "Mrs. Fox, your husband may be a philanderer but he's not a criminal. We have the serial killer in custody and we have absolute proof that he is solely responsible for the dancing-shoe deaths starting with Nan Sheridan."

"Thank you. I guess you can understand what this means to me."

"Who was that?" Doug had stayed home from work. He felt lousy. Not sick, just lousy.

Susan told him.

He stared at her. "You mean you told the FBI you thought I was a murderer! You actually thought I killed Nan Sheridan and all those other women!" His face darkened in incredulous rage.

Susan stared back at him. "I thought that was a possibility, and that by lying for you fifteen years ago I might also be responsible for those other deaths."

"I swore to you that I never went near Nan the morning she died."

"Obviously you didn't. Then where were you, Doug? At least level with me now."

The anger faded from his face. He looked away, then turned back with a cajoling smile. "Susan, I told you then. I repeat it. The car broke down that morning."

"I want the truth. You owe it to me."

Doug hesitated, then said slowly, "I was with Penny Knowles. Susan, I'm sorry. I didn't want you to know because I was afraid of losing you."

"You mean Penny Knowles was about to get engaged to Bob Carver and didn't want to take a chance on losing out on the Carver money. She'd have let you be accused of murder before she'd speak up for you."

"Susan, I know I played around a lot then . . ."

"Then?" Susan's laugh was harsh. "You played around *then?* Listen to me, Doug. All these years my father has never gotten over the fact that I perjured myself for you. Go pack your clothes. Move into your bachelor apartment. I'm filing for divorce."

All day he begged for another chance. "Susan, I promise."

"Get out."

He would not leave before Donny and Beth came home from school. "I'll see a lot of you kids, I promise." When he walked down the driveway, Trish ran after him and grabbed his knees. He carried her back and handed her to Susan. "Susan, please."

"Good-bye, Doug."

They watched him drive away. Donny was crying. "Mom, last weekend. I mean, if he was like that all the time . . ."

Susan tried to blink back her own tears. "Never say never, Donny. Your father has a lot of growing up to do. Let's see if he can handle it."

*A*RE YOU GOING to watch your program?"
Vince asked Nona when he phoned Thursday afternoon.

"Absolutely not. We prepared a special wrap. I wrote it. I lived
it."

"What do you feel like eating tonight?"

"A steak."

"Me too. What are you doing over the weekend?"

"It's supposed to be mild. I thought I'd drive out to the Hamptons. After the last few weeks, I must go down to the sea again."

"You have a house there."

"Yes. I think I'm changing my mind about buying Matt out. I
love my place and he really is very forgettable. Want to come
along for the ride?"

"I'd love to."

*C*HRIS BROUGHT AN antique cane for Darcy to
use while her sprained ankle mended.

"It's very grand," she told him.

He wrapped his arms around her. "Are you all set? Where are
your things?"

"Just that bag." Greta had phoned insisting that Chris bring
Darcy to Darien for a long weekend.

The phone rang. "I'll skip it," Darcy said. "No, wait. I tried to reach my folks in Australia. Maybe the operator finally caught up with them."

It was both her mother and father on the line. "I'm absolutely fine. I just wanted to say . . ." She hesitated. ". . . that I really miss you guys. I . . . I love you. . . ." Darcy laughed. "What do you mean, I must have met somebody?"

She winked at Chris. "As a matter of fact, I have met a nice young man. His name is Chris Sheridan. You'll approve. He's in my business, only upscale. He has an antiques gallery. He's good-looking, nice, and has a way of showing up when you need him. . . . How did I meet him?"

Only Erin, she thought, could really appreciate the irony of her answer. "Believe it or not, I met him through the personal ads."

She looked up at Chris and their eyes met. He smiled. I'm wrong, she thought. Chris understands too.